LATE HARVEST

LATE HARVEST

Fiona Buckley

This first world edition published 2016
in Great Britain and the USA by
SEVERN HOUSE PUBLISHERS LTD of
19 Cedar Road, Sutton, Surrey, England, SM2 5DA.
Trade paperback edition first published
in Great Britain and the USA 2016 by
SEVERN HOUSE PUBLISHERS LTD

British Library Cataloguing in Publication Data

Buckley, Fiona author.
  Late harvest.
  1. Smuggling–England–Exmoor–Fiction. 2. Great
  Britain–History–George III, 1760-1820–Fiction.
  3. Historical fiction.
  I. Title
  823.9'14-dc23

ISBN-13: 978-0-7278-8594-4 (cased)
ISBN-13: 978-1-84751-697-8 (trade paper)
ISBN-13: 978-1-78010-758-5 (e-book)

All Severn House titles are printed on acid-free paper.

Severn House Publishers support the Forest Stewardship Council™ [FSC™],
the leading international forest certification organisation.
All our titles that are printed on FSC certified paper carry the FSC logo.

Typeset by Palimpsest Book Production Ltd.,
Falkirk, Stirlingshire, Scotland.
Printed and bound in Great Britain by
TJ International, Padstow, Cornwall.

Dedicated to the memory of

PETER ANDERSON

A much respected colleague
whose work saved lives.

He loved Exmoor too.

Prologue

Once more, it is June. In this year of Our Lord 1860, I am approaching eighty years of age. I can no longer walk far. I can't now make my way down the winding sunken lane that leads from Standing Stone farm, my home now for a good thirty years, to see the combe below. I see the lane in my mind's eye, deep and rutted between its steep banks. Dog roses are in bloom, tangled with the hedges atop the banks, and the banks themselves are thickly grown with long grass and tall foxgloves and sorrel, with golden buttercups and the red and white and pink of clover and valerian, overhanging the lane, all heavy with the warm scents of summer.

The lane is a path of reddish earth that leads down into the combe and climbs the ridge of moorland on the far side. It isn't yet time for the heather to be out, so the moors are still mostly dark velvety brown, though splashed here and there by patches of long tawny grass, and the bright green of marsh or young bracken or the bright gold of the gorse, which is always out somewhere.

The track leads over the ridge, to descend towards Foxwell, the farm where I was born and where my son William still lives with his wife Susie. The window by which I sit for most of my time looks that way, and in clear weather I can see the sea, the Bristol Channel, framed in the dip.

That view of the sea holds memories. Oh, such memories! There are two nights that I recall especially. On both of them, the moonlight was so bright that the Bristol Channel could have been made of molten silver. On one of those nights, a child was conceived. On the other, a man died.

I am well looked after here, by my daughter Charlotte and her sensible husband, Rob Weston, and I am mostly happy – except for my arthritic hips and, of course, my sorrow for Ralph, a sorrow which will not leave me while I live. We should have had a lifetime together. I am glad of the years we did have but . . . if only, when we were young, our elders had let us alone.

I live very quietly and many of the things I did, in past years, are not known to the world outside. Which is just as well, because if they were I would be known in virtuous circles as that wicked old woman at Standing Stone and there would be some truth in that. I did, when younger, do a number of things which many people would consider to be horribly wrong. I flouted the laws of God and man, and I don't deny it. Nor do I repent. I feel regret for those I hurt but if I had not acted as I did, others would have been hurt instead. It was never a matter of whether to cause harm; only a choice of who should suffer. Not that I thought of it that way in those days, but it's true, all the same.

It is a pity that my other daughter, Rose − who knows much of my past and to this day remains scandalized by it − still refuses to have anything to do with me, but to her chagrin, her children and Charlotte's have made friends. There will be no continuing feud.

I grieve for what Ralph and I were denied, but yes, I rejoice in what we did have, and I will not apologize because I fought for it. Rest in peace, my dear love, and I shall not forget you. Nor will I forget how and where and when it all began, on that misty January morning in the year 1800, at my father's funeral. When Colonel Danworth's staghounds were running on a hot scent.

It occurs to me that if I have a strain of lawlessness in me, well, I may have inherited it from my father. He didn't exactly set me a good example. Thank heaven.

People Like Us

I was christened Margaret, but I was usually called Peggy, Peggy Shawe, of Foxwell farm on Exmoor. I was a disappointment to my father, who had wanted a son and never got one. I gave considerable trouble, I gather, when I entered the world and afterwards, my mother was never again able to conceive.

Foxwell was – and is – a prosperous place and it was unusual in that we had the freehold. We were not part of the crown lands as most of the Forest of Exmoor was, nor did we belong to any of the other great estates, such as the Luttrell or the Acland lands, but owned our property outright. It went back to some service or other rendered by one of my ancestors to Charles the First during the Civil War between the King and Cromwell. We had been granted the freehold as a reward.

Now, for the first time, there was no son to inherit, only me, a daughter and the only child. Not that my father showed it in any unkind way; indeed, he was careful to see that I had an education. I attended a small school in Exford, our nearest village, about three miles away. It was run by the Reverend Arthur Silcox, an ordained vicar although he had decided to turn to teaching for a living, and his wife Amelia. They were good teachers and did much to widen the horizons of the dozen or so local children, sons and daughters of tradesmen and farmers from round about, who were their pupils. They not only taught us to read, write and add up; they also instructed us in a certain amount of geography and history. They had a globe, showing us where the continents and the various countries were; and we learned something about the products of those distant countries, and the strange beliefs held by the people there. We learned too that we lived on a planet spinning round a sun, and that the stars that studded the sky on clear nights were also suns, far away in space.

And we were told stories about the Egyptians and the Greeks and the Romans, about the Roman emperors and Antony and

Cleopatra, and how the barbarians burst in to destroy that ancient world, and how civilization flowered again after the Dark Ages. We learned about William the Conqueror and Queen Elizabeth and Shakespeare, and even read parts of his plays, including *Romeo and Juliet* and *Antony and Cleopatra*.

It was a wide education for our district, though not detailed, since most of the pupils would spend their lives tilling the land, serving behind shop counters or simply cleaning the home and raising children, and would have no need of so much knowledge.

Some parents doubted that there was any sense in us learning so many things that would be of no use to us and it was rare for any pupil to stay beyond the age of fourteen, while most were taken out of school at twelve. I enjoyed school and persuaded my father to let me stay until I was fourteen, but after that, he insisted that I left. I was to inherit Foxwell one day, and he had hopes that I would marry a local lad, perhaps a younger son, who would be happy to join me there, and that in due course I would have a son to follow me. He even had a prospective husband in mind for me, though I knew that he would not press me against my will. What he did insist on was that I should now concentrate on learning how to be a farmer's wife – or, if necessary, a farmer in my own right.

He died in January 1800, when I was in my twenty-first year, the result of an accident when his pony slipped on an icy track and threw him, causing him to crash headfirst into a rocky outcrop beside the path. And that is where my tale truly begins.

The day of the funeral wasn't icy though it was cold, with a sharp wind and an iron-grey sky. A sad little procession set out from the farmhouse, bound for the church of St Salwyn, half a mile or so beyond Exford. We used a handcart to transport the coffin. Wheels are often a trial on Exmoor, what with the steep gradients and the frequency of mud, but we had some small carts and wagons at Foxwell, as well as a light trap. However, none of these seemed quite right for a coffin, or for those who accompanied it. Somehow, the handcart for the coffin while the mourners went on foot seemed more respectful. Bearers would take over at the Lychgate and carry the coffin inside 'in a seemly fashion' my mother said.

At least, that was the original idea. In the event, things didn't work out quite that way.

In the lanes through which the bier had to be taken, there were none of the summer's dog roses or foxgloves, only tired grasses and straggling weeds. A considerable crowd set out from Foxwell, for Mr Samuel Shawe was well known locally. People from several farms round about came to us that morning to accompany us to the church. Among them were a gnarled widower, Ned Bright from Marsh Farm, a couple of miles north of us, together with his two grown sons, John and James.

John Bright, one day, would take over the tenancy of Marsh and it was the younger son, James, that my father hoped would in good time marry me. No formal words had ever been spoken, but the understanding was there. James and I were friends, though there was no great passion involved. He was a four-square, tow-headed, blue-eyed lad a couple of years older than I was; I was a brown-haired, brown-eyed wench with a good complexion; both of us types seen often in our district. I had known him all my life. I had shared a bench with him at the Silcox school and because our backgrounds were so alike, I thought of him much as though he were my brother.

It would be a very suitable alliance, however, and the prospect clearly appealed to my father. As I said, he never pressed me, but he did sometimes refer to it in a casual way. I had overheard him once say to my mother, *One day, I fancy our Peggy and Jim Bright'll make a match of it;* another time, he said to me, *Seen aught lately of young Jim from Marsh? Nice lad, that. Make some wench a good husband one day, I shouldn't wonder.* A week or two after that, he remarked to me: *Saw Mr Bright at the market yesterday; says young Jim's been axin after 'ee.* I had never objected. One day, James would no doubt make me a formal proposal and we would be married at St Salwyn's and he would come to live at Foxwell. Everyone would approve. It was a thing that was going to happen, but I had few feelings, let alone emotions, about it.

Our two maids, young Betty Dyer and stout Mrs Page, who was married to our placid middle-aged cowman, Bert Page, did not come to St Salwyn's with us, but stayed behind to put the finishing touches to the hospitality that must be offered when the ritual was all over. Mother and I had made the cold dishes beforehand but the hot dishes required on-the-day attention. Bert Page came with us, however, and helped with the handcart. Bert had a rim of grey beard round his jaw which made him resemble a sailor, but if anyone said so, he replied that he preferred the company of cattle to the hazards of the sea. He had a deep, soothing voice that the cows seemed to like.

Father's closest friend, Mr Josiah Duggan, would be among those meeting us at the church, my mother told me. Mr Duggan was a shipbuilder at Minehead, which was and is a port on the coast about twelve miles away from Foxwell as the crow flew, but a good bit further on horseback.

'He'll have his two boys with him,' Mother said. 'He's got a daughter as well, but she's married on the other side of Somerset.'

'I see,' I said, not very interested. I had only met Mr Duggan senior a few times and then very briefly. In fact, I had only recently come to understand the link between him and Father, although I had long known that Mr Duggan, or sometimes a messenger from him, arrived at Foxwell now and then bringing supplies of brandy and tobacco. I had gradually come to realize that these goods were contraband, and had been smuggled into Minehead by Mr Duggan without paying duty. I also understood that one never talked about these things – just in case a Revenue man should be within earshot.

Other mourners met us as we came into Exford, including Mr Silcox, tall and thin and sympathetic. His wife Amelia had died not long before and his grave face told my mother and me how well he understood our feelings. It was a really big crowd that approached the old bridge that Mr Silcox had once told his pupils was built in the Middle Ages. We should have continued over the bridge and past the big village green and up the hill on the far side, but just as the handcart was about to be trundled on to the bridge, we heard the cry of a hound pack. Everyone stopped, turning their heads.

The hunt was running over the upward sloping fields behind us. An antlered stag was racing ahead, with the hound pack pouring in pursuit. The horsemen came after, pink coats bright, the man in the lead riding a big piebald, striking even at a distance. The rest of the field streamed in the rear, strung out.

'That's be Colonel Danworth's pack from Devon!' James exclaimed. 'I know that patchwork animal in front! That be Colonel Danworth atop 'un!'

Other exclamations followed.

'They'm closin' in . . .!'

'They'll get 'un soon . . .'

'Poor old Samuel: he'd have loved to be following; he followed the Danworth hounds, he did; not fair, him lying on that there bier . . .'

'Let's see the end of it, we can make it on foot, up to where we can *see*, even if we can't be right there. Let's do it for Samuel . . .'

'Vicar won't mind . . . follows hounds hisself when he gets the chance . . .'

'You won't mind, either, Jenny Shawe – your old man loved the chase . . .' That was the gnarled Ned Bright. My mother, looking bemused, said faintly: 'Yes, yes, I know. I don't mind.'

It didn't look as though it mattered much whether anyone minded, the vicar or my mother and certainly not me. The mourners had made their minds up already.

'Samuel, he'd have said yes, go after 'un; I can hear 'un cheerin' us on . . .'

'We can leave 'un on 'un's cart, under the shelter of the bank yur; he'll come to no harm . . . you'll stop with 'un, maybe, Mr Silcox, seein' as you don't hunt . . . you can stop along with Jenny and Peggy here, you can go on to the church and wait; we won't be that long . . .'

'Quick, or they'll be out of sight . . .'

And it was done. The handcart, complete with the coffin, was pushed close to the bank at the side of the track, and the mourners were gone, running and scrambling up towards the fields, finding their way through hedges and up rabbit tracks, tearing uphill in pursuit of the hunt, aiming to find a vantage point from which they could see the kill. I saw Ned Bright forcefully widen a gap in a hedge and with waving arms beckon John and James to follow him, which they did without a backward glance.

In a few moments, my mother and I were alone with only Mr Silcox and an elderly man, Mr Eastley, who had once been a grocer in Exford but now took his leisure while his son and daughter ran the business.

It was Eastley who said: 'I'll stop yur with the coffin. Mr Silcox, do 'ee take the ladies into my shop. Fire's banked in the parlour at the back; keep 'un warm there.' He cocked an eye towards the receding crowd of mourners. 'My boy and girl be up there with the rest: shut the shop today, we did. Here's my keys.' He pulled them out of a drooping, overused pocket in his fleece-lined coat, thrust them at Mr Silcox, and then from the same capacious pocket tugged out pipe, tobacco and tinderbox and settled himself in the shelter of the hedge, alongside the bier. 'Go on with 'ee now!'

'You can't stop here under that hedge in this cold! You'll catch your death!' protested Mr Silcox.

The retired grocer wrapped his stout coat more firmly round him, yanked his best black hat down almost to his eyebrows and said: 'No, I shan't. Been up at dawn all my life and out in all weathers; we've allus had geese and hens and a pony along of the shop. You'll be the one catching your death, not me. Go on with 'ee now!'

Mr Silcox took the proffered keys, and we went.

The place was empty. We seated ourselves in the back parlour and Mr Silcox, leaning forward to poke the fire back into life, said: 'I was a bit shocked, ladies, seeing the Brights go off like that, without a by your leave. Young James didn't as much as glance your way, Peggy, and you two are supposed to be half engaged! I shall have a word with that young man. He was once a pupil of mine, same as you, and I hoped I'd taught my boys and girls good manners!'

'It's all right,' I said uncomfortably. 'They're like that. We're all like that, suppose. I might have rushed off with them too, only it's my father out there on that cart.'

'We understood,' my mother agreed, warming her hands as the fire responded to Mr Silcox's urging. 'Maybe Samuel is up there, lookin' down on it all and cheering them all on. He'd have done the same, in their place, I've no doubt of it.'

'I was born in Bristol and sent to school in London and

then to Oxford,' Mr Silcox said ruefully. 'Maybe I don't fully understand the folk hereabouts. It's as if Exmoor's a different country with its own customs! All the same, good manners are good manners in my opinion and I *shall* have that word with James – and his father too. If you and James are serious, Peggy, it's time to settle things and today is no bad day to start the process. Your life, and yours, Mrs Shawe, won't be the same now and today is none too soon to think of the future.'

'I dare say you're right,' said my mother. She looked tired and her widow's black didn't suit her. Like me, she had a good complexion, but today, for the first time, it was showing lines, and her eyes were heavy, as though she had cried in the night and perhaps she had. 'But I can't think,' she said. 'Not yet. Not till this is over.'

'No more can I,' I said. 'Later, Mr Silcox. Not today.' I looked at him, meeting his kindly grey eyes, and added: 'I know we'll need help, a man to take charge and give the orders and so on, but somehow I'm not sure I'm quite ready to marry.'

'Ah.' Mr Silcox, much as Mr Eastley had done, pulled out a pipe and tobacco, fished further into his pockets and came up with a piece of paper, which he twisted into a spill and lit from the fire. His face had a reminiscent expression. When his pipe was drawing, he said: 'I can remember, when you were at my school, Peggy, how you used to enjoy hearing the stories I used to tell, about people in times past. It was a way to keep you all interested, to make you understand that in the past, people were still people, like us. Your eyes used to brighten so.'

'Yes,' I said. 'I loved those tales.'

'I know, and I sometimes wonder,' said Mr Silcox, 'if I was wise to fill your heads with them. Because quite often, the men and women whose names have come down to us in stories were *not* people like us. They were important people, powerful folk. They didn't live like us. They did heroic deeds, fell madly in love and died for love or made wars because of it – I told you of Helen of Troy, didn't I, whose beauty caused men to fight over her? And I told you about Antony and Cleopatra, and how Shakespeare wrote a play about them, and I recall one year, I made my class read through *Romeo and Juliet*.'

'I remember that,' I said, and for a moment I forgot how sad a day this was and my voice became eager. 'I really did enjoy those tales!'

Mr Silcox shook his head. 'I know; I saw it. But maybe I should have told you then – the real world, the here and now, our world, is nothing like that, young Peggy.'

'I should think not!' said my mother. I had repeated the plot of *Romeo and Juliet* to her and it hadn't found favour. 'Daft young things,' had been my mother's verdict. 'Life's hard enough and death comes untimely quite often enough as it is; no point in rushing on it headlong all over some dreams about true love. Juliet should have listened to her parents and married Paris. She'd have forgotten Romeo fast enough when she had a baby to rear and a good man to look after them both.'

Now, she said: 'Mr Silcox is right. Today's not the day to talk of such things but quite soon, yes, I think the banns should be called for you and James. All these great love stories be pretty tales enough but not for people like us. Folk like us take what's to hand and suitable and mostly it works out well.'

'I know,' I said soberly. 'I expect I'll feel ready to settle things before too long. My father, having that accident . . . it's been a shock, that's all. So much to do, to think about . . .'

'The spring is coming. Everyone feels differently in spring!' Mr Silcox said encouragingly.

'We'll have to keep wearing black for a while,' my mother said. 'But for you, Peggy, three months will be enough. You'll leave off your black in April and I'm going to see as you go to the May Day dance here in Exford. James will escort you. And maybe . . .'

Her voice tailed off, though the unspoken words were audible to us all. On May Day, perhaps, James would propose and I would accept and there would be an announcement. I tried to imagine it, but it refused to seem real. By some kind of tacit agreement, we began to talk of other things. And eventually, the mourners came back. We went out to join them.

They were excited, having witnessed the kill, and the last trudge up the hill to the churchyard gate was none too dignified because they were all chattering eagerly about the chase. The stag had been a twelve-pointer, apparently, a fine head and one of the huntsman had said he'd given the hounds a splendid run. However, at the gate, the vicar met us, clad in his clean white surplice, and the somewhat dishevelled cortege reorganized itself into a semblance, at least, of propriety.

Six bearers, John and James Bright, Bert Page and another of our farmhands, the Eastley son and Mr Silcox, took the coffin from its handcart and bore it into the church in the proper manner, where it was laid on a high trestle, and the service proceeded. Then we followed it out and it was lowered into a newly dug grave. My mother and I held each other and turned away as my father, hitherto such a power in our lives, was lowered into what I could only think of as a nasty wet hole.

Reverent words were said, a clod of earth was cast on top of the coffin and I saw that it was done by Mr Josiah Duggan, who had been already in his seat in the church when we arrived there. I noticed that he had two younger men with him though from where I stood beside the grave, I could only see them in profile. They would be the boys that my mother had mentioned to me. The Brights stood opposite to me and my mother, facing us, and this time James did catch my eye and gave me a slightly apologetic smile.

Then we must all turn away, and begin on the long trudge home, where there would be cold ham and hot pies, both fruit and meat, and freshly made bread with butter and honey, and to drink there would be not only hot tea, but also brandy and mulled wine, most of which had been delivered by one of Mr Duggan's men two days previously.

The Brights walked with Mother and me, and James, gruffly, said to me: 'Sorry we all rushed off after the hunt like we did. Mr Silcox has spoken to me, says we shouldn't have done it. But your dad would have done the same – wouldn't 'ee, now?'

'Yes,' I agreed. 'He probably would,' and my mother, over-hearing, sighed.

I had no feelings about the incident. Nothing mattered except that my father had been left behind in the churchyard, in that hateful wet hole, and we had had to turn away and go home without him. And the wind was so cold. We would all be thankful to get back to Foxwell.

Our farmhouse was old, thatched, built of reddish-coloured stone and looking more as though it had grown out of its hillside than been constructed there. Dormer windows peered from the roof, somewhat overhung with thatch, as though the roof needed a haircut; there was a massive front door which was so rarely used that we had had to oil the hinges so the coffin could be carried through it in proper formal fashion. Most of our indoor life took place in the enormous kitchen. The parlour was usually ignored and had had to be cleaned and dusted specially for this sad occasion.

The parlour, however, was also big. In previous generations, the Shawe family had often been large and the parlour had been extended at some time, so that it could be used for sizeable gatherings, with space for dancing. It had a fine hearth, and the maids had a good fire going, for the parlour was where the food and drink was set out. As soon as we were within, I ran upstairs to shed my outdoor things and then hurried back down, to help with the hot dishes. Then, along with my mother and the maids I began to move about in the throng, offering plates of this and glasses of that, until I was intercepted by Mother, who was talking to Mr Duggan.

He and I exchanged polite greetings, and my mother said: 'Well, it's just me and my Peggy now, and neither of us will be wanting much in the liquor way in future, but we'd better always have a keg of brandy to hand, in case of someone needing help after an accident, and we'll have to have supplies of tea. If someone can call now and then, we'll let you know what's wanted.'

'It will be my pleasure,' said Josiah Duggan, and then, looking round him, said: 'Where are my boys? I dare say one or other of them will act as my messenger sometimes.' He reached out with a long arm and pulled a youth, who was talking to someone else, unceremoniously away. 'This is Philip, my younger lad. Philip, meet Mrs Jenny Shawe and her daughter Peggy.'

Mother and I dutifully acknowledged bows from a round-faced young man who said he was pleased to meet us. Neither he nor his father offered any explanation for the curious fact that he had a black eye.

'Now, where's my eldest?' Duggan said restively. 'I can never keep track of him. He's just done a boatbuilding apprenticeship up north – a much better idea than training him myself; sending

him away meant bringing new ideas back, and that I'm all in
favour of. And he'd get no favouritism in someone else's yard,
and that's healthy. But he's come home mighty independent.
I can never put my hand on him . . . There you are, Ralph!'
He caught a passing elbow and pulled a second young man
into our group. More introductions were exchanged.

The elder Duggan son had a head of thick, rather untidy
black hair and a lean brown face. As we looked at each other,
he smiled at me, with a glint of beautiful teeth. His dark eyes
took part in the smile, glowing with it as they looked into mine.

And the whole world changed.

Recognition

When I was at school, one of my fellow pupils was a girl called Emma Sands, the same age as me. We left school together. Two years later I met her by chance in Exford, and she told me she had fallen in love. It was instant, she said, between one moment and the next, like falling down a well, except that the well was full of stars and wild, glorious music. She had never known it was possible to feel like that. Her parents didn't approve of the young man but she hoped to talk them round. She would beg and plead, she said, for he was the only man for her.

I never found out why her parents disliked him, or even who he was but I did learn, some months later, that she had run away with him. I never heard any more. Perhaps she was happy, perhaps it was all a disaster. I shall certainly never know now.

My experience of love at first sight was nothing like Emma's. I did not feel that I had fallen down a well; stars and wild music – or any sort of music, come to that – were entirely absent. Instead, it was calm and warm. It was the same feeling that people have when, unexpectedly, they meet an old friend whom they haven't seen for years and there is the pleasure of recognition, the desire to sit down together and talk and talk, to catch up with all that has happened since last they met.

It was the same for him although he didn't tell me so then. He simply said: 'Miss Shawe, here you are handing dishes round but you must be exhausted after such a sad morning. I have heard how you and your mother were left deserted while the rest went off after the hunt. I'm appalled.' Like his father and brother, he had the Exmoor accent, but used words in an educated fashion, as Mr Silcox did. 'Let me help you to some of what I believe are called the baked meats.'

Mr Duggan, having introduced us, was telling my mother

how disappointed he was that his younger son wasn't interested in shipbuilding and shaking his head at an embarrassed Philip. Ralph drew me away and I don't think any of them even noticed us go. I was escorted to the laden table and there Ralph competently loaded plates for us.

'And here's some mulled wine,' he said, dipping glass beakers into the bowl. Mrs Page had thoughtfully provided a pile of trays, augmenting ours by lending three of her own and borrowing more from the Brights. Armed with a tray each, we could carry our booty with ease. Ralph led me out of the crowd. 'Now let's sit down and eat and talk.'

The parlour had wide window seats. We sat down on one, as easy together as though we had known each other all our lives. 'Tell me,' I said, 'how did your brother come by that black eye?'

'Now, if my father had given it to him, that would be a tactless question,' said Ralph, grinning.

'In that case, I think your father would have tried to explain it – told us a tale about an accident of some kind, I dare say,' I said.

Ralph laughed. 'You're right, at that. No, Philip's been in a fight. Over a girl. A very tiresome and silly girl, too. I said to him: you might at least squabble over a worthwhile wench and not that daft Maisie Cutler.'

'Who is Maisie Cutler?'

'Seventeen-year-old lass who works on a smallholding just outside Dunster. Ever been to Dunster? Where the Luttrells' castle is – it overlooks the village from a hill.'

'Yes, of course. There's a regular yarn market at Dunster – Mother and I have bought yarn there. It's that village a couple of miles from Minehead,' I told him.

'That's it. Used to be a port, once, but it got silted up. The sea's retreated. Avill Smallholding, where Maisie works, is just outside, at the inland end. A few cows, a few pigs, a lot of vegetables. Not much of a place but Maisie's employed for the house and the dairy and she does a bit of hoeing and weeding, Philip says. Probably doesn't work any harder than she has to. She's pretty and plump and as vain as a peacock, and flirting's the only idea she has in her little golden head, and Philip's mad for her. Only he has a rival.'

'And the rival blacked his eye for him?'

'That's it. Laurence Wheelwright, farmhand, from a place near Timberscombe – you know, the village further up the Avill valley. He'd be a good match for her,' said Ralph, becoming thoughtful. 'Said to be saving up for a place of his own, and got half of what he needs already – a legacy from an aunt or something. He's dead serious about her. He and Philip came to blows two days ago. She didn't turn up to meet Philip somewhere and then he came face to face with the two of them, out walking near where Laurence works. Well, there was trouble and Philip lost the fight. You should have seen the state he was in when he got home! No, maybe you shouldn't. According to him, Maisie just stood back beaming, loving it because two men were fighting over her.'

'That didn't change his mind about her?' I asked.

'Not a bit of it. He still thinks she's wonderful. She's young, he said, almost cooing; all that'll pass. Philip is more interested in agriculture than shipbuilding. He looks after our little patch of garden very well, I admit – he's got green fingers, for sure. He said if only Dad would help him set up in a smallholding of his own, he'd put a ring on Maisie's finger the next day.'

'Would she let him?' I enquired.

'That's just it. Dad thinks she wouldn't, and he won't come across with any money to help Philip get the likes of her for a wife. What are we talking about Philip and Maisie for? Let's talk about us. I hear there's to be a May Day dance here in Exford. Will your mother let you come – I mean on account of being in mourning, and so on.'

'Yes. She's already said so. She . . . she will expect me to be escorted by James Bright. That's him, over there.' James and his brother John were together, deep in talk with Bert Page. A few words drifted towards us, something to do with a promising Red Devon bull calf, a likely future sire that somebody called Francis Quartly had for sale, except that apparently he wasn't willing to sell it. 'Got ideas about using it hisself,' James was saying. 'Wants to improve the breed, so he says. Reckon he's just tryin' to push the price up . . .'

'James' father farms not far from us,' I said. 'It would be suitable, everyone says, and we were at school together and . . .'

'I know,' said Ralph. 'There is supposed to be an under-standing that you and James Bright will marry. The Fellow – Mr Silcox – who told my father about the way you and your mother were left deserted by the roadside, also told him that. Mr Silcox was horrified because even the young man who is supposed to be interested in marrying you still ran off to watch the hounds, leaving you and your mother and the coffin under a hedge. I assure you that if I had been there, I would not have abandoned you to go after the hunt.'

'I understood why it happened,' I said lamely. 'Even my father himself might have done the same thing . . .'

'You are very forbearing,' said Ralph. He became serious. 'Listen, we've only just met but somehow . . . I want to get to know you better and you've a lot to find out about me. My father's a free trader, for one thing. I'd better tell you that straight away.'

'You mean a smuggler.'

'We call ourselves free traders. I'll be in it too, I expect, now I'm back home. Will you mind?'

'Will *I* mind?' I didn't add *Why me?* because I knew already why he had asked. But it was far too soon to say so. 'I've never thought about it,' I said. 'Everyone does it – or buys the goods, anyway. My father did.'

I faltered as I spoke of my father, remembering once more that I would never see him again. I gave Ralph a slightly watery smile. 'My mother's already arranging with your father for deliveries of tea and occasional brandy, for medical purposes.'

'Good. That will keep our families in touch. You and I must meet and talk a time or two between now and May Day. Peggy – may I call you Peggy? Miss Shawe sounds so prim.'

'Yes, you may. If I can call you Ralph.'

'Tell me about yourself,' Ralph said.

I tried to oblige, and he listened with attention, though an account of life at Foxwell wasn't exciting. It was inter-rupted, anyway, because James now broke away from the discussion about Red Devons, and came over to us. He was frowning. I gave Ralph a quick smile and went to meet him before the two of them could come face to face. 'Good day, James. I just sat down for a while and Mr Duggan kindly came to talk to me. I feel as though I've walked a hundred miles today. What was all that about a bull calf?'

'My father's heard of a good one, over the other side of the moor – South Molton way. He didn't like seein' you chattin' with they Duggans. Free traders, they are, and us Brights don't hold with 'un. It's breakin' the law, whatever pretty names they call it. Oh, I know your dad used to buy from them and I expect your ma will too – she'll want the tea, like as not. We shan't interfere. But we wouldn't like to see either of you makin' friends with that family, just the same.'

And who are you or your father or brother to tell us what to do? I'm not wearing your ring yet.

'Your glass is empty,' I said. 'What are you drinking? Mulled wine?'

'Yes, if you please. You talk like Mr Silcox,' said James restlessly as we moved towards the table. 'Learnt more from him than I did, I reckon. We Brights are plain farm folk.'

'So are us Shawes,' I said calmly, and dipped a glass of wine for him.

Other people came up to talk to me; in a few moments, I was once more separated from him and I let myself drift back to Ralph, who was still on the window seat.

'You'd best not hang round me too much just now,' he said, though with another of his beautiful smiles. 'I know the Brights don't hold with the Duggans. But Peggy, use your mourning as an excuse if you need to, but I beg you, settle nothing with James Bright that you went to school with until I have danced with you on May Day. I'll make excuses to ride out here a time or two before then. You see . . .' He was totally serious, almost pleading. 'When we first met today, I felt as though I'd always known you. I want, I need, to know you better. I felt – I feel – as though something extraordinary has happened.'

Perhaps it was not too soon after all. I opened my mouth to tell him that I felt the same, but once more we were interrupted, this time by Josiah Duggan. He was a big, heavy man, his dark hair and beard turning grey, and small broken veins in his nose signalling that he enjoyed his own illicit wares. Ralph had inherited his colouring, I thought, while Philip was a diluted Duggan, with mousy hair and light brown eyes.

Josiah looked down at me and said: 'This is a sad, sad day, Peggy Shawe, but I've got something for 'ee that'll maybe help. Step out into the front porch for a moment. Follow me out. Don't look as if you're with me.'

I stared at him in astonishment but Ralph gave me a nod, as much as to say, *Yes, go on, I know about it*, so I let Mr Duggan senior saunter away ahead of me and after a few moments, I followed as instructed.

A woman I hardly knew, the wife of a farmer from some distance, accosted me with condolences but I shook her off, murmuring that I badly need a breath of fresh air; the parlour had become so hot, what with so many people in it and such a roaring fire. Seconds later, I was in the porch, beside Josiah. He pushed the massive front door to behind us and drew a package from within his black jacket.

'Take this.' He thrust it into my hands. 'Let no one see, not even your mother. Open it in private and show it to no one. *No one.* It's heavy but I see you've a good big pocket in your skirt. Put it in there, take it straight upstairs and hide it till you're free to attend to it. Now I'll go back indoors. You wait a bit before you come back inside.'

Then he pushed the door open again and vanished through it. I was left clutching the package, which was in the form of a heavy leather drawstring bag. It was *very* heavy, astonishingly so. When I put it into my pocket, the pocket sagged and bulged, weighing my skirt down.

Puzzled, I once more waited for a little, then went quietly indoors, letting my right hand hang, casually, I hoped, over the burdened pocket. I went upstairs and straight to my room, where I pushed the package into my bed, well down under the covers. After that I went back to the parlour to re-join the throng.

Wondering.

I opened the package after I had gone to bed, and studied the contents by the light of a candle.

They consisted, at first sight, of two letters, one folded into the other, and of a second drawstring bag. This was what had given the package so much weight. I spread out the letters first. One, which had the words *Read this first* on the outside, bore the signature of Josiah Duggan. It bore a date nearly two years in the past, and it said:

> *My dear Peggy Shawe, your father asked me to write this for him as he's no hand with a pen. He dictated, I wrote. I tidied up his wording somewhat but left enough of how he really spoke and sounded, so it will seem to you as though it's him talking to you. I have kept all this secret as he wished, except that Ralph knows your father left something with me for you. I had to make sure someone could take the job on if I weren't there to. You never know what may chance to happen. I can trust Ralph and so can you. Please understand – here I repeat your father's request – KEEP WHAT'S IN THIS PACKAGE A SECRET. No one but you must know it exists. NO ONE. EVER. Or not until the need to use it should arrive. I herewith pass on your father's love and care for you. Josiah Duggan.*

Bewildered, I opened the second letter. It was in the same handwriting but it bore the signature of *Samuel Shawe.*

> *My dear little Peggy, I've allus wished I had a son but that don't mean I haven't loved you and worried for you, more than you've ever guessed, I fancy, for I've never been one for putting my heart where everyone can see it. But it seems to me that women can have a hard time in this world if things go amiss for them. You and your ma'll be safe enough while I'm here but things happen. You never know.*
>
> *I hope you'll be happy, my dear, and safe, married maybe to James Bright, as is a good young man if a bit over-virtuous, the which he gets from his father who won't buy as much as a keg of brandy for Christmas if it comes from free trading. But he'll make an honest husband, if you like him, only don't marry him if you find you can't like him enough. That's up to you. There'll be others! I've left your mother the farm and most of all I own, except there's a bit of money for you – official like. But I've been thinking, when you get wed, no matter who to, all you own becomes his and then if things ever go badly wrong, where might you be? That's a bad law, that is.*

Like I said, you never know. I'm getting on in years now and who can tell how long he'll live? I don't want to get caught out. When I go, I want to know you're protected. Since, under the law, if you are married, what's yours wouldn't be yours but his, I beg you to make sure he don't know of this and best make sure no one else knows of it either and to hell with the law.

I'm trusting Josiah Duggan with writing this and getting it to you if anything happens to me, because he don't worry too much about the law either and he'll see there's someone to take over from him. You hide this where you can always put your hand on it but no one else'll ever find it. It ain't for frittering; now you mind on that. I want you happy and safe, my wench. Your loving father, Samuel Shawe.

Blinking away tears, I at last tackled the heavy little bag. Inside it was yet another bag, linen this time, and tied together with string, very tightly. I realized why when with the help of my scissors I finally got it open. It had been fastened so securely in order to stop it from clinking.

It was full of coins, a mix of values. There were shillings, crowns and half-crowns, all squeezed together in yet another little linen bag. They were silver. But the rest was in gold: half-sovereigns, sovereigns, double sovereigns. I counted it and was astounded. The gold alone added up to two hundred pounds. No wonder it weighed so much.

Dancing in the Spring

There were no safe hidey-holes anywhere under our roof. Mrs Page in particular, took a real delight in turning out cupboards and no loose floorboard would ever escape her, either. If I were to hide the money as instructed, it would have to be somewhere outside.

But I knew of a place. We had an old barn, quite near the house. It was immensely sturdy, with stone walls a couple of feet thick, and stout oak doors, grey and dry with age but hard as iron. It was a useful place for storing things like farm equipment and fodder. My father had always seen that its thatch was regularly renewed.

I did not know just how old it was and nor did anyone else, but it was believed to date from the twelfth century. If so, one could assume that since it had withstood centuries of wind and rain (we have plenty of both on Exmoor), it was unlikely to fall down in the near future.

And it had a hidey-hole.

I had found it when I was a child of eight. I noticed one day that a stone at the outside of one corner seemed to be poking out. I pushed at it with inquisitive fingers and found that it was slightly loose. I wiggled it and it came away in my small hand, revealing quite a large cavity behind it.

I have often wondered how the cavity came to be there. Carelessness by some medieval builder long ago when the barn was first constructed? Or made deliberately at some time when someone – like myself just now – wanted somewhere to hide something? Anyway, I pushed the stone back, firmly, so that it no longer showed, but I made a little scratch on it with the edge of a trowel, to help me remember which it was. Later, I sometimes made use of the hidden space.

My father had had me educated but he was never too pleased to see me reading books at home; there was always what he called too much proper work to be done – hens to feed, shirts to be patched, pastry to make, a million things. Well, the Silcoxes used to lend their pupils books at times, and when I borrowed one, I sometimes put it in that cavity, wrapped in a piece of old towel or something like that, to keep it clean, and took it out to read whenever I could. I hadn't done that now for years, but I hadn't forgotten it. I thought the hole would be big enough, just.

I always rose early, anyway. This time, I made a special point of being the first downstairs, again carrying my heavy secret in my pocket. In the kitchen, I shifted it into an egg basket which had a lid to it. Then I went out, gave the poultry their breakfast, strolled round the barn to the corner I had in mind, which luckily couldn't be seen from the house, and crouched to fiddle with the well-remembered stone.

It resisted me at first; I hadn't touched it for a long time, and on the last occasion I must have thrust it home very firmly. It had settled and stuck. Making sure that I was unobserved, but keeping my basket jealously on my arm, I slipped round into the barn to find some kind of lever. I took down an old scythe that was hanging on the wall, went back, and applied the blade round the edges of the stone. It came away at last and yes, there was comfortable room for the leather drawstring bag with the letters and coins inside. I rammed it in and put back the stone, taking care that it shouldn't be noticeable, but could be pulled out if necessary. I understood what my father had meant about not frittering the money. This was for emergencies, and an emergency could demand speed.

From the very moment when there began to be talk of James and me, it had always irked me that if we married, then one day, in the nature of things, I would inherit Foxwell, only I wouldn't, because it would pass at once to James. Every single thing I owned would become his and he would be entitled to do what he would with it without even asking me. Resentment of that had lain, niggling, at the back of my mind. It must have niggled at my father's mind, as well. I was glad of this hidden hoard; a windbreak against the possible storms of life.

Oddly enough, I did not feel the same way about Ralph. His father had said that Ralph could be trusted. I believed him. If I married Ralph, I somehow I did not think that he would high-handedly claim his rights, snatch things away from me and never ask my opinion. And somewhere in my mind, a small, cautionary voice said: *But James might.*

I met Betty as I came out of the barn after returning the scythe to its hook. Her bright brown eyebrows went up. 'What be doin' in that old barn, Miss Shawe?'

She meant no harm, but she was just naturally inquisitive and also just naturally impertinent.

'Looking for the black hen,' I said. 'She's forever wandering off and laying eggs where she hopes we won't find them. I've found her in the barn before.'

That was a lie, but I hoped Betty wouldn't realize it. She, however, had noticed something else and pointed at it. 'Why, there's the black hen, there peckin' away at the grain like the rest!'

'So she is.' I expressed surprise. 'Well, she wasn't there a minute ago. Or else I'm going weak in the head.'

'And you with your dad just gone and the buryin' only yesterday. Not to be wondered at.' Impertinent and inquisitive she might be but she was also kind. 'You come indoors now and I'll make 'ee a nice cup of tea, and then you set down while I do breakfast. Have 'ee got eggs in that basket?'

'No, I was just about to start collecting them.'

'Let's both do it, then thy ma'll be down and I'll see to breakfast for both of 'ee. Fresh eggs and hot bacon, nothing like it.'

I remember the May Day dance on Exford Green vividly. The Brights came to join us first so that we could all go to Exford together, with James as my official escort. I recall that, encouraged by my mother, who insisted I leave off my black, I had bought some buttercup yellow material and green-gold trimming and made myself a new dress for the occasion, while she herself had progressed from black to lavender. It felt strange not to be in mourning any longer.

I can see the five of us gathered in the big square kitchen of Foxwell. It was a friendly place. I see the whitewood table laid for the late supper we had planned. I see the rows of pans hanging on one wall, and the massive old dresser laden with plates and cups on the opposite one. I see the hams hanging from the ceiling beams and, poignantly, Father's battered old basket chair by the hearth, padded with cushions for which Mother had knitted covers in red and blue, and Ned Bright sitting there instead of Father.

I see the deep brick fireplace and the fire with the trivet in place over it, ready to cook the supper stew. I remember that the evening was warm so that the fire made the kitchen very hot. I remember the Pages and Betty coming in to join us, and how the sweat dripped off plump Mrs Page's temples.

It was such beautiful weather.

Mother and I, along with Mrs Page and Betty, went in the trap, drawn by one of our sturdy Exmoor ponies. On this occasion it was our youngest gelding, Spots, called so because in some lights one could see shadowy dapples under his bay coat. We had the right to run some ponies on the moor and we always had three or four on the farm, bred from our own herd and trained by us from infancy. Bert Page was riding another of them. The Brights all preferred full-sized horses, but we liked the Exmoors best, since for all their small stature, they were immensely strong and as surefooted as tightrope walkers.

Exford's village green was – and is – a fine big one, with plenty of room for dancing, and where there were trees beside it they cast shadows across the grass, as though someone had been busy with a paint pot of a darker shade. By the time we arrived, a crowd had already gathered and we could hear the band tuning up.

It was many years ago and I don't now remember all the musicians. Whoever they were, the band still exists and some of their grandsons are the music-makers now. I can't recall who was playing the big drum, the flute or the cello but I do remember the mighty trombonist, Ezra Kent, the brawny Exford blacksmith, and I remember Peter Shearer, the lame lad whose widowed mother ran a haberdashery shop just beside the green. Peter couldn't dance but he played the fiddle superbly and was ably seconded by aged Mr Eastley, who had guarded my father's coffin while everyone else went a-hunting. There was a clarinet as well, skilfully handled by short, round, jolly Mr North, who, improbably, was the Exford undertaker. Mr North did gardening and house repairs as well, because, as he frequently said, with a merry chuckle, ours was a healthy community by and large and people didn't die often enough to keep him alive, let alone his wife and large brood of offspring. All of them had been at my father's funeral, and there were kindly smiles for me and my mother, welcoming us out of seclusion and back to the merry world.

We settled our horses and the trap beneath some trees, and went to join the throng. The tuning up finished. Mr North, who was also the master of ceremonies at the Exford dances, had stepped out on to the green and was bidding everyone welcome and announcing the first dance. Only the people nearest to him could hear what he was saying but we all knew it word for word, anyway, and when the band struck up, everyone recognized the tune and therefore, the dance.

And, of course, James Bright turned to me at once and said: 'Peggy! Want to dance? That's a pretty dress you're wearing!' and then seized my hand before I'd had time to answer and led me off. As we went, I saw his father and my mother, smiling fondly after us. None of them aware that I was looking round for the Duggans. And especially for Ralph.

I knew they would be there. I had seen Ralph three times since the funeral. Twice he had ridden over with his father to discuss what were tactfully called matters of business with my mother; once he came on his own to deliver some tea. Each time, we had managed to have some private talk, and on the last occasion, he had told me that his father would not object to our marriage. That was the first time the word *marriage* was mentioned between us, and it sent a frisson of joy down my spine, and yet it seemed as natural, as normal, as birdsong. He had added that if we married, the Duggans would help my mother out by paying for an extra hand or two to keep Foxwell in good order. He had also promised to see me at the dance.

My mother as yet knew nothing of all this and in fact had eyed Ralph askance and said to me, after the third visit: 'Why does the Duggan son keep turning up? I hope he hasn't got his eye on you, my girl. You're as good as settled with James

Bright. Farming families should marry into one another. The sea and the land don't mix.'

Now, as James and I took our places in the set, I wondered if I should have talked to my mother as Ralph clearly had to Josiah. Her idea had been that James should wait until I was out of mourning, but that was officially happening today. Here and now, in fact! What if James proposed to me at once, on this pleasant evening, in the middle of this very dance, before I'd had a chance to speak with Ralph?

'Thank the good Lord it's grand and sunny,' James said, as the dance began. 'Bit of luck, that. When it rains, the village hall's all right, but it's not the same as dancing on the grass, out in the sun.'

'No, I agree. The hall always seems so shadowy,' I said dutifully.

'Did your dad decide on sowin' wheat this year?' James asked. He had asked the same thing at last year's May Day dance. Once again, I said yes and told him which field. It was the same conversation, word for word. As we parted to revolve briefly, hand in hand, with other partners before returning to each other, I wondered if his next remark would be another enquiry about our wheat. It had been, last year.

It was.

'How do you fancy the crop's coming along?'

I found something new to say. 'Very well, and I just hope that stags won't get into it, the way they did last August. Father was very upset.'

'Aye, they're as big a nuisance as bad weather. Can't go after them with a gun, though; the hunt won't have it.'

'The wheat crop's important. Maybe we should go after the hunt with guns!'

'*What?*' said James in an outraged voice.

'I didn't mean it. I was making a joke.'

'Oh. I see,' said James, who obviously didn't. He had little sense of humour, I thought. The dance separated us again at that point, but a few moments later, when we were hand in hand once more, he began to talk about the trouble his mother had, keeping things cool in her dairy during hot weather. I said: 'I agree,' again.

Conversation with James was heavy going. It wasn't just that he said dull things; his voice was monotonous too. And then he said something that wasn't dull at all, but on the contrary was what I had been dreading.

'Peggy, now 'ee's wearing colours again – and that there dress is pretty; a proper picture, that's how 'ee looks – well, b'ain't it time we talked about marriage? I know your mother last year was still sayin' you were young yet and she didn't want to lose your help round the place, either, but time's goin' on and my father's been urgin' me on and I've had a hint or two from your mam too. She's got good sense and she knows it's time to let 'ee go. What do 'ee say?'

So here it was, as I had both expected and dreaded. Now what was I to do? At that moment I caught sight of Ralph, along with both his parents and his brother Philip; they had just arrived. I smiled at James, feeling sorry for him, knowing I was going to hurt him, trying to hold him off for just a little while, until I was sure, and knowing in my heart that I was sure already.

'It *is* time for us to talk, James, but not in the middle of a dance! This evening I just want to enjoy myself. Life has seemed so serious for so long. Today I just want to be a filly in a field, kicking up my heels and being gay and giddy.'

'I see,' said James. I heard the disappointment in his voice.

I was thankful when the dance ended and he led me back to the side of the green, where we found my mother and the Duggans together. Mother was talking animatedly to Mrs Duggan, who was Welsh-born and whose first name was Bronwen. We had met her on a few occasions. She had been on our side of the Bristol Channel for long enough to have lost much of her Welsh accent, but there was still a trace of lilt and an occasional Welsh turn of phrase to remind people.

Bronwen Duggan was dark-haired, dark-eyed, stocky and full of vitality, and had a lovely smile when she was happy but when we joined them on the green, she was clearly holding forth on something that displeased her. The dark eyes were flashing but the smile was not in evidence.

'Philip ought to take a stronger line, indeed he ought, if he wants to wed that Maisie Cutler, not that I'd worry if he picked someone else. She's as good-looking a lass as ever I saw, and healthy, but look at her now! She comes to the dance with Philip, and then poor Phil turns his back for half a minute to say good day to someone and up comes that Laurence Wheelwright that was hanging round her already when Phil met her, and off she goes to dance with him! And who is he, compared to Phil? That's what I'd like to know!'

'Attractive,' said Mr Duggan. 'And with ambitions he might well achieve. He's foreman now on that Aclands farm where he works and he's said to have a bit of money behind him. Don't care for him myself – pushy, I call him – but he's got a way with the wenches, and Maisie's fallen for it, by the looks of things.'

James was still beside me, ready to lead me out to the next set. I turned slightly away from him and with a show of interest, asked Mrs Duggan what Maisie looked like.

'Fair hair and big blue eyes and she's mighty proud of them,' said Bronwen forcefully. 'But not much sense, I'm sorry to say.'

'She's just young,' said Philip sharply, and then, as another dance was announced, swung away from us, grabbed a girl apparently at random, and departed into the set.

'Trouble is, Philip's wild for her, and now he's miserable,' said his mother crossly. 'Look at him now, dancing, yes, but with a face like a tombstone. All in the dismals, indeed he is, and all because of that little flirt. That's her, over there, and that's Laurence. They're not dancing now. Wooin', more likely. Look how he's got his arm round her!'

I looked. The couple in question had sat down on the grass beneath a tree. Maisie was indeed pretty, a buxom lass with a cloud of pale hair, as Bronwen had said, and a flawless complexion. I didn't greatly admire the supposedly attractive Laurence, though. He seemed to be a wiry type, not very tall, with untidy light-coloured hair. Though just now, he was being amused by something Maisie was saying and I saw that he had a pleasing, monkeyish smile and splendid teeth.

Ralph said: 'Peggy, would you like to dance? The set's just forming up.'

'Let's!' I said thankfully.

I took his hand. From the corner of my eye I saw James

turn abruptly away and I heard him inviting Bronwen Duggan. As I went on to the green with Ralph I caught sight of Ned and John Bright, frowning. And then we were in the dance, skipping to the music, and Ralph was saying: 'If you're still of the same mind, Peggy, my love, what if we announce our engagement when we get back to our parents? I keep being afraid that James Bright will get in before me.'

'He already has. I put him off,' I said.

'You . . . you mean it, then? It's you for me and me for you?'

'Yes, if you mean it too.' One, two, link hands with each other and the adjacent couple, and round in a circle we go. Briefly, we exchange partners. Then I was back with Ralph, who said: 'I've meant it since the moment I saw you, at your father's funeral, looking so sad. Lovely brown hair you have. Beechnut colour. I want to wake for the rest of my life to see that brown hair straying over my pillow.'

I laughed. 'It will turn grey one day. Will you like it so much then?'

'By then we'll be so much one person we won't notice things like that and I'll have turned grey too, anyway. If I haven't drowned at sea or been caught by the Revenue. You'll be marrying into a family that takes risks. You do understand that?'

'Yes. I understand.' I spoke soberly, knowing that he spoke the truth. But he was Ralph. We belonged together.

'I will marry you,' I said. 'I will . . . be like Juliet and follow you, my lord, throughout the world.'

We were going down the set, hands clasped and held high. His grip tightened. 'I will do all I can to make you happy and keep you safe. Peggy, sweetheart, let's get it settled. There won't be any trouble with my parents; I told you, my father is agreeable and my mother knows her boys will go their own way, anyhow!'

'My mother may not be so agreeable.'

'We'll talk her round.' The dance was ending. The set broke up. Hand in hand, we walked back to our families, who were still together in one group.

'Will she worry because you're marrying a free trader?' Ralph asked and then answered his own question. 'I suppose she might. She doesn't disapprove of free trading, though, does she?'

'I don't think so, no. The Brights do but I think Mother might just be anxious in case my husband got caught.'

'I worry more about my father than about me,' Ralph said. 'I'm afraid of *him* getting caught. I don't think he'd survive in prison, not at his age. What do *you* feel about us?'

'I just haven't thought about it much. But so many people seem to have a share in it, don't they? It seems odd that just importing goods and selling them can count as a crime.'

'It isn't a crime. The crime is the enormous duties the government charges. If the duties were more reasonable, free trading wouldn't be half as popular, though a lot of us would probably do it for the excitement. It's why we still bother to bring in tea, even though the government has actually reduced the duty on it. But some of the other duties are sheer extortion. Ruling folk never understand what ordinary people will put up with and what they won't. We're not wicked, my lass. Not Dad and me, anyhow. I wouldn't be so sure of some of the men in the trade, I grant you, but we Duggans have never murdered anyone or harmed any Customs man beyond a punch on the nose or a shove into the harbour once in a while. Well, here we are. Here they are.'

They were indeed. My mother, the Duggans and the Brights were all close to each other, watching us as we approached. 'I'm nervous,' I admitted.

'I dare say. Your mother won't like it at first and the Brights won't like it at all. We may have the devil to pay!' His hand tightened on mine. 'Don't worry. I'm here. Peggy, you are sure? Say it to me, darling. You are sure?'

'I am sure.'

I was. My future path lay before my feet. I would travel it with him and I could not even think of walking on through life in any other direction or any other company.

We were back with our families and friends. Ralph beamed at them. 'That was a lively dance, Father, Mrs Shawe. And now we have something to tell you. Peggy and I,' said Ralph, as easily and calmly as though he were commenting on the weather, 'had a little talk while we were dancing. We are happy to announce that we're engaged.'

Paying the Devil

There was the devil to pay, all right. It started with a triangular shouting match, then and there, between my mother, the Duggans and the Brights. James, his face red with humiliation and fury, and his eyes as hard and round as blue marbles, declared half a dozen times that I couldn't do this to him, no I couldn't, I was engaged to *him* and he'd not stand being jilted.

My mother cried and said I was a foolish girl and didn't know my own mind and didn't I know that James was the one for me and it had been understood for years, only she and my father had thought me too young for marriage and been too fond to let me go before they must. She then rounded on Josiah Duggan and demanded to know how he could let his son behave like this. Then, glaring at Ralph, she told him to go away, to leave her daughter alone. 'Don't you dare come near Foxwell or my Peggy again!'

Josiah Duggan looked amused, if anything. Bronwen Duggan shook her head at us but smiled, which caused Ned Bright to ask her what she thought was so funny. Philip Duggan, who had rejoined his family, attempted to say: 'If they're in love, what does it matter?' and was trounced in a furious chorus by James, Ned Bright, John Bright and my mother.

Ralph and I held on to each other, tight. People nearby were turning round and staring, and some of those who had made out what it was all about, were grinning.

Finally, Josiah Duggan somehow managed to convince the rest that this was not a subject for discussion under the trees round Exford Green in the midst of the May Day dance. Wouldn't it be best if we all met quietly at Foxwell tomorrow morning, and talked things over like sensible folk?

This was finally agreed, though not before Ned Bright had thrown a punch at Ralph and had it neatly parried. Ralph said: 'There, there,' whereupon, John and James caught hold of their father to stop him from further violence. They had noticed Exford's constable making his way towards us. The ugly scene broke up.

It was resumed, with vigour, at ten of the clock on the following morning.

John Bright didn't come ('It b'ain't rightly his business,' said his father grimly), but Ned Bright and James were there in good time, both glowering. A few minutes later, the Duggan family arrived in force. 'What's *he* doing here?' Ned demanded, on seeing Philip.

'We spent the night at the inn in Exford. We'll all go home together,' said Josiah mildly. 'Philip won't interfere.' The Brights scowled more than ever.

Then the business of the meeting began.

It was like a parody of a social occasion. We sat glumly in the parlour while Betty and Mrs Page, supervised by my mother, offered cider and tea, chicken and bacon pies and fresh baked scones, refreshments which were scorned by the Brights but partaken of cheerfully by the Duggans.

'Now, let's all be reasonable,' said Josiah. 'It seems we've two young folk here who've fallen suddenly in love and we all know what that's like. The days are gone by when parents arranged these things. It's for the youngsters themselves to decide, surely we all agree there.'

'The youngsters did decide, after listening to their elders first, and that's how it should be!' barked Ned Bright. 'And then your son – oh yes, he's good-looking – comes and pushes in and turns the wench's head. No, I don't blame 'ee, Peggy; you're too young to know your own best interests but . . .'

'That's what I say!' My mother had her handkerchief out and was dabbing her eyes. 'Peggy's not yet twenty-one and until she is she can't wed without I say so, and I *don't* say so, not unless it's to James like it ought to be!'

'When's your birthday, my lass?' Josiah enquired, turning to me.

'August the tenth,' I said.

'And what age would you be now?'

'I'm twenty!' I said defiantly. 'So I'll turn twenty-one this coming August and it's only a bit over three months away!'

'We can marry on the eleventh of August,' said Ralph calmly, stretching from his chair to mine to take my hand. 'And there's none can gainsay us.'

'I was goin' to ask 'ee at the dance, and you went on about wantin' to be fancy free for the evening and all the time . . . all the time . . .' James choked and stopped. I saw with distress that his eyes were wet.

'I know, James. I'm sorry. This . . . just happened.' I really was sorry. James is one of the people I hurt, and hurt badly, in the course of my life. Yes, I do regret it. But . . .

At the time, everything I did seemed inevitable.

Josiah tried to be a calming influence. 'In my view,' he said, 'James and Peggy here ought to talk to each other alone for a bit. The rest of us ought to go to the kitchen and let them stop here till they've done.'

Ralph's grip on my hand grew stronger. 'There's nothing Peggy needs to say. It's all been said.'

'No, Ralph.' Bronwen was firm. 'She do owe James a word or two. They should talk. My husband's right.'

'It's all right,' I said to Ralph. 'Don't worry. I do need to say sorry − in private, as it were.'

Everyone got up except James and myself. Ralph was reluctant and looked at me anxiously but he went out with the rest. I looked at James.

'How could 'ee, Peggy?' he said. 'How *could* 'ee treat me like this? All the years we've known each other . . . I've had hopes, ever since I wur a boy at school with 'ee . . . how could 'ee hurt me like this?'

The anger and injured pride had gone, to be replaced by bewilderment and pain. 'I'm so sorry,' I said miserably. 'I'm so sorry. But I *can't* marry you, James. I . . . would you want me to, would you really want me to stand beside you at the altar and take those vows and all the time be wishing you were somebody else? That's how it would be.'

'Not for long, I promise 'ee. You'd forget soon enough. We're well suited; you know we are. What would 'ee do in a boatbuilder's family, and they're what they call free traders, too! You shouldn't be mixed up with the likes of they . . .'

'James, please . . .'

'I'd be coming to Foxwell to live. There'd be little ones to
bring up and we'd always be busy, working together here,
there's a heap of things I can think of to do. Look at that herd
of Red Devon's 'ee's got – fine animals but your bull's gettin' on,
and Bert Page thinks he knows where we can get a young
one, ready for work in a couple of years, if they Quartly
brothers over Molland way, will just let go of that half-grown
calf they're so wild about. You heard us talking about it, at
the funeral. Look, love, bemused 'ee've been, well, it happens,
but think ahead, think of the future, think about they Red
Devons . . .'

It was so exactly like James to go on about improving a
herd of cattle, when the real subject under discussion was his
own marriage. His mind was for ever trapped in the practical.
I had hardly ever heard him laugh, in all the time I'd known
him. He was so dull, I thought, that I could not now imagine
how I had ever thought I could marry him. I hadn't realized,
not until I looked into Ralph's eyes, just how tedious a lifetime
with James Bright would be. And now, he had made it clear,
by accident but quite definitely, that he had already been
thinking of Foxwell as his.

'I'm sorry, James. I can't. It's Ralph for me now. I'm sorry,
sorry, sorry. But there's many a fine young woman on many
a farm on the moor; you'll find someone else and soon you
won't even remember me. It'll work out well in the end.'

'Peggy . . .'

'No, James. No, please, don't say any more. Please.'

'All right,' said James, now much on his dignity. 'I've seen
a ring in Minehead. Just one diamond, but it was pretty. Still,
I dare say a family of free traders can manage a whole circlet
of them.'

'James, don't! I'm not like that. You know I'm not like that.'

He got up and came over to me, looming over me as I sat
in my chair, and reached out as if to pull me up into his arms.
I held myself away and said: 'No, James, please. It won't do
any good.'

Anger flickered in his eyes then; for a few seconds I was
almost afraid of him. Then his face softened and he stepped
back.

'All right. Sorry. Listen, Peggy, I'm here. If things don't turn out right . . . if you change your mind . . . I'm still here, though it's goodbye just for now.'

He went out of the room. I sat on, trying not to cry. Ralph mustn't see me crying because of James.

In fact, as my mother told me afterwards, they all stayed on in the kitchen for a while in case I needed to do a bit of weeping. 'I told them it would be natural; you're not heartless,' she said to me. 'Just a pity you're senseless instead!'

When they did come back, it turned out that they too had done some talking together. Bronwen Duggan, who had much of the peacemaker in her mentality, had suggested that I should spend a month staying with the Duggans in Minehead, to see how well I would adapt to life there, and to give Ralph and me a chance to get to know each other a good deal better than we did now. My mother now replied to this and her answer startled both Bronwen and me.

'Make it six weeks,' Mother said grimly. Her usually gentle features had hardened. 'Six weeks, from the end of May. The two of them had better not see each other for a month; let them cool off. But if they're still of the same mind then, Peggy shall come to you at the start of June and stay till halfway through July. Let her find out, thoroughly, what it'll be like, livin' in a world that b'ain't hers. Farming folk and seafaring folk don't mix, never have mixed, can't ever mix. They'm different worlds. She'll want to come home before the six weeks are out, mark my words, but *don't you let her*. Let her find out the hard way that your life b'ain't right for her. I want her *pleading* to come home.'

We stared at her and she stared at me. 'But if you don't change your mind, then come home in July and we'll start seein' to your brideclothes and you'll be married from here and that'll be it. I'll do right by 'ee, never fear.'

I said nothing, but I was thinking. *I need only wait till May is out and then, for six wonderful weeks, I shall see Ralph every day.*

It was settled. The Brights, sullen and still scowling, took themselves off. I was bound to have a lot of baggage for a six-week stay, Josiah said. When the time came, I should travel by

sea. He and Ralph would meet us at Porlock, the nearest port
to us, and they'd get there in their own small boat.

'We've a fine little boat,' he told us, 'and if we call it the
Bucket that's just our fun. We'll sail you back to Minehead.
You can shift your things by trap to Porlock; it's no more than
a few miles. And you can start getting used to the idea of
marrying into a seafaring family!' he added.

And from Minehead, Ralph would take me to Taunton,
where the shops were better than in Minehead, and he would
buy me a ring.

The Duggans' boatyard was familiar to me. Father used to
take us all to Minehead once in a while. We would have an
overnight stay at an inn, and at some point during the visit
we usually called on the Duggans. Josiah wasn't always there,
but we would take tea with Bronwen, in their tall house just
beside the yard. To my life's end, I will remember that mingling
of hammering from the yard with the cry of the seagulls that
whirled and called overhead, and the smell of seaweed from
the harbour.

Minehead was small but it was growing. It wouldn't be long
before it did have shops to rival Taunton's, and when the tide
was out, it had beautiful sands where, as a little girl, I sometimes
enjoyed a scamper.

There was plenty of room for scampering, for the Bristol
Channel tides went out a long way; at their lowest point,
getting to the edge of the sea felt like setting out to walk to
Wales. The town was overlooked by a towering headland called
North Hill, and the boatyard lay just below it, between the
foot of the hill and the harbour, which had a curving quay
like a beckoning forefinger, and offered a protected mooring
place for the fishing fleet that plied out of it.

In those days, we always rode, sometimes taking the route
down the Avill valley, through the villages of Wheddon Cross,
Timberscombe and Dunster and then turning south-west for
the last two miles to go through little Alcombe hamlet just
outside Minehead. On other occasions, given pleasant weather,
we took a track that went over Grabbist, the hill overlooking
Dunster, and led down into Alcombe. But when I went to

make my stay with the Duggans, things were different. Mother and I went to Porlock in the trap with my trunk and we met the Duggans there: Josiah, Ralph and Bronwen.

'So here we are,' Bronwen said. 'To welcome my future daughter-in-law. I'm glad the weather's calm. I'm no sailor.'

'It's too calm!' said her husband. 'Sailing to Porlock with hardly enough wind to tack against took half a century and it won't be much better going back even with the wind behind us. We started at dawn!'

Ralph and I took little notice of all this. We were embracing. We hadn't seen each other for a month.

I said goodbye to Mother at Porlock and she cried a bit, even though I'd be coming home again in July. The journey to Minehead by sea was all new to me and I sat in the *Bucket*, looking about me, fascinated. Across the channel, Wales was visible, rather too clearly, as too much clarity probably meant rain before long. I had seen views across the channel often enough before, however; what I watched with so much interest was the coast of Somerset sliding by, the towering cliffs with the surf breaking on the rocks below, the clouds of seabirds that had nests on the ledges, and the dark, inaccessible cave-mouths here and there.

We heard the sound of hammering even before we were properly round the end of the quay. 'We're busy,' Josiah told me, 'now that we're at war with France. We have space enough to assemble small warships. I trained, and Ralph here did the same, in big shipyards up north. This very week, I've landed orders for two brig sloops to help fight Napoleon off if he gets any ideas. They'll be valuable, in a war. Small, swift vessels, they're to be – that can sting like wasps and get out of the way fast.'

I nodded. We got the news regularly in Exford. After his sermon, the vicar usually told us something about events in the world outside. I knew quite a lot about Napoleon Bonaparte.

According to the vicar, Napoleon was a Corsican who had risen to prominence during the Revolution that had shaken France so horribly eleven years ago, and now called himself First Consul of France, and clearly had ambitions to become a man of power. He didn't seem to like Britain. He had lately been to Egypt, where he had tried to form an alliance with a potentate with the object apparently of interfering with England's trade route to India.

Having failed in this attempt, he had come home to turn himself into this First Consul, whatever that might be, and promptly led an army through the Alps to Italy, where an area formerly under French control had lately been seized by Austria. He was determined to get it back and by the sound of it, was succeeding.

'There's trouble coming and it's not too far away,' Josiah Duggan remarked as he secured the *Bucket* to her mooring. 'That man's had his eye on England since he set off for Egypt with harming our trade in mind. He means business. Pity an asp didn't get him.'

'What's an asp?' Ralph enquired, as he helped me out of the boat on to the foot of some steep stone steps.

'It's a poisonous snake,' I said. 'Mr Silcox, my schoolteacher, told us about it. Cleopatra used one to kill herself, when she knew she and Antony had been defeated, and she'd be taken to Rome and made to march in a Triumph, and maybe executed.'

'There, Ralph. There's more to education than how to lay a keel, as I've told you often enough before,' said Bronwen, laughing.

'Not fair,' said Ralph. 'I've had an education too. Careful of those steps, my love. Tide's going down and it's left some slippery weed on them. My schoolmaster did tell us about Cleopatra and said that she killed herself; he just didn't say how. Sounds nasty. A snake! Ugh! Give me your hand, Peggy. I'll see you don't slip.'

The Duggans' house was completely different from Foxwell's farmhouse. Foxwell was long, low and rambling, though very strongly built, with walls that in places were three feet thick, stout stairs and beams of solid oak. The oak, said to have come from ancient ships, had been hardened in sea water to the strength of steel. By contrast, the Duggans' house was tall and narrow, with four storeys as well as a cellar, which had steps down from the kitchen, and an outside hatch as well, leading to a chute. It had a slightly rickety air. The stairs were narrow; the timber of doors and window frames creaked loudly in every gale.

It had a lovely parlour, though. I had always enjoyed taking tea there. Our parlour was frankly uninspiring and rarely used but Bronwen's furniture was always polished, and there was a tall clock with a deep tick, bright covers for its comfortable array of chairs and sofas, and pretty ornaments on the mantel-piece – two silver candlesticks, a little horse in white china, and a silver snuffbox with a lid patterned in silver and red enamel. Bronwen called it cloisonné-work.

None of the Duggans used snuff but she had bought this, she said, because she liked it. The house had a small flower garden behind it and Bronwen kept vases of flowers about the house, something else that didn't appear at Foxwell.

One thing that I did find difficult to get used to, though, was the noise. The adjacent boatyard was never quiet during the day, except on Sundays. There was always that sound of hammering and sawing and men calling to each other. I would have to accustom myself, I supposed, and wondered how long this would take.

At supper on my first evening there, I learned a few more things about the family I now expected to join. There were three maidservants but they did not live in. They were the daughters of fishermen from the cottages by the quay and slept at home. I realized later that this was deliberately planned.

Philip was there but soon would not be. For the moment, he was helping in the boatyard, but was candid about the fact that he didn't like the work, was happy for Ralph to be its heir, and intended very shortly to join his Great-Uncle Stephen, who had a farm, Standing Stone, out on the moor, and begin learning the work of agriculture.

I knew of Standing Stone, which was not so far from Foxwell, but I had never been there. It was a hill farm, perched high, which on Exmoor was apt to mean thin soil and poor productiveness, and on a ridge behind its farmhouse there was one of the single standing stones that are found here and there on the moor, set there by some long-ago people for reasons now unknown. It was eight feet high, with a slight list towards

the south. Mr Silcox had once told his class that it might well
have been a primitive signpost used by those long-departed
peoples.

That was all I knew about it. I had never seen Stephen
Duggan and all I knew of him was that he was in late middle
age, and was reclusive. He didn't attend the gatherings that
drew people together from neighbouring farms, to celebrate
weddings or christenings or Christmas, or to show their respects
at funerals. He worked the land with a few farmhands, who
did his marketing for him. They turned up now and then at
inns in various villages and if at Foxwell we ever had any news
of Mr Duggan of Standing Stone, it came through them. There
hardly ever was any news, anyway. But I now learned that
once in a while, Josiah Duggan and Philip would visit him,
and that Philip intended to join him there this year.

In my first week with the Duggans, I accompanied Josiah
and Philip on one of their visits. 'You'd best get to know your
prospective new relatives,' Josiah said jovially. We were quite
pleasantly greeted; Stephen Duggan had help in the house from
some of his farm workers' wives, and we were entertained to
a good dinner. He looked very elderly, being mostly bald, with
gaps in his brownish teeth and a beard in which grey and
brown hairs were mingled. He smiled amiably enough though
not prettily, owing to the teeth.

On the ride home, Philip and his father revealed to me things
concerning Standing Stone, that I hadn't known before.

'That Laurence Wheelwright, that's after my Maisie, worked
there once,' Philip said. 'It's just as well he moved on to that
place near Timberscome. I couldn't go to Standing Stone if he
was there.'

'Thank heaven for that,' Josiah said. 'If you're set on farming,
Philip, Standing Stone could turn out to be a good thing for
you, since Great-Uncle Stephen happens to be a childless
widower. My poor uncle had no luck with his children. None
of them lived past twenty. It's a cruel world sometimes.
Anyhow, I hope the end will be that you're provided for,
Philip. Not what I'd choose myself, but if you really want to
plod about before dawn, in the mud, milking cows, that's your
business. Though we could do with an extra pair of hands in

the boatyard now there's all this extra work to be done, building vessels for war. If you were to change your mind, now . . .'

'You can hire better hands than mine for the work and as for milking cows and mud, that's no worse than sailing all night and getting wet through when it's rough and the sea's crashing aboard, and it's no worse either than risks with the law,' said Philip, somewhat sullenly.

Josiah, though, seemed unable to resist making a dig or two at this strange son of his who preferred milking cows to laying keels and free trading. 'I'd like to feel you really are provided for, Phil, as I fancy you'll want to get wed before long. How near are you and Maisie now to settling things?'

'Not yet. Not quite,' said Philip and his face became even more sullen, though he made himself brighten it and added: 'I think she's a bit too young, not eighteen till autumn. Best let it be for a while.'

'She's a flighty piece,' said his father candidly. 'I've heard she's still being seen around with Laurence Wheelwright.'

'Where did you get that from?' snapped Philip.

'Two days back, your mother met Mrs Spears that Maisie works for at that Avill place near Dunster. According to her, Laurence collected Maisie on her afternoon out last week.'

'*What!* She told me she couldn't meet me last week because she was visiting her parents!' Philip almost shouted it.

'Let be, let be.' Josiah, having troubled the waters himself, now strove to pour oil on them. 'The girl's young, like you say. It's a pity Standing Stone isn't nearer to Dunster, though.'

'I'll see Maisie soon,' said Philip, quite menacingly. 'And I'll have a word or two to say to her!'

'Careful! Don't make the girl resent you,' said Josiah. 'Make her think you're better company than that Laurence. Now, here's a nice stretch of track. Let's get a move on, and canter.'

As time went on, I learned the ways of the house, the times of meals, the ins and outs of the kitchen, the kind of food preferred and how it was prepared. Friends came to dine now and then. I particularly liked Harriet and Edmund Baker, a brother and sister who lodged in a fisher family's cottage quite nearby. Harriet taught in a small school in Minehead while Edmund was a curate working at St Michael's Church, up on the side of North Hill. They were such a frank and open pair. Edmund was a pleasant-looking young man, but Harriet was almost a beauty, shapely, graceful in her movements, neither too short nor too tall, with lovely chestnut hair and eyes to match. She also had the good complexion so typical of our west country, where the damp air is kind to our skins. Ralph warned me, though, never to mention free trading when the household had outside company. 'One never knows, and though he's never said so, I don't think Edmund cares for our – *other* way of earning a living. In that case, Harriet may not care for it, either.'

I noticed also that there was something that Mr and Mrs Duggan didn't care for, and that was leaving me and Ralph alone together. Perhaps they were wise, since whenever we did have a few private minutes, we were apt to slide into each other's arms. However, they did once or twice let Ralph take me out for a sail in the *Bucket*. Whichever of them saw us off always said, *Mind you behave yourself, Ralph*. Ralph taught me how to row a gig out to the *Bucket* when she was anchored in the midst of the harbour, and I learned a little, too, about managing her sails.

He took me out into the channel and he told me the names of the two islands that jutted from the water to the north-east. Flatholm was, appropriately, the flatter one, Steepholm the one that rose from the sea like the back of a gigantic whale. On another of these expeditions, we went along the coast, right back to Porlock, and he pointed out the remains of an old land-slide from the cliffs, which had blocked what he said had once been a most useful path for free traders, since it slanted up, right to the top of a cliff, from a cave which was above sea-level and at low tide had a small sandy cove below it. 'Until – before I was born, it was – a chunk fell off the cliff in a storm and dumped a great big boulder on the path and made it useless!' said Ralph.

Ralph was an interesting talker. He told me about his time in the north, where the people and the accent and what he called the atmosphere were so different from ours that the north of England sometimes seemed like a foreign land. He really had been well educated, even if he didn't recall how

Cleopatra had killed herself. Apparently, he hadn't read that particular play but he could recite long quotes from other works of Shakespeare, as well as knowing the names of many stars and constellations, too. Conversation with Ralph was never dull.

Sometimes I wondered how we would ever endure the waiting until our marriage in August or how I would bear being separated from him in July. But at least, for the moment, we were together. It was a time, I remember, of enhanced awareness of everything about me. Ralph's nearness was like a magnifying glass, making every experience bigger, stronger, more full of meaning. The sun was brighter, the smell of the sea more invigorating; the seagulls whiter, their cries more wild and passionate. When a gale arose, the wind was like a living thing that wailed while it shook the house. Every one of my senses was wide awake, showing me the world in a detail and clarity I had never known before.

At the end of my first two weeks, there came a night when Ralph and his father were out of the house from evening until daybreak. I saw them go out after supper. They had not said where they were going, and Bronwen behaved as though she hadn't noticed their disappearance.

In the night, I was wakened by sounds outside, and looked from my window to see shadowy figures moving about below. I opened my window a little and heard men speaking to each other in low tones, though I recognized a voice or two and picked out a few names.

I recognized the name Barney; that must be a fisherman called Barney Oates whom I now knew by sight, a slow-moving, slow-spoken man with a grizzled beard. I also heard Josiah addressing someone as Luke, and briefly glimpsed a silhouette I thought I knew. I had seen Josiah talking to him on the quay; a lean, bleached man with a harsh face. Ralph, who was with me on that occasion, had said it was someone called Luke Hatherton, adding that he and Josiah were friends but that he personally didn't care for Luke, or for his son Roger, who was just a younger version of him.

'They're a ruthless pair and not to be crossed,' Ralph had said, and I remembered how once he had remarked to me that though the Duggans had never done serious harm to the Customs officers, there were some among the smugglers who might – or possibly, had.

Leaning on my sill, intent on what was happening below, I heard another name spoken. Someone called Daniel was being told to fetch something or other over here. I caught a reply in a young man's light voice, though I couldn't make out any words. Whoever Daniel was, he sounded nervous.

Then I withdrew, feeling somehow that I shouldn't be listening, or watching, either. But as I closed the window, I heard a familiar sound. It was the noise the cellar hatch made when it was raised, and it was followed by a rumble which was not quite the same as the rumble of a coal supply being tumbled down the chute.

Josiah and Ralph were at breakfast the next morning, dressed in the breeches and old shirts and salt-stained leather coats they wore for sailing, and looking tired. Again, Bronwen made no comment.

Nor did I. It had dawned on me in the night why the Duggans didn't want maidservants sleeping in the house. I was glad that Ralph had taken me to Taunton to buy my engagement ring. I knew that my beautiful South Sea pearl was not smuggled goods. I was glad of that.

Life with the Duggans was not confined. They kept several horses in a small stable yard on the other side of the house from the boatyard – so that the noise wouldn't disturb them too much, Josiah told me. Bronwen, who had grown up on a Welsh farm, rode well. Sometimes we rode out together. She showed me a track up North Hill that led out on to a path along the crest of the coastal hills.

This led to a steep dip into Porlock, and over to our right, poised upon the cliff, was a high point known as Selworthy Beacon. 'There'll be one there ready to light if the Frenchies look like invading,' Bronwen said.

We never went on to Porlock but would turn then and ride back. Up there, the sky seemed very big and the surrounding valleys very deep, and all around was the same moorland heath that encircled Foxwell, with its stretches of heather and pale gold moor grass, patches of bracken and clumps of gorse. I did miss the open moors round Foxwell. To find moorland within reach was welcome news to me.

My first two weeks with the Duggans were very happy. Until that warm and sunny June morning, when things began to change.

Kingfisher

That was the day when, over breakfast, Josiah remarked that he had business in Dunster with one of the Luttrells' foresters. I was interested, since the Luttrells owned the castle at Dunster and were among the most important folk in the county, though the village itself was a poorer place since the sea receded and Dunster was no longer a port.

'The Luttrells have been felling some pine trees,' Josiah said. 'Nothing like a good straight pine to make a good straight mast. Best trees of all grow in deep valleys. They reach upwards to the light, a hundred and fifty feet tall, sometimes. Well, these are pines like that. I fancy doing a deal. The Chief Forester's got authority to fix sales. Jim Sadler, that's his name. Lives in Dunster, two doors from the Luttrell Arms. Fancy riding out there today to see him, Ralph? I've too much on hand and it's a dead nuisance, losing Philip.' Philip had left three days ago to begin his new life with his Great-Uncle Stephen at Standing Stone.

'I've told Sadler,' said Josiah, 'that one of us would call on him today and he said that he would wait at his house, it being a matter of business. Take Peggy along. Let her see our business in action.'

It looked like a pleasant expedition. Ralph took the horse his father usually used, a big flea-bitten grey called Flecks, while I rode the gentle chestnut mare, Tansy, Bronwen's favourite. 'I don't need her today,' she said. 'You take her and welcome.'

The ride was only a little more than a couple of miles and we took it easily, trotting mostly through a lane shadowed by trees. The weather was sunlit and breezy, and at first there weren't too many flies. It was growing hot, however, by the time we reached the village, and Ralph got ciders for us at the inn, the Luttrell Arms. There was a tethering rail for our horses and we could drink our ciders inside, in the cool.

After that, we left Tansy and Flecks where they were and strolled along the street. I noticed with regret that the cobbles

were in need of attention, and that there was weather damage
to the roof of the yarn market that was built over a hundred
years ago and where my mother and I had sometimes bought
yarn for our knitting. It's circular, with a counter running
all the way round it, and the roof is there to protect the yarn,
the sellers and the customers alike from rain. Mr Silcox had
told his pupils about it. He said that there was probably no
other just like it in the country. I thought this interesting, and
wished the market was being better cared for. It was as though
bygone times still existed, all around us, preserved in the things
our ancestors had built. I wonder, sometimes, whether the
people who put up the standing stone on Stephen Duggan's
land were our ancestors too, even though they lived so very
long ago.

But the whole village had a neglected air. The cottages
were well-built, mostly dating back centuries, but many of
them were now in need of repair. Dunster has become more
prosperous nowadays and all those repairs have been done. I
am glad of it. However, even then, the Sadler cottage was
decently maintained and we found Mr Sadler at home and
waiting for us with his wife. We all sat in the little parlour
and listened while Ralph and Mr Sadler, a brown, burly man
who actually smelt of timber, haggled over quantities and prices,
Ralph insisting that if the Duggans placed a big enough order,
a discount was customary, and Mr Sadler disagreeing with
Ralph's interpretation of the words *big enough*.

The haggling, I thought as I listened, was as much a pastime
as serious business. The two of them were enjoying themselves.
They reached agreement at last, and we accepted cups of tea
and then returned to the cobbled street.

Ralph said: 'If we walk through the village to the other end
and turn left down a little lane towards the old mill, we'll
come to the Avill River. There's a medieval packhorse bridge
there, built for the times when merchants came here to buy
wool and took it away on packhorse trains. The wool industry
isn't what it was. But the bridge is a pretty spot. Shall we take
a look?'

We strolled companionably through the village and turned
into the lane. It ran alongside a swift, narrow stream that Ralph

said was the leat that powered the local watermill and then turned again, to come to the main river and step on to the bridge.

I hadn't seen it before. It was a peaceful place. Upstream of the bridge, the river ran smoothly under the shadow of over-hanging trees but downstream, the current was strong at first on the left, but to the right there was a pool where trout lurked, making rings on the water now and then as they surfaced. A yard or two further on, the river widened into a ford and the current slackened. The brown-tinged, peaty water glinted in the sunshine. After the ford, the stream narrowed again and flowed away round the foot of the castle hill and out of sight.

The bridge itself was of solid grey stone and it was narrow and high-sided. Wheeled traffic and people on horseback mostly used the ford. We stood, resting our hands on the coping of the downstream side, and looked at the pools and the current, and then turned to look upstream, where the water was inky in the shadows.

'My love,' said Ralph suddenly. And kissed me.

It was the first time. Hitherto, we had held hands, and embraced, but never as yet had he pressed his mouth on mine and . . .

It was extraordinary. The sense of companionship and friend-liness was still there, but now it became like an underground stream, while above it . . .

For the first time I was fully aware of Ralph's body, of his physical being, of his warmth and strength and his need, and aware too of my own need, which came on me from nowhere, astonishing me by its force. I had never known such a feeling before though I knew at once what it was. I wanted him as much as he wanted me. I wanted union with him, completion, the blending of our two bodies into one. My arms slid round him and just as his kiss seemed to be ending, I responded to it in a way that made it start again.

When at last we broke apart, I felt strange, almost shy, as if he, or I, or both of us, had just turned into other people. I wanted to say something but didn't know what. Ralph's eyes were smiling. If he had suggested, then and there, that we lay down on the bridge and made love forthwith, I would have done so willingly.

He didn't, of course, suggest any such thing. He just stood smiling at me and then, something like a brilliant blue arrow plunged from the trees to the water, reappearing a moment later and revealing itself for an instant of time as a kingfisher, with a little fish in its beak. There was another blue flash, hurtling upwards this time, and the beautiful thing was gone, and a tiny fish which, a moment ago, had been happily flicking its tail as it swam through the waters of the Avill had been snatched to its death without warning.

I remembered that, later.

'We'd better go back,' Ralph said, and took my hand. As we strolled back off the bridge and started for the village, he added: 'I wish we could bring our wedding day forward. Shall we try and talk your mother round – or get my dad to talk to her?'

'I don't think it would be much use,' I said doubtfully. 'She . . . she does feel strongly. It isn't so *very* long now. Just till August.'

August. Only a couple of months away. A couple of centuries. Two thousand years.

'We'll have to live with my parents at first,' Ralph was saying, 'but I think we should have a home of our own as soon as we can. Somewhere near the boatyard, of course. If one of those cottages by the quay should come vacant, that might make a start for us, though we'll probably want something still bigger and better before long – at least, I hope we will.'

Of course we would! Children! I felt myself blushing and Ralph saw it, and laughed.

A few minutes later, we were back in the main street and nearing the yarn market. Then we saw that something unusual was afoot.

The first thing I actually noticed was the horse that was tethered to one of the uprights of the market. I recognized it because it was distinctive. It was a dapple grey and it had an extraordinary shape. To create it, an Arab stallion had assuredly got together with a carthorse mare. This horse had a solid body and a thick, heavy neck and on the end of the thick

neck was unmistakeably the delicate dish face of the Arabian
breed, lustrous eyed and with a skin so fine that at close quarters
one could see the network of veins below. I knew it because
it belonged to Mr Silcox. Then I saw Mr Silcox himself. He
was standing foremost of a crowd of people, his silvered head
visible above the people in between us. The crowd had gathered in front of a cottage, a few doors away from the inn, and
Mr Silcox was talking to a couple on the cottage doorstep.

'Something's happening,' said Ralph, and we quickened our
pace. 'We'd better find out what. I'm not mistaken, that's the
cottage where Maisie Cutler's parents live.'

Mr Silcox caught sight of us as we approached, and called
to us. We joined him and the crowd let us through. It seemed to
consist of people drawn together by the signs of disaster. The
forester and his wife were there, their faces full of concern,
and so was the manager of the Luttrell Arms, and four or five
anxious-looking housewives with shopping baskets. The couple
on the doorstep were presumably Mr and Mrs Cutler. He was
a square-built fellow in the garb of a labourer; she was a plump
woman like an older version of Maisie. Both looked distressed;
Mrs Cutler, indeed, was crying. When they saw Ralph, whom
they evidently knew, they called to him and he called back.
We came to a stop beside Mr Silcox.

'What's happened?' Ralph asked, outright.

'It's Maisie, their daughter,' said Mr Silcox. 'I've just heard.
I rode in to Dunster about other business, but when I saw there
was trouble at this house, I came to see what was wrong. I had
Ernie Cutler in my class long ago, didn't I, Ernie?'

'Best man at my wedding, you were,' said Mr Cutler.
'As for what's happened now, Ralph, it's Maisie! Our girl! She's
disappeared.'

'She were to come and see us yesterday,' said Mrs Cutler
tearfully. 'But she never. She's never done that afore and not
let us know. She'd always find someone to bring word if she'd
said she'd visit and then couldn't.'

'Yes, and once she pretended she'd promised to see us, as
an excuse to put your brother off, Ralph, so as she could walk
out with that Wheelwright man we don't like!' barked Mr
Cutler. 'But she didn't make any false promises to us – only

to Philip. Oh, she told us about it! Little minx! She laughed. I said to her, no good'll come of all thy flirting . . . but this time she really was coming to us. She'd never play games with *us* . . .'

His voice trailed away.

'She'm only seventeen!' wailed his wife. 'What's a girl to do, when all she wants is a bit of harmless fun, and the fellows will get so earnest and solemn? But Ernie's right; she never let *us* down, never. She promised to come yesterday and we waited all day and no word and no Maisie, and this mornin' . . . this mornin' I got up and walked all the way to the Avill Smallholding to find her and ask what had gone wrong and . . . and . . .'

She dissolved into tears again. Mr Silcox said sombrely: 'She meant to come to Dunster to her parents. She told her fellow servants so. She set off. She never arrived. She's vanished off the face of the earth.'

Inquest

The Cutlers had apparently just returned from their fruitless visit to Avill smallholding and had been asking their neighbours if anyone had seen Maisie, which accounted for the way the news had spread and the crowd had collected. Someone had meanwhile sent for the local constable, who at this point arrived to take charge. He declared that a search must be organized and Ralph said that he must stay and join in. I must ride straight back to Minehead to tell his parents and ask them to send word to Philip.

The constable was already sorting his volunteers into groups to search various areas. I made haste to untie Tansy, and get on to her back. As I left, I heard someone consoling Mrs Cutler, saying that it would be all right, she'd be found; maybe she'd been out somewhere and had an accident, but it was dry last night; she very likely hadn't come to much harm. I hoped that this was the answer, but an uneasiness deep inside me said that it was not. Philip was going to be badly upset, I thought.

When I got back to Minehead and told my tale, Josiah set off at once for Standing Stone. After that Bronwen and I endured a weary day without news, until the evening, when Josiah and Ralph returned. They had been with search parties in different areas and had finally met in the Luttrell Arms ('Where else,' said Bronwen, 'and what of us, all awaiting news at home?') where the searchers got together when at dusk the task was called off. Josiah told us that Philip had thrown a saddle on one of his uncle's ponies and rushed away to join the hunt, and that Stephen Duggan, though grumbling at the loss of working time had nevertheless summoned his farmhands and arranged a search of his land and its immediate surroundings.

'But nothing's been found. Not a sign of her,' Josiah said wearily, sinking into an armchair in the parlour. 'And when Philip got to Dunster and was looking for someone to tell him where he could be most useful, the constable pounced on him and marched him into a back room at the inn and questioned him! It seems that that fellow Laurence Wheelwright was questioned too, since they were rivals and she was a silly girl, the sort that plays with fire.'

'But Philip would never . . .!' Bronwen left the end of the sentence in the air.

'Let's not pretend,' said Josiah wearily. 'There's no knowing what passionate young men will do if they're stirred up enough! What do you say, Ralph?'

'I can't believe it of Philip. He's my brother! I know him! I'd put my money on that Wheelwright fellow.'

'It seems that Wheelwright can account for himself while Philip can't,' Josiah said. 'I gather that the day the girl vanished, Philip was out nearly all day, on a pony, moving sheep from one Standing Stone pasture to another. On his own. All there was on his side was the fact that the sheep had been moved all right and Uncle Stephen would confirm it. No one has said he was seen near Dunster or anything like that, but he could have been there. Poor lad thought he'd be arrested straightaway!' Josiah groaned. 'I think they let him go because there wasn't really anything against him and they still had Wheelwright in view!'

Laurence had also been released after questioning and joined the hunt, but had voiced his indignation all over Dunster and when Josiah reached the Luttrell Arms that evening, was holding a wrathful court. He had, he said, been in company all of the day when Maisie vanished, repairing a barn roof in a field belonging to the farm – it was called Alders – where he worked.

'He said another fellow was working on the barn roof with him,' said Josiah. 'Young Daniel Hopton. Well, I know Daniel. So does Ralph here.'

'He's not a special friend of Laurence's,' said Ralph. 'Wouldn't lie for him, I think.'

I remembered, on the night when strange things were happening in the yard below my window, hearing someone call the name Daniel, and a youthful voice replying. Josiah and Ralph no doubt knew Daniel Hopton very well indeed.

The days went by. The search was repeated, when men could

spare the time. We heard nothing from Philip. June was passing. The search was given up. Prayers were said for Maisie in St Michael's at Minehead and St George's in Dunster but few really believed she was still alive, although somebody did suggest that she had got herself into such a tangle between Laurence and Philip that she had run away.

There was some exasperated comment about that theory. *Silly girl*, people said. *What's she to do, all on her own?* Others said, *She'll have gone to hide in Taunton* (Somerset's populous county town) *but fancy giving up a good place at Avill? Silly girl, silly girl.* The majority, however, said: *No, she'm dead, that's what she be. Or her parents'd have heard from her. She were always a good girl that way. It's one of they two boys, Duggan or Wheelwright, mark my words.*

On the last day of June, after a five-day stretch of hot, dry weather, Mr Stark, the farmer at Alders, took a young sheepdog out on Dunkery, the highest point of the moor, to work on training the animal to obey commands. Mr Stark went up to the great heathery slope called Codsend Moor. It is wild and bleak up there and there are bogs. They spread and overflow in wet weather, but the heatwave had shrunk them considerably. Mr Stark came back faster than he had gone, with his dog on a leash and his face bloodless under its outdoor tan. Josiah, who had been in Dunster that day, arranging for some more pine logs, came home with a grim face. Dunster was brimming, he said, brimming with news, bad news.

He told us: 'They've found Maisie Cutler.'

The young sheepdog had found her, to be precise. Josiah actually met Mr Stark in Dunster's main street the next day and heard it from him, first-hand. The animal had gone running ahead of his master − 'I'm having a right old time,' Mr Stark said, apparently, 'tryin' to teach 'un to do as I tell 'un; I were whistling for 'un to come back but would he come? No, he wouldn't. Kept on runnin' and nosin' and then sits down and lets out such a howl, I thought he'd hurt hisself. So I start running too and oh my God . . .!'

The dog was howling because he had found human remains and somehow known them for a tragedy. He was crouched by a shrunken bog, all among the shrivelled reeds round its edge. The dry weather had done its work and the bog had yielded up what it had been hiding.

The inquest took place in the Luttrell Arms, in a big upstairs room with a medieval ceiling, whose beautiful carved beams drew my eyes at once, though not for long. The business in hand was too serious for that. All the Duggans attended, including myself, as an honorary member of the family, so to speak, and also including Stephen Duggan, who had abandoned his reclusiveness for once to give Philip his support. I recognized some of the jury but I can't remember the name of the coroner, though he was an impressive man with a military air, probably an Acland or a Luttrell. He was past middle age but straight in the back, with a ginger moustache and what is called Presence. He was not the kind of man who is ignored.

There was no doubt, it appeared, that the body was that of Maisie Cutler. It must have been a horrid sight. Mr Stark's description and his pallor as he recited it, were evidence of that, and so was the haggard face of her father as he confirmed his formal identification.

Both he and his wife had identified the good leather shoes, complete with brass buckles, which they had given her last Christmas, and there was a seed-pearl brooch and a little matching necklace that Philip, his voice taut with unhappiness, said he had given her for her seventeenth birthday the previous November. They were shown to him and he recognized them. Most of her abundant fair hair was still recognizable too, or so her father said, crying.

There was little doubt either as to the manner of her death. A bone in her throat – a doctor testified that it was called the hyoid bone – had been fractured and that was a sign of death by strangling.

Evidence was taken from Philip, from Laurence Wheelwright, and from Daniel Hopton who had worked with him on the barn roof on the day when Maisie was last seen. He was a skinny lad, no more than twenty, I thought, with large ears and a dust-coloured tuft of unruly hair just above his forehead. He had sounded nervous when I heard him speak that night in Minehead and he sounded nervous now. I recognized his voice. This, for sure, was the same man.

Their evidence repeated what they had said before, and the whole community knew what that was. Daniel swore that neither he nor Laurence had left the roof that afternoon. Laurence, still exuding indignation, said that the roof had been completed and couldn't have been if he had spent the afternoon murdering Maisie and transporting her, dead or alive, to Codsend.

Philip swore that he had been with the Standing Stone sheep all that day. He wasn't that clever at the work as yet and had taken a young dog that needed experience as well, and the task had taken longer than it normally would. His Great-Uncle Stephen testified that the sheep had been moved in accordance with his orders. He had not noticed the time of Philip's return though he agreed that it was quite late in the day. On the face of things, as Philip was mounted, it was possible that he had finished with the sheep quickly and then gone on to Dunster.

It was agreed that no one had seen Maisie with either Philip or Wheelwright and that no one could possibly have intercepted and quarrelled fatally with her and then got her body to Codsend in broad daylight, without someone noticing. *But*, after a fatal quarrel somewhere near Dunster, her body could have been hidden and then moved after dark. The movements of the two young men that evening had to be established.

It transpired that both young men had been in company. Laurence had been with friends in the inn at Timberscombe and Philip had been at supper with everyone else at Standing Stone. Either, however, could have crept out at dead of night, and got back unnoticed. Mr Stark glumly admitted it, and so did Stephen Duggan though with such reluctance that the coroner fairly had to drag it out of him. Beside me, Bronwen wept quietly during Uncle Stephen's testimony and Philip's face was like white marble.

The jury, however, took some time to reach a verdict and when they did, they were cautious, which was natural enough since they were local men and well acquainted, therefore, with many of those present. Josiah whispered to me that two constables were in the room. One was the man who had organized the search, a tall individual with a craggy face. The other was burly, with a beard. They were not sitting together. The room had two doors and the constables were strategically placed, one close to each of them. Josiah did no more than say who they were, but I knew at once, with a cold worm of fear in my stomach, that they were there to make an arrest if required.

Finally, however, the foreman of the jury stood forth and explained, in rather convoluted terms, that it was known to them all that the poor young woman had had a flirtatious nature, the which was not to be wondered at in a girl only seventeen and said to be pretty, and it was known that two young men, not so long ago, had fought over her, but where there were two there might be three or even four and whatever some of them might think privately . . .

One of the other jurors muttered something which was inaudible and the foreman broke off to glare at him.

'Your verdict, please,' said the coroner, becoming impatient.

'We won't name names,' said the foreman, glaring again at the man who had muttered. 'It's murder by a person or persons unknown.'

'What was it that man was mumbling, who interrupted the foreman?' Mrs Duggan said as we were filing out.

'My name or Laurence's, I should think,' muttered Philip bitterly. 'Well, we all know where Laurence was when Maisie vanished. Up on a barn roof with Daniel Hopton! And where was I? Moving sheep on Standing Stone land and who's to say I didn't sneak off to meet Maisie? I'd known for a few days that I'd be told to move those sheep, and I knew when. I could have fixed things with Maisie beforehand, talked her into *not* keeping her word to her parents for once and met her on the moor.'

'But you didn't!' said Bronwen nervously.

'No, of course I didn't! But I could. I could have met Maisie and quarrelled with her over the way she's been seeing Laurence – she might have laughed about it to me, just for the fun of seeing me get wild with her! She'd done that before and it made her giggle, can you believe it? And then I could have got back and no one the wiser. I could have slipped out at night and taken her to the bog . . . Oh, dear heaven, as if I'd have done that to Maisie! I'd never have hurt her, never, no matter how wild she made me! Poor Maisie, she must have been so frightened!'

By then, we were standing beside our tethered mounts. Momentarily, Philip buried his face in his pony's mane and as he straightened up, he used the mane to wipe his eyes. Defiantly, he said: 'I *could* have done it. Only I didn't. Didn't. Didn't. Oh, poor Maisie, my darling, if only you'd let me marry you and keep you safe! I loved her,' he said bitterly.

Josiah said: 'Best not worry about it. That foreman was right. Where there's two there could be three – or four or five. I don't mean to hurt your feelings, son, but could be she wasn't the best wife for you. It'll all smooth itself out, you'll see.'

Escape

After the inquest, Philip went back to Standing Stone with Stephen Duggan and for a while we heard nothing from him. I was now preparing to go home to Foxwell, dreading the parting from Ralph, but also looking forward to being with my mother again – and planning for my wedding and thinking about my bride clothes.

And then came a day that I still recall with pain.

We'd done plenty of talking about the inquest, of course, but on that day, I don't think it was mentioned. At supper that evening, Ralph remarked that a merchant brig, the *Sheila Marie*, was expected into Minehead harbour in a few days' time and Ralph was interested in her because when he was in the north, he had helped to build her. She was bound for Antigua, he said. He had learned of her impending arrival from a sailor whose ship had just arrived at Minehead from Bristol where, at the moment, the *Sheila Marie* was preparing for her voyage to the New World.

At Bristol, it seemed, she had picked up a cargo of luxury goods for the owners of sugar plantations – 'things like expensive chess sets and good bronze and earthenware and fine furniture and some oak timber as well' – and in Minehead was to add a consignment of ironware. 'Then she's for the high seas and the West Indies. One of these days, I'll make a voyage like that.'

He saw me looking at him and laughed. 'But not yet, my love. And maybe when I do go, you'll come with me.'

We all laughed then, and went cheerfully to bed.

In the depths of the night, I woke to the sound of a furious hammering on the door. I heard Josiah going down the stairs, shouting to know who it was, heard Ralph echoing him as he hurried from his own room to follow his father down, heard the front door bolts being drawn back and then recognized Philip's voice, exclaiming: 'Dad! Oh, Dad!' in such agonized tones that I had sprung out of bed before I even knew I meant to. It was cold. Hastily, I pulled on a robe and a shawl, thrust my feet into slippers and ran from my room, almost colliding with Bronwen, similarly clad and clutching a candle. We sped downstairs together.

Moments later, all five of us were gathered in the parlour, staring at each other in the light of a three-branched candlestick that someone had put on the table, and Josiah was twitching the window curtains to make sure that no lights showed outside. Philip was there, pale and dishevelled, trembling visibly and saying, over and over: 'They came for me. They *came* for me.'

'Who did?' asked Josiah, turning away from the curtains. 'Sit down in that chair there, son, and tell us what happened.'

'They came to arrest me! Constables. To Standing Stone. Just on dusk and pounding on the door as if they wanted to break it in – Uncle Stephen was furious, went to the door shouting at them to wait, he was coming, what did they mean by carrying on as if they were an invasion of Frenchies . . .'

Bronwen handed him a mug of cider and he gulped it thankfully. Josiah said: 'Go on. You got away – how?'

'I were upstairs,' Philip said. 'Supper were done. Uncle and me meant to play a game of backgammon. I'd gone up to fetch my set. I heard the men downstairs, saying they'd got a warrant to arrest me . . . for the murder of Maisie Cutler!' His voice broke and the candlelight showed the glint of tears. Philip was younger than I was and I was not yet twenty-one. What was it like, at our age, to face death by hanging?

'I got out of the landing window,' said Philip, wiping his eyes and trying to command himself. 'Didn't stop to think; I was so frightened. That window's just over the kitchen roof. You know Uncle had a new kitchen built on, just one storey?'

'Yes, yes, go on!' Bronwen urged him.

'Well, I got out. I slithered to the ground from there, ran to the stable. Uncle's got four ponies there and his heavy horses. I just bridled one of the ponies in a hurry – no time for a saddle – picked the pony with the white sock; he's the fastest – and got out of the place. Didn't know where to go, so I came here. Dad, I didn't do it, I didn't. I'd *never* have hurt Maisie; it's unthinkable. I might have murdered that Laurence

Wheelwright,' said Philip, a gleam of spirit returning. 'But never Maisie. Never Maisie.'

'Don't worry about that,' Josiah said shortly. 'Whether you did it or not, you're our son and your ma and I'll look after you. Where's the pony now?'

'Out there, tied to our gate,' said Philip, jerking his head. 'It was an awful ride,' he said miserably. 'Took hours. I didn't dare go down the Avill valley, through all those villages. The men that came to Standing Stone would guess I'd make for home and chase me down the valley because it's the obvious way, and for so much of it there's no getting off the track; it's nigh on straight up one side, and straight on down to the river on the other . . .'

'That's my boy,' said Josiah soothingly. 'Always try to think what the enemy might do and then fool them. You came over the moor, I suppose?'

'Yes, over Dunkery. The night's clear and there was a half-moon but it made everything look so weird; I felt I were being hunted . . . I came past Codsend; awful, I saw it in the moon-light, that bog poor Maisie was found in; gave me the shivers; I thought what if her ghost rises out of it and comes after me . . .'

'Steady, lad!' said Josiah.

'After crossing Dunkery I came down into the woods, and then through all those tangled lanes, into Minehead. It was as creepy under the trees as out on Codsend! I was frightened all the way! All the time I felt there were . . . beings I couldn't see, all round me, watching. Never believed in piskies before but . . .'

His young voice was terrified. I looked at him with pity, realizing that he was little more than a child, and how fright-ening it must be, to be hunted by the law and then driven out alone to the midnight moors and woods.

Josiah took control. 'I shouldn't start believing in them now,' he said. 'All your imagination, that was. Imagination and panic. Now then. We'll have the law here, sure as sure, once they know you've bolted. You're right – they'll guess you'd make for here. So we've to get you out of sight, and that pony, too. Well, I've had it in mind that something of this sort might happen. I knew if you got warning in time, you'd likely turn up here. Ralph!'

'I know what to do,' Ralph said. 'The *Bucket*'s been ready for days.'

'I'll pack the hamper,' said Bronwen, turning towards the kitchen.

'You'll be needed for getting rid of the pony,' Josiah said to her. 'There are folk enough in Minehead, including two constables, that know quite well how many animals I've got in my stable, and know I don't keep ponies and certainly not a pony with one white sock and the Standing Stone brand as well. You'll have to swap its bridle for a halter, lead it from Tansy and . . .'

'We ought to turn the pony loose on Dunkery, but it's too far,' said Bronwen, sounding exhausted. 'I couldn't get there and back before dawn . . .'

'No, I know.' Josiah sounded like someone who was thinking fast. 'Best go up North Hill and along to Selworthy Beacon. That'll have to do. Then take the halter off the pony and scare it away. Let it wander till it finds its own way home or someone notices it and takes it there. Since it does carry the Standing Stone brand, it'll be got back home in the end. I'll let Uncle Stephen know what we did with it. Get dressed now, hurry with the hamper while I saddle Tansy. I'll halter that pony and hang up its bridle among the rest of my tack. Bronwen, I'm sorry, but I can't deal with the pony myself; I've got to be here when the law arrives and that might be any time soon! I've got to keep my finger on what's happening.'

'Muffle their hooves,' said Philip. His young face was drawn with fear, and the candlelight accentuated the lines it had made. 'I came through Alcombe slow, so as not to make too much noise and I think no one heard me but you'll be passing St Michael's and the cottages near it and you *mustn't be heard*.'

'All right.' But I heard the weariness in Bronwen's voice. She could still enjoy a ride on a sunny morning, but the clock on the mantelpiece said half-past three, and she had been dragged from her bed into the midst of a crisis and she was no longer young.

'I can take the pony,' I said.

It was as if, until that moment, none of them had realized that I was actually there. They all turned towards me.

'You?' said Josiah. 'You oughtn't to know anything about all this. You ought to be in your bed, fast asleep and innocent as you should be. No, you get upstairs and get under the covers and stay there till the right time for rising. You've heard and seen nothing, understand?'

'I think of myself as part of this family,' I said. 'I will be truly part of it soon. I want to help, and Bronwen is tired. It'll seem a long way, in the dark.'

There was a silence. Then Ralph said: 'Good girl. You see, Dad, how well I've chosen? Peggy's part of us already. Let her do it.'

Josiah and I stared at each other. His eyes had narrowed. The shadows thrown by the candles had changed him too, making him seem taller than he was. He looked, suddenly, remote and formidable and oddly calculating. For a moment I was almost afraid of him.

Then he said: 'Very well. Go and dress, Peggy. Fast. Bronwen, find her a pair of Philip's old breeches. She'd best go astride. Then see to that hamper. Put a ham in, apples, bread – anything you can think of that'll last a few days. And a knife and some salt and water bottles and ale. Quick now, both of you.'

We were quick, but by the time I was downstairs again and out in the stable yard, Josiah and Philip had attended to the saddling and haltering and – I noticed this with interest – had from somewhere produced sets of what seemed to be thick felt socks for Tansy and the pony. It was plain that muffling horses' hooves was a task with which the Duggans were familiar.

I got astride Tansy, and Josiah pushed the pony's lead rope into my hand and said *Godspeed*. Then we were away.

It was a strange ride in the night, up the steep and winding way past the church to North Hill and along the lengthy track to Selworthy Beacon. To save time, I cantered where possible but I was not used to leading a second animal and feared to lose control if we went too fast.

The half-moon was still there, in a clear sky, so I could see where I was going but the pale light made the world look mysterious, haunted. I could understand Philip's fears. Once a sinuous shape, probably a stoat, rippled across the track, to pause for a moment and look at me and I saw the moonlight reflected, greenish-white, in small, fierce eyes. Then it was gone, but then, somewhere out in the heathland, something squealed wretchedly. A rabbit, perhaps, dying in the fangs of the stoat or a fox.

It was then that I thought of the kingfisher and the little fish in its beak, and now I felt a very real, spontaneous pity for Maisie. Like the fish, she must have known unspeakable terror before she died.

I came at last to the top of the path down to Porlock, where I drew rein. Tansy snorted, with disapproval, I felt. She probably hadn't wanted to be dragged out of her doze and her comfortable stable in the middle of the night to be saddled and put to work. I patted her, murmuring a few soothing words. There was an awkward time after that, when I had to dismount and without loosening my grip on her reins, remove the muffling socks from the pony's feet. Luckily, the pony was tired and put up patiently with me while I fumbled at the straps round its fetlocks.

I got the socks off at last, crushed them into my breeches' pockets, took off the halter and used the lead rope to rouse the pony into throwing up its head and cantering off towards the Porlock track. It flashed indignant heels at me as it went and the moonlight gleamed on its shoes. I climbed back on to Tansy and started for home.

The return journey was different. The moon was westering now and the haunted feeling of the small hours had gone. There was no sign yet of dawn, but it couldn't be far away. I could go faster now that I only had one horse to manage and Tansy, sensing that she was now headed home, moved quite briskly. I was tiring, though. I was thankful when at last I was riding down past St Michael's and its neighbouring cottages, because it meant that I was nearly home. I realized that I had come to think of the Duggans' house as that. At last I was down on the shore road and passing the boatyard entrance and turning in at the little private gate to the house. Josiah emerged from the shadows at once.

'I'll see to Tansy. All well?'

'All well. She's not sweating.'

'Go indoors, into the parlour. I'll come when Tansy's settled.'

There was no one about when I went in. Kitchen, parlour, the dining room were all empty. There were still candles alight in the parlour, however. I sat exhaustedly down, until Josiah appeared, with a bottle of wine in one hand and two glasses dangling from the fingers of the other. 'We both need this. My thanks, Peggy. You just got back in time – there's dawn in the sky now. It would have borne hard on Bronwen to do that ride. She's asleep now.'

'Where's Philip?' I asked as he poured the wine. 'And Ralph?'

'Ralph's taken him off in the *Bucket* with food enough for several days. We're going to hide him till I can get him away.' He handed me my glass. 'See here, my girl, do you realize that what you did tonight was commit a crime? You've helped to get a wanted man away. That means I can't tell you things, because if you talk, you'll land yourself in jail.'

'I wouldn't talk anyway,' I said. 'And I don't believe Philip did it!'

'I don't think he did either,' Josiah said. 'Not like him at all, I'd say. I'm not sure, mind you, young men in a state of jealous passion . . . Well, it doesn't matter anyway; he's my son and that's enough for me. But you are not my daughter.'

'I soon will be.' I sipped the wine, glad of its warmth in my gullet.

'Not as soon as you think. Now, you listen to me. Your mother'll blow the top of her head off with rage when she gets to know that the family you're supposed to be marrying into is mixed up with murder – and there's a warrant out for your intended's brother. She'll withdraw her consent, mark my words . . .'

'She can't!' Weary as I was, I sat up straight and angrily. 'We delayed the marriage until I came of age. After that, she can't stop me.'

'But I can. I don't want you estranged from your own kin, my girl. No. *Listen!* I have to get Philip away overseas. Never mind where or how. He's young and tough and I'm sending him to kinfolk, but they're not close kin; maybe they won't take him in though he'll carry a letter from me, begging them to. And since I can't risk him being stranded in a foreign land on his own, Ralph's going with him, to see him settled,

somehow or other. Ralph's older and a lot more worldly wise.
He'll see Philip right. By the time Ralph comes back, well,
maybe all this will be settled down and half-forgotten and then
perhaps you and he can start again. But for the time being,
the engagement's broken, understand?'

'No! *No!*' I was on my feet, horrified, knocking over the
wineglass that I had put down on a low table, sending the
wine over the table on to the carpet. 'The engagement isn't
broken! I'm going to marry Ralph!'

'One day, maybe, but not yet. Sit down. Sit *down*, I tell you!'
Josiah picked up my fallen glass, which had come to no harm
on the carpet, and refilled it. 'Here. Now then. You're due to
go home in a week anyway, but I'm sending you back early,
doing right by you in your mother's eyes. Not today – you're
worn out. But tomorrow. The sooner you're out of here, the
better. As it is, we'll have the law at this door any moment!
Everything has to look as it should.'

'But I want to stay my full time. I'm marrying Ralph and . . .'

'You are *not* marrying Ralph. Not now, anyhow. Didn't you
hear me? He's bound abroad, on my orders, and you'll do as
you're told, same as he will. I had a right barney with him
while you were out. He doesn't want to go overseas; said I
ought to go. But I made him see different. I'm sending you
home and you'll put it about that you can't wed into a family
with so much scandal all round it. No one'll be surprised at
that. Tomorrow, I'm taking you and your luggage round to
Porlock in the *Bucket* and I know who'll lend us a cart in
Porlock to get us to Foxwell. I'll give you a chance to say
goodbye to Ralph. He'll be back here presently, once he's
settled Philip in hiding. Meanwhile . . .'

'Say goodbye? To Ralph?' I didn't know how to cope with
this. I really was afraid of this new, overbearing version of
Josiah Duggan, and I couldn't see how to defy him. I felt that
he was quite capable of taking me home by force. I was too
tired, anyway. I wanted to curl up in a corner and cry.

'You need sleep,' he told me now. 'Today you'll rest upstairs.
But first, dress yourself in proper clothes. Get out of those
breeches and into a lady's gown. Then you can sleep on the
bed but you'll still look normal if the law comes here and

wants to talk to you. If you're questioned, you know nothing. You hear me? You slept all night. There were no disturbances. You got up as usual this morning and everything was just as it always is. You're puzzled and surprised to be questioned. You've no idea where Philip is; you thought he was at Standing Stone and you're shocked to hear he's a wanted man. You're *horrified . . .*'

'Well, so I am but that's because I'm sure he didn't do it . . .'

'You can say that if you want to. Say you can't believe it, not Philip! Run out of the room in tears if you like. Then tomorrow, back you go to Foxwell and soon the world will know you've abandoned your engagement. You wouldn't dream of going to the altar with one of us questionable Duggans!'

I tried once more. 'But Ralph and I love each other and whatever Philip's done or not done, it's nothing to do with Ralph!'

'It is now,' said Josiah. 'And tomorrow, even if I have to knock you on the head to do it, you go home to Foxwell, and you stay there.'

Leaving It To Nature

It was ten in the morning when two Minehead constables, backed up by a couple of soldiers, arrived at the Duggans' door.

The three maidservants had come as usual and been told that I was resting because I was unwell. Bronwen brought me some breakfast in my room. She looked wan but she was fully dressed and said she would be in the kitchen, helping one of the maids to peel potatoes for the midday meal. The other two girls were busy about the house with brooms and dusters. 'Everything looks ordinary,' she told me.

Ralph was not yet back. Josiah was in the boatyard, from which, as ever, came the clamour of tools and voices. I had changed my clothes as bidden and I had also done my hair. I hoped I wouldn't be summoned but Bronwen called my name after only a brief wait. I put my shoes on and went downstairs.

The constables did the questioning politely enough and I was, I trusted, the perfect bewildered innocent. No, I had not seen Philip and no, there had been no disturbances in the night that I was aware of. I had slept the night through just as usual though this morning, I said delicately, I was a little out of sorts. As I had calculated, the constables retreated courteously from the obvious implication.

I exclaimed in horror when they told me that Philip was to be arrested for the murder of Maisie Cutler. I couldn't believe such a thing of Philip, I said. I was sure there was a mistake. Oh, how dreadful! Oh, dear. I was so overcome that one of the maids offered me some smelling salts though at that point, remembering that I was a strong girl from a farm and not a swooning miss in a romance and that the constables probably knew it, I waved them impatiently away.

Josiah, who had been summoned but had insisted on finishing something in the boatyard before answering any questions, came in just then and was irritable with the intruders.

No, he hadn't seen his younger son and would have had something to say to him if he had, getting himself suspected of murder! Damned young fool! Not that Philip could possibly be guilty. Young fool, he might be, but not to that extent. Where was Ralph? Took the *Bucket* to Porlock this morning to see about getting a bill paid, some customers were mighty slack over paying for work. Keen enough to get it done but when it came to opening their wallets . . . He launched into a tirade about bad payers and the constables had to interrupt him twice before he could be distracted from it.

The law left at last, still suspicious and dissatisfied but without finding any sign that Philip had come to us last night. It was another two hours before Ralph came home. I was upstairs again when I heard his voice below, and once more I hurried down, to meet him just as he came in through the kitchen door.

'All's well,' he said. 'Philip's safe enough now though in a state. I'll have to go back to him later; don't want him left alone too long. I'll get some sleep first, though. Dad says the constables have been and gone.'

I said: 'Ralph!'

'Parlour,' said Bronwen, appearing from the kitchen with a bowl of batter in her hand. She went on beating it as she talked. 'Go on. You need a bit of time to sort things out between you.'

In the parlour, with the door closed, I said: 'Your father says he's taking me home to Foxwell tomorrow but why should I go? Why can't we go on with our plans? Your father says you're going abroad with Philip but do you really have to? If so – you'll come back, won't you? I'll wait. It won't be that long, surely!'

'You have to go home because otherwise your outraged mother would probably fetch you,' said Ralph grimly. 'Dad's sure of it, once the news gets to her. Let her daughter marry into a family with a charge like this hanging over your future brother-in-law! She'll have none of it! Dad says he knows her well enough for that. Look, Peggy . . . Oh, my darling Peggy; don't be angry with me; it's no fault of mine . . . but I can't tell how long I'll be gone. I've got to see Philip safe and

settled before I can leave him. I *must!* and it could well take
some time. Years, even. It wouldn't be fair to leave you –
bound. Keep my ring if you wish, but . . . regard yourself
as free.'

I stared at him and saw that, just as with Josiah last night,
he had become remote. Physically, he was standing only three
feet away from me yet I felt him withdrawing, and it was
dreadful, as though a wall, a buttress, some bulwark on which
I had come to depend to guard me against storms or enemies,
had crumbled before my eyes.

'Why can't your father go?' I demanded angrily.

'Simply because it may take time. He can't leave the business for so long and besides, Philip's got to disappear quietly,
so as not to affect our family or the boatyard too much,
and . . .'

'No one has ever been *really* happy about our engagement,
not even your father, at heart,' I said bitterly. 'This is a golden
opportunity to separate us.'

'No, Peggy, that's not so. My father likes you. He wants to
protect you and now that you've actually taken part in Philip's
escape and you're on the wrong side of the law yourself . . .'

'I'll still wait!' I said. 'Ralph! Don't you want me to? Don't
I matter to you any more?'

'Of course you do. Always and for ever.' His voice shook
and yet he still seemed remote, and he was holding himself
stiffly, his hands at his sides. 'But I can't hold you to an engagement that may go on and on . . .'

We had never quarrelled before, but we quarrelled then. I
threw myself at him, seized hold of him, shook him, demanded
to know why if he had to make a long stay abroad with
Philip, I couldn't come out to him, to marry him wherever
he was.

He in turn shook me, telling me that I didn't know what
I was talking about, that he had no idea himself what kind of
world he'd find on the other side of the Atlantic, that my
mother would be frantic whether I was twenty-one or not,
that we'd got to be sensible, and if I thought he didn't care, I
was wrong, and if I wanted to know, he'd come near to hitting

his father last night, when Josiah ordered him to break off with me.

I said I didn't believe it; that it was obvious that he just wanted to jilt me and was seizing this chance to go adventuring as an excuse . . .

I knew in my heart that that wasn't true. In the deepest recesses of my being was a certainty that Ralph and I were meant to be a unity and that he knew it just as I did, but I wanted to sting him, to rouse him, to make him fight for us. To some extent, I succeeded, for he became furious and shouted that it was a lie, and one day he would come back and if I were still unwed, then we'd begin again but it was all uncertain, like sailing into a fog, and he couldn't and wouldn't leave me alone and yet bound. I shouted something back – I forget what – and then we were holding each other and we were both crying and he wasn't remote any more, but real and warm and strong . . .

And about to be taken away from me.

In the end I broke free, still crying, and fled from the parlour. I ran upstairs and locked myself in my room. It was evening before at last I let Bronwen in to comfort me. She brought food on a tray and said it was best that I should not see Ralph again, adding that he was in the worst mood she had ever seen him in, and in her opinion, this was a tragedy, but it was nevertheless right that I should go home.

'No one can make you marry anyone else if you don't want to. You can wait for Ralph if you choose, *cariad*.'

'What?'

'It's a Welsh endearment, my sweet. I don't want him to stay away long, either. Bad enough to have one son in exile, never mind both.'

So I stayed where I was till morning, though I didn't sleep. I crawled down to breakfast and Bronwen said that Ralph had left early, to see the master of a ship that was now in Minehead harbour, about getting Philip away. Then Josiah came for me.

I was beyond protest by then. I packed my things as bidden. I let Josiah take me to Porlock in the *Bucket*. I don't think I exchanged one word with him, though, all the way. It was a warm day and I sat on deck and watched the cliffs go by, towering massively on our left, their feet littered with the debris of old rock falls, like dark teeth sticking out of the water while the waves, breaking over them, threw up great plumes of white spray.

We passed the old landslide that Ralph had told me about, that had blocked a useful path between a cave and the clifftop, a path the free traders had once used. I remembered him telling me. I could hear his voice in my head. To be with Ralph was always to hear something interesting. I did not know how I would live without him.

By midday, we were at Porlock and Josiah was arranging, as he had said, to borrow a pony and cart. We drove back to Foxwell, through the same lanes that had seemed so beautiful on the day of the fair. Now I noticed only the ruts in the track and the tangles in the long grasses and the brambly banks.

My mother, all distraught, met us at the gate of the farmyard.

'I've heard!' she said shortly. 'I gave 'ee a day to send her back; otherwise I'd have come to get her. Glad 'ee's had a bit of sense, Josiah. Well, come in and have a cider. I won't ask 'ee where Philip is, though I don't doubt you know well enough. Here's Bert Page. Bert, see to this pony and cart and then carry Peggy's things up to her room. Peggy, come inside; I'm that thankful to see 'ee home! What a mercy I said 'ee shouldn't wed until August. What a mercy I held out. If 'ee'd been wed already – oh, the shame of it! Oh, I'm sorry, Josiah but when it's one's own daughter . . .'

'I understand. Why else would I have brought her back?' said Josiah. We all went inside. I cried as I crossed the threshold of my own home. It felt like entering a prison.

The days that followed are a blur in my memory. I wept often, I know. I also kept on wearing my pearl betrothal ring, which made my mother angry. Those things do stand out from the blur, like the top of Dunkery Beacon standing clear of low cloud. Particularly my mother's wrath about the ring.

'But it's my engagement ring,' I said. 'I'm still betrothed to Ralph.'

'Oh, no 'ee's not and don't put on that fine young lady voice with me, either. You'll never marry Ralph and that's final.'

'I've promised to wait for him. He'll come back one day and . . .'

'You'll not wait for 'un; he'll be gone years, mark my words, and life b'ain't like that. Wenches b'ain't like that and that means you!'

'When I'm twenty-one, and it won't be long, I can marry whoever I like and wait for whoever I like, as well!'

'That's enough!' We had been at breakfast but now my mother was on her feet, coming at me round the table. Betty was in the room and cried out in protest but my mother ignored her. She seized my left wrist with one hand and with the other tried to tear the ring from my finger. I clenched my fist in resistance and she hit me across the side of the head, so that my ears rang and pain exploded through my skull. Bert Page, breakfasting with us as usual, exclaimed: 'That's enough!' and came to my aid, seizing my mother's arm and breaking her hold on me.

'Let the maid be! Oh come, Mrs Shawe, come, the wench has only just been parted from the man she was to marry; be gentle, I beg 'ee, be gentle . . .'

'Take that ring *off*!' Mother shrieked, crimson with fury. But Bert had drawn my mother away and although I was still seeing stars, I sprang up and ran for the door, and the stairs and my room, where I locked myself in. Below in the kitchen, I could hear my mother weeping wildly and crying out that if only my father had lived, nothing like this would ever have happened; he'd never have let me even think of marrying into the Duggans, not right, it wasn't, the Duggans being what they were and all very well to buy a few free traders' goods but when it came to *marrying* such . . . and I could hear Bert Page's deep, steady voice trying to calm her.

Trembling, I sat miserably down on the edge of my bed, my left fist still closed to protect my ring. I heard Mother come upstairs, sobbing, and go into her own room. At length, cautiously, I made my way downstairs again and found Bert still in the kitchen, sipping a fresh mug of tea.

'I were waiting for 'ee,' he said as I came in. 'Tell you what, maid, best take that ring off or we'll all be frazzled afore long. She'll carry on like that whenever she sees it. No one'll have any peace.'

'I won't take it off! I *am* still engaged to Ralph and one day . . .'

'I didn't say otherwise,' said Bert pacifically. 'But why get thyself knocked about over it? Keep the ring, but not where she can see it. Wear it in bed! Hang it round thy neck under thy dress. But in the name of peace and quiet, hide it. Maybe the day will come to bring it out again. Meanwhile, life's got to be lived and I like to eat breakfast in quiet. Don't do the digestion any favours, all this to-do.'

'Mother'll think I've given in, abandoned Ralph and I haven't, I *haven't!*'

'Say so if you must,' said Bert, 'though in your place I wouldn't. But hide that ring.'

I didn't take the ring off at once, but when Mother eventually came downstairs, to eat the midday meal that Betty and I had prepared, she stared at it all the time, her face so angry and bitter that I couldn't bear it.

That night I took the ring off and put it on a string. Next morning at breakfast, when I saw Mother's eyes on my ringless finger, I said: 'I have removed my engagement ring as you wished. But please understand that I have not ceased to be engaged.' The ring was lying over my heart. It would stay there, I told myself, until the day when once again, it could grace my hand.

Bert at this point made some commonplace remark about the farm work and Mother said, quite quietly: 'Folk ought to stick with their own kind. I've been relying on thee to bring a useful son-in-law here. And don't go thinkin' you've a broken heart. Them Cleopatras and Heloises of legend can have broken hearts; common folk have tougher ones, and any little bits of damage,' she finished, on a note of grim amusement, 'soon get cured by hard work.'

I said nothing, but I left the table as soon as I could. As I went out of the kitchen, she added, quite mildly: 'You'll see, love. Nature'll win 'ee round, given time. You'll see.'

Nature would do nothing of the sort, I said to myself. Nor time.

But I had left one thing out of my calculations. I hadn't reckoned with Ralph himself.

Wearing Away

Hard work, my mother's recommended treatment for heart-break, is easy to come by on a farm. Throughout the rest of the year 1800 I must have done plenty of it, though I recall few details. But the harvest had to be got in and sheep had to be moved about and presumably these things were done. Pigs must have been slaughtered for there were hams and bacon for us women to prepare; muck had to be spread on the fields ready for next year's crops; stock sold at markets.

News filtered through, concerning the aftermath of Philip's disappearance. Stephen Duggan's pony somehow found its way home and was discovered one morning standing hope-fully outside its stable. As far as I ever heard, the constables who came to arrest Philip never realized that he'd taken a pony at all. No one knew how he'd got away or where he'd gone.

And then, it was Christmas, and the Bright family came over from Marsh on Boxing Day and dined with us, which meant facing James Bright. I had of course seen him since my return home, when he paid a civil visit one Sunday and told me, in a formal sort of way, that he was sorry to hear of my broken engagement.

'It isn't broken,' I said, ignoring my mother's angry expression and slipping a hand under the shawl I was wearing, so that I could feel the pearl ring on its string. 'But the wedding has had to be delayed. Ralph Duggan has had to make a business trip abroad.'

'Ah, yes. I heard something about that, at the market in Dunster one day,' James said. 'I came across Josiah Duggan. He's telling people that there'd been talk of it some time ago but it was all set aside once plans began for Ralph to get married.'

I could guess what kind of tale Josiah was putting about. Philip's disaster had caused my mother to end the engagement,

Ralph had taken himself off to foreign climes after all, and if I persisted in saying we were still engaged, well, wenches are sentimental creatures but the truth was, the betrothal was over.

In the spring of 1801, I had a letter from Ralph.

It began, encouragingly, with the words *My darling*, but the rest of it was like the tolling of a knell.

I am sorry to tell you that I cannot return to England soon. I hope this won't be too much for you to bear. I can but hope that by now, what I have to say won't hurt you too much. It hurts me, my love, more than I can say but I am helpless.

Philip and I are in Antigua. I came with Philip to see him settled but it has proved difficult. Our relative – George Duggan, the son of a second cousin of Dad's – has a sugar plantation here. He lives in a fine house with his wife and four young children. In this part of the world, the workforce is mostly slaves, and sometimes there's cruelty, yes, on the Duggan plantation too, that I won't tell you about, as it sickens me and yet it's all legal – and in England, Dad and I could have been imprisoned or transported as criminals for landing a few kegs of cheap brandy!

The Duggans here see nothing wrong with slavery but they were appalled to hear of the accusation against Philip. My father sent a letter with me, that I was to give to Cousin George. It explained the circumstances and declared every confidence in Philip's innocence. But Cousin George and his wife were so shocked that they wanted to put Philip on the first ship home! They only agreed to keep him if I stayed too and 'kept watch over him' and let them know at once if he gave any trouble.

They wrote to my father, saying that they would harbour Philip (that's the way they put it) if I agreed to stay for five years, and Dad wrote back to me, saying that I must consent. He told me that if I set foot in England even one day short of that, I would never inherit the boatyard – he'd leave it to Luke Hatherton's son. Roger Hatherton has joined the boatyard now, I gather, and is doing well. I have been so angry! I've never liked the Hathertons. But here I have to stay, like it or not.

If I come home and throw my inheritance away, I still couldn't marry you for what would I have to offer you? I am no farmer and in any case, I could not bear to live at Foxwell at your expense. Also my father truly thinks it isn't fair to you, to expect you to marry into a family as tainted as ours now is. And also, of course, he respects your mother and her wishes. What can I do? The power is in his hands.

I'm bitter but helpless. I hate Antigua, but for the time being I must stay. Philip and I came out on the Sheila Marie, the merchant brig that was due to call at Minehead before leaving for Antigua. I think she was mentioned to you. Her master and Dad knew each other as boys.

George Duggan is regarded as a decent man. He does see that his slaves are tended if they're ill and he won't break up families. The slaves can't marry but they pair up and he won't sell off one of a pair without the other. But slaves they are, just the same, and if one of them displeases him . . . God help the poor creature.

Philip's not so sensitive. He's learning the sugar business. So am I. Dad sent some money with us and as long as Philip behaves himself, George may be willing, later, to help the two of us start up on our own. He is gradually warming to Philip, whose behaviour is exemplary. I think Philip hopes I'll stay for good, once I'm used to the place.

I don't want to do that, but the five years must be served before I can think of coming home. I can't ask you to wait. Find a good man, Peggy darling, don't waste your life waiting.

My father has written to me that one of his fears for you was that one day, you'd find yourself with a husband in prison or worse and have to beg charity from your family, or else you might be caught up in lawbreaking yourself – as you already have been (destroy this letter and show it to no one!). There's something in that, I suppose. It is why I've always worried about Dad. He'd never survive being shut up in prison; he's a man of the open seas. I worry even more now I am so far away.

Peggy, love, find a husband and have children. I don't say forget me. I won't forget you! But it was just a dream that couldn't come true. My dear love you will always be. Be happy, darling.

Goodbye, your loving Ralph.

I read the letter sitting in my room, by candlelight, one evening. I had kept it by me all day, waiting to be alone and private before I opened it. I read it twice and then I wept. And raged. And next day, I went to my mother and said, very calmly, that I was now of age and could not be kept from marrying where I chose. I said I wished to go out to Antigua to marry Ralph. My mother burst out into harsh laughter.

'You'll need money for that! Fares to Antigua can't be any too cheap. Well, 'ee needn't think I'll pay!'

There was work that day, in the lambing pens, but I ignored it. At a moment when the kitchen was empty except for myself, I kissed Ralph's letter and then, as he had so wisely advised me, tore it to pieces and fed them into the fire. When I was certain they were utterly destroyed, I took a pony and went to Exford to see Mr Silcox.

I told him what was in the letter (except of course for the reference to my own lawbreaking). Mr Silcox was kind, sympathetic, and a broken reed.

I arrived just after I reckoned he would have stopped teaching for the day. He took me into his parlour, gave me a glass of wine and explained that there was no possibility whatsoever of my getting to Antigua without money, and that even if I had money, he would do all he could to stop me.

'I wouldn't send you or any young woman off on such a journey, all alone. You can hardly work your passage as a sailor, either,' he added ironically.

'I might get employment with some family that's going out there,' I said, suddenly inspired. 'As a companion or a children's nurse. Aren't there agencies in Minehead and Taunton, that find such posts for people?'

'And how often would you have to go to Minehead or Taunton to see if there were any offers? You'd be back and forth every other day. And you'd have to pay fees to the agency. And when you got to Antigua safely, and it's not a journey anyone would recommend for a girl on her own, do you even know the name of the plantation or how to find it? Your young man is right. He sounds a decent fellow but he's out of reach.'

'We're in love. You don't understand!'

'Yes, I do. But it's like a fever and people can recover. Many

a fine marriage has been made between people who weren't
in love, but were alike enough to make good partners. As you
well know,' said Mr Silcox, filling a pipe with a rich-smelling
and probably smuggled tobacco, 'there's a farmer's son called
James Bright who'd marry you tomorrow if you'd give him
half a chance. Take him, Peggy. You'll be safe. You won't even
have to leave your home! You'll be where you belong and I'd
take my oath that before long, you'll be as happy as any woman
in the world. Take my advice.'

I thanked him for the advice and went miserably back to
Foxwell, where I was again summoned to help with the lambing.
If Ralph was helpless, so was I. I could do nothing without
money . . .

I did think, then, of the cache I had hidden in the wall of the
old barn. I could use that!

And then I knew the bitter truth. I wasn't brave enough
to go to a shipping agency by myself and try to find a passage to
Antigua or anywhere else. I hadn't the confidence or the
experience.

Ralph was lost to me.

The year wore on. The Brights came to Sunday dinner twice,
and we went twice to them. Nothing of significance was said
but I saw James Bright's eyes on me, again and again. Seasons
changed. Haymaking came round again, in collision with sheep
shearing, as usual, and we were all busy. The June weather was
good and the hay must be cut while we had the chance.
Neighbours rallied round to help each other. Stephen Duggan
never made an appearance on these occasions, but he always
sent two or three men to lend a hand, and the Brights turned
to, as well. In a very short time, our hay was in and the fleeces
were off our sheep; then, in turn, we helped at Marsh and
Standing Stone. My mother, along with the wives of the various
farmhands, provided refreshments and I worked at piling the
mown grass into haycocks until it was dried right out and
ready to be built into ricks. We were making haycocks at
Marsh when James, who had been at the far end of the field,
where scything was still in progress, found someone to take
over from him and came back to me.

'Peggy,' he said, 'you look hot and thirsty. So am I. Let's get ourselves some cider and take a few minutes' rest.'

There was a clump of trees at one corner of the field and in their shade was a barrel of cider and some tin cups. I was indeed thirsty and I did as James suggested. The sun was very warm and I was far too hot for comfort, even in my thin linen gown. James, in shirt and calf-length breeches, was probably hotter still. There was a beading of sweat on his temples and forehead, where a lock of his tow-coloured hair was stuck to the skin. His eyes were the same blue as the clear sky above us, and their expression was friendly. It was also remarkably adult. I had known him all my life and yet, now, there seemed to be something unfamiliar about him, as though he had changed in some way while I wasn't looking.

'It's time for us to talk,' he said. 'I reckon, Peggy, that you know well enough how I feel about 'ee, and your ma and my dad know too and like the notion. It's a happy thing, for a couple to marry and have their families round them all smiling and pleased. It's a good start, that is. No, don't say anything yet.' I had opened my mouth to say something about being still engaged and how much I cared for Ralph, but James hadn't finished.

'I was sorry for 'ee when I heard things were broken off with Ralph Duggan, for it was plain enough 'ee didn't want them broken. But they are, and he's far away and not likely to be back any time soon. So your mother says. Is she wrong?'

'No,' I said. 'But I said I'll wait and . . .'

'Wait for what? What if he never comes back? Folk often don't, when they go abroad and make new lives in foreign places. I'm here, and ready to marry you tomorrow if only you'd say yes. I'm healthy and my mother always said I was good-natured; I'll do right by 'ee.'

'And you'll come and live at Foxwell. You'll gain Foxwell into the bargain, one day,' I said cruelly.

James was unconcerned. 'Yes, and why not? Got to be practical, in this old world. It's that or the army, fighting the French, but I'd as soon not be sticking bayonets into other men or firing cannonballs at them. I'd sooner plough and sow and reap the corn to feed folk. Yes, Foxwell's my opportunity, but I wouldn't want it if I didn't like 'ee so well. I wouldn't wed a girl I couldn't care for, even for a farm of my own.'

'What if the girl doesn't care for you?' I sounded harsh. It was because I was afraid of myself. Inside me, something was giving way. Hope was fading and worse still, so was the memory of Ralph. He was no longer as real to me as he had been. It wasn't as easy as it used to be, to conjure him up in my mind's eye. Reality was the hot sun and the hay that threw off pollen that dried the throat and made one sneeze, and the sound, somewhere, of a cuckoo calling and this sunburned young man sitting in front of me and talking, his voice low and warm and full of the familiar local accent.

'You'll care, given time,' he said. 'It'll come natural. You'll see.'

I shook my head. I said I was sorry, but no, no, it would never do, Ralph was different; Ralph was special. I was grateful for the compliment and I understood that James had paid me a great honour but I loved Ralph and always would.

'And 'ee'll die an old maid for 'un?' asked James, looking infuriatingly amused.

I didn't know what to say to that. I sprang up and ran away. He didn't pursue me, but I heard him laugh.

The year went on. James' brother John got married, to a girl called Becky Stannawood, whose parents kept a haberdashery in Exford. Mother and I attended the wedding, in St Salwyn's church. The bride wore a beautiful dress of silk, pinky foxglove colour. It was much admired, and at the reception, in the back room of the haberdashery, there was much laughter and joking and people saying to me, *When will it be your turn, Peggy? Don't leave it too long, now!* I smiled in answer and said things like, *Well, I'll have to see. I'm still only twenty-one.* And got back disconcerting answers such as, *Time goes quicker than you know, maid.*

And I admit it, I did feel envious of Becky, in her foxglove silk with its flounces and embroidery, cosily cocooned in the approval of both families, I wished it could be me, beautifully dressed, standing beside Ralph . . . going home that night with Ralph, to be united with him in the secret consummation of our vows.

Harvest time came and we held a harvest supper at Foxwell. There was dancing in the evening, outside at first, until clouds swept over the moon and it started to rain. I ran for shelter in the house, but was caught by James and pulled aside into a barn. I found myself being firmly and efficiently kissed, and I heard James say: 'Come on, Peggy. Isn't it time you made your mind up? You're keeping me on edge and I'm losing my patience. There are other girls in the world – only I'd rather I had you.'

I made one last feeble attempt to resist. 'And you'd rather you had Foxwell too?'

'Yes. Why not? I've a life to live and with you alongside, I can make something of Foxwell. Give me an answer, Peggy. Now. Yes or no?'

The rain rattled on the roof of the barn. The place felt cold, but James's arms were warm. I found myself leaning against him. I still loved Ralph; for a moment, my memory of him regained its old clarity. I saw his unhappy face when we were quarrelling. But I was tired, so tired, of holding on. My last lingering hopes had been wearing away, bit by bit, for a long time now. There was a wrenching, tearing moment, a feeling in the pit of my stomach that was not physical but felt as though it was, felt like pain. Then I turned away from Ralph, dragged myself free of him and said yes to James.

Before the wedding, I put Ralph's pearl engagement ring in a little box that had once held a brooch, a Christmas gift from my father. Then I went to my hiding place in the barn wall and put the box in with the money. It would always be there. I would not forget it. But I would not look at it again.

One month later, I stood before the altar at St Salwyns's, and Margaret Hannah Shawe said *I will* to James and became Mrs James Bright.

Weregild

'If my rheumatics get much worse,' my mother grumbled, 'I'll not be able to get out of this old chair once I'm sat in it.' She eased a cushion into a more comfortable position behind her and settled back into the basket chair that had once been my father's. 'Pour me a brandy, will 'ee, Peggy. No good asking *you* to share it, I suppose, James. Ah well, you're a good lad mostly, if only 'ee weren't so prim as a young lady's governess about free trading.'

'I never interfere with your private business,' said James. 'As my mother-in-law, I respect you too much for that. But you know my feelings. That brandy comes from France and bringing it in without paying duty on it is not lawful. What's more, just now, it puts money in Boney's pocket as well, and now we're at war with him, that won't do. The government's going all-out to put a stop to it and no wonder. That Revenue cutter the *Shark,* she's swallowed a good few contraband-runners and she'll swallow more afore she's done. And quite right too. There won't be much more cheap brandy or silk for anyone.'

'I laid in some silk cloth *and* a good lot of brandy and wine when I saw the beacons being built on Dunkery and Selworthy,' said Mother. 'Liquor keeps my old bones warm, so it does.'

Since my marriage, she had taken to drinking a good deal on most evenings. 'I can please myself now 'ee's wed and not my responsibility,' she said to me once when I queried the amount she was consuming. She now gave James a grin from which he visibly recoiled. She had lost several teeth of late and the grin was positively witchlike.

'I've enough to last a good few years,' she said. 'And if 'ee don't want any of my nice drinks, James, my stock'll last the longer. Can't 'ee keep those children quieter, Peggy? Look at Will, there, banging 'un's spoon on the table for more. He's had his supper! Either give 'un more or take 'un out. And

there's Rose howling – this here place is Bedlam sometimes!
You never made such a din as I remember. Wish 'ee'd made
another boy instead of Rose. We need sons in this family.'

'I didn't have any say in the matter,' I pointed out.

'And I wanted a daughter. That's a good family, that is,
one boy and one girl,' James said, backing me up. I gave him
a smile.

It was February 1805. We had been married, by then, for
a little over three years. Our son, William, was now two and
his sister, Rose, was nearly a year old. My married life was
working. James had been a cautious and careful bridegroom
and if my introduction to married life had been without
excitement, it was also without pain, and I had my children
easily. William, four weeks early, was tiny. For some reason,
no more had followed but William and Rose were both
healthy and there was plenty of time, James said
unconcernedly.

I got on well enough with James. He worked hard and
expected me to work hard too, but he was also careful of
me. It was from James that I acquired the habit, when walking
or riding out alone, of always taking a knife with me. Having
a knife had once saved his life, he said. He had been cutting
back some undergrowth near a river and he had slipped and
fallen into the water, catching his left foot in a tangle of
brambles.

'I were slidin' backwards and couldn't lift myself anyways,'
he said. 'I could reach my foot, just, but not untangle it. Only
I had my good sharp knife on my belt, so I got that out and
I could just about stretch far enough to do some slashing. So
slash I did and the foot came free and I ended up in the river
and got mighty wet, but I didn't drown. You never know.
Things happen.'

I took his advice and barely a week later, when out on the
moor, gathering whortleberries, I found one of our sheep
caught in a gorse patch, trapped by its thick wool. I had
encountered this sort of thing before, more than once, and
scratched my hands and arms badly while releasing the animals.
With a knife, the task was much easier. The same thing
happened again about a year later. James was a careful farmer

and a careful husband and if what I felt for him wasn't love, it was respect and in due course, affection.

We argued sometimes, but not often, not after the time when I disagreed with him over which field to plant next year's wheat in, and he reminded me, very forcibly, that one day the farm would be his. It would never be mine, even if Mother were to will it to me. Whatever a wife earned or inherited belonged automatically to her husband and I shouldn't forget it. I was angry, saying that I would expect a say in decisions all the same, and he slapped me. That was when I began learning to be a little wary of James.

But he was essentially kind and wanted to please me. He had let me choose the name Rose for our pretty baby daughter, even though he would have preferred something more work-aday. I was grateful for that.

It was shortly after that conversation about my mother's supplies of drink, and the government's determination to stop free trading, that my mother's strength began to fail. The stiff joints she had complained about suddenly grew stiffer and she became breathless after climbing the stairs. Her skin developed an odd orange flush, not the healthy pink of her former outdoor life. A week after that little spat with James about free trading, she suddenly died.

She was in the dairy at the time, trying to help Mrs Page to churn butter, in our West Country way, rolling the butter churn back and forth between them, in a sling, rather than spinning it by a handle as I have since learned is the manner of it elsewhere. She said she could manage as long as she could sit down, and we put a chair in the dairy for her.

Suddenly Mrs Page cried out my name and brought me running from the kitchen, to find my mother lying on the floor while stout Mrs Page stood by looking terrified and begging her to speak. I knelt down beside her in alarm, and then understood that she was dead.

Foxwell seemed strange now that I was alone there with James and our children. The farm was prospering in his care, but he was very careful with money and we didn't have as many hands as we really needed. Betty had left us to marry, and pale little Annie, who replaced her, was a fifteen-year-old waif from an orphanage in Taunton, which to James meant that he could pay her much less than Betty had ever been paid. As a result, I worked harder than ever and rarely left our land. I heard little of the Duggans, except an occasional snippet from Mr Silcox who had formed the habit of occasionally riding out to dine with us. From him we heard that in Minehead, Josiah Duggan had cut back on his free trading, partly because of the dangerous Revenue cutter the *Shark*, but partly, said Mr Silcox, because he didn't care to swell Napoleon Bonaparte's coffers. James and Josiah were in agreement there, I thought.

When I heard these occasional mentions of the Duggans, I tried to give no sign, but always, something moved in the pit of my stomach. Something I could not control; something that I did not think would ever die away. I took care not to let it show.

1805 passed and 1806 set in. As William approached the age of four, he put on a spurt of growth. He became quite useful at small tasks round the farm. At supper one evening, James commented on it, with approval.

'He's interested in the sheep. Before long I'll get him a puppy of his own to train. Boy and dog'll grow into shepherding side by side. Though he'll need some schooling. I know you set store by schooling, Peggy, and that's right enough. I've often been glad of my own. When he's a bit older, he can go to Mr Silcox's school, same as we did. And Rose too, later on. I've actually talked to Mr Silcox about them – I saw him when I went to Exford today. Met him in the White Horse Inn – he were having a pint of cider. I've asked him to dinner tomorrow as there's something he wants to talk about. He's takin' on an assistant so as he can retire in a year or two, it seems. He's already thinkin' about our William there. Collectin' pupils in advance so as his replacement'll have a good full classroom to start him off.'

I had just finished giving Rose her supper. I leant back in my chair, feeling her relax sleepily against my shoulder. Times were changing, I thought. Bert Page had died just after the previous Christmas, and Mrs Page seemed to age overnight, going suddenly from stout but brisk middle age to a hobbling crone, and then she had left us to live with a married daughter in South Molton on the other side of the moor. We had had to find replacements for the Pages. Fred Webster was a large, quiet, good-natured man in his thirties, with a large, quiet, good-natured wife called Mattie, about the same age, and three children so far, though they said candidly that they hoped for more. James had a sharp tongue at times but none of them seemed to be in the least impressed by it. Fred would listen when James berated him, say: 'As you wish, zur,' and tug his forelock and then go on imperturbably doing whatever he'd been doing before.

This irritated James at times, but on the other hand, Fred was competent. He was very good with our Red Devon bull. Mr Francis Quartly of South Molton had finally relented and let us invest in one of his fine young bulls but though a splendid sire, Foxwell Sandy had an unreliable temperament. We were glad to have Fred's help in managing him, and I was certainly pleased with Mattie's assistance in the house. She was a good cook and skilled in the dairy, too.

I sat there, patting Rose's back, and looking into the fire and thought: well, this was life. Changes were bound to come. Mine was not the life I had chosen but Ralph was far away, and I was turning into a typical placid farmer's wife and careful mother, with my waistline not what it was and my dreams laid by.

But not thrown away. No, never that, though only I knew it. And if I didn't go to the market, the Websters brought back gossip. One of the things I had gleaned from them was that Ralph was still in Antigua.

But one day, he might come home, said a renegade little voice within me. He might. If only I could see him again. Just once. That would be enough. It wouldn't be wrong to wish for that, would it? Just to see him, to exchange a few words! Just to look on his face again and feed my hunger for him. To renew my memory of how he looked, the way his hair grew . . .

Ralph.

Aloud, I said: 'William can't very well go to school in Exford before he can sit a pony on his own.'

'Ah. Ponies,' said James. 'All ours are gettin' on in years. I've been a bit slack over this,' he added thoughtfully. 'Exmoors can live a good few years past twenty but they don't all. I should have picked out a couple of our foals two or three years ago. Nothing like a pony you've handled since it was six months old. You know them through and through and they know you. Well, at next autumn's Pony Fair in Bampton, I'd better keep one or two of ours out of the sale and try to buy a couple of full-grown ones as well; there always are some. I just hope all ours last that long.'

I had actually tried, once or twice, to remind James about the advancing need to replace our ponies, but he didn't like it when, as he exasperatingly put it, I tried to make decisions concerning the farm. Foxwell was his, not mine. I said nothing.

Everything was normal that evening. Except for my secret dreamings, the past was asleep.

It woke up, abruptly, when Mr Silcox came next day to dine.

I welcomed him, as usual, into the parlour. It was no longer dismal because when I took over the running of the house, I had remembered the polish and flowers and ornaments of Bronwen Duggan's parlour and tried to recreate it at Foxwell.

Flowers were not feasible, since we didn't grow them and wild flowers don't last well in vases, but I had brought in some little ornaments, taken to polishing the furniture at least once a month and added colourful cushions and a mantelpiece clock with a pleasant tick. James let me keep some of the money I made from the butter and eggs that were my province more than his and I used that. These simple things had altered the whole atmosphere of the room from neglected to friendly.

Mr Silcox's grey horse had long since died, and he now had a placid brown mare, a plump-sided creature with a maternal air about her, as though she regarded her riders as children in her charge. James unsaddled her while I showed her owner into the parlour and offered him wine. I noticed as I did so, that he was growing visibly older, with new lines on his long-chinned face and a thinning of his silvery hair. He seemed active enough, however. He accepted some white wine, though I saw him glance doubtfully at the French label on the bottle. 'My mother bought it before the war started,' I said. 'We wouldn't want to trade with Boney's country now.'

'Quite. There's not much free trading these days,' said Mr Silcox. 'And a good thing too, in my opinion. I never thought the government was right to put so much duty on so many things, but breaking the law is still to be deplored. Peggy, I want to talk to you about the future. And I've a piece of news, too, that I didn't have when I saw James yesterday . . . Ah, here *is* James. Good.'

Over the wine, Mr Silcox explained his plans. 'I'm taking on an assistant. He used to be a curate at St Michael's, but he's taken to teaching. Edmund Baker, his name is.'

'I remember him. He and his sister Harriet used to lodge by Minehead quay. They came to the Duggans' house sometimes while I was staying there,' I said.

James frowned. He always did if I made even the slightest, most oblique reference to the days of my first engagement. I think he sensed that I still remembered Ralph with tenderness. For this very reason, I sometimes made casual references to those former days, hoping that because they were casual, they would reassure him. I wanted him to think that they were just a part of my life that I still remembered, but not with any special feelings. If I kept it up for long enough, I hoped this would actually happen. His knotted brow at this moment suggested that so far, it hadn't. I pretended not to notice.

Mr Silcox hadn't noticed, either. He went cheerfully on. 'Edmund does indeed have a sister called Harriet. She teaches at a little school in Minehead. It was she who interested Edmund in education and now he particularly wants to bring it to the children of the outlying areas, such as up here on the moors – just as I have been trying to do for most of my life. Edmund Baker is leaving his post at St Michael's and is joining me next month. I think he'll be a good teacher – he's a patient fellow and very well informed. And I'm doing my best to see that he has a class of a worthwhile size to teach. Now, when I saw you last, James, you said you were interested in sending me your children?'

James said yes, and I began to talk of my son's good health and rapidly developing intelligence. James agreed, though he said that he hoped the school would concentrate on common-sense subjects and not go off into that there Latin and a lot of silly talk about folk like that Romeo and Juliet, who wrecked their lives for the sake of what they called love. 'I mind on your telling us about they things and it was all mighty interesting, but it's not much use on a farm. Hope I don't give offence.'

'Ah,' said Mr Silcox. 'But even if you don't have a use for such things, you know them, don't you? I told you about them. And there they are, stuck in your head and something to think about when you've nothing else on your mind! Once you know something, you can't stop knowing it. Doesn't mean you have to imitate it. No harm in pondering on how other folk lived in other times. Knowledge can be a kind of amusement. Never mind. Now, my other bit of news, that I couldn't tell you yesterday, James, as I didn't know it then myself. It's about the Cutlers – the parents of that poor girl Maisie who was found in that bog on Codsend all those years ago. Remember?'

'Not the sort of thing most folk would forget,' said James. I was silent. I wouldn't forget, either. If Maisie hadn't been murdered, I would not be here now. I would be with Ralph. Ralph. *Ralph.*

'I've always been friendly with the Cutlers,' Mr Silcox said. 'I go to see them now and then and yesterday, after I saw you in Exford and I'd gone home, James, *they* came to see *me.* Fact is, after all these years, Ernie Cutler still asks my opinions on things, as he did when he was a young man, just out of my schoolroom. I remember he asked me, when he was courting Lilian Summers, that's Mrs Cutler now, if I thought he was marrying too early. He was twenty, then. Well, he had a good job working in the grounds of the castle, so that he could look after her and that being so, I said the rest was up to him. Anyway, yesterday, only half an hour after I left you, Ernie and Lilian were at my door. They'd borrowed a horse – courtesy of the Luttrells and their head groom – and come twelve miles up the Avill valley to talk to me, riding double. You'll never guess what's happened.'

No, we couldn't. We waited for him to tell us.

'It seems,' said Mr Silcox, 'that two weeks back, they woke up in the morning and opened their front door and found a package on the step. It was heavy, Ernie said. They opened it, and there was five hundred pounds inside, in high value coins. There was no letter with it, no sign where it came from. But there it was. Five hundred pounds.'

'I don't understand,' I said, bewildered. 'Why should anyone . . .?'

'Maisie,' said James, sharper than I was. 'That's what you mean, don't 'ee, Mr Silcox? Blood money, from her murderer.'

I sat up straighter in my chair. 'Then it couldn't have been Philip! He's abroad.'

'You can't know that for sure!' said James rather snappily.

Mr Silcox shook his head. 'Come, James. The whole of Minehead knows that the Duggan boys are both in Antigua. The Cutlers know – they said as much to me. Peggy has it right. Whoever presented the Cutlers with that money, it wasn't the Duggan sons.'

'Josiah could have put that money on the Cutlers' doorstep, trying to clear Philip's name,' said James. 'I wouldn't put that past him.'

Mr Silcox laughed. 'The Cutlers talked to me of that, as well. The first thing they did was go to the village constable and tell him, and the upshot was that there's been an enquiry, with the magistrates looking into it. Someone did suggest Josiah had done it. But I gather that Josiah was at the enquiry and nearly blew the top of his head off, he was so angry. Said he'd always known his son was innocent and the boy was doing well where he was and he – Josiah, I mean – would be a fool to stir all that old business up now, when folk were starting to forget it and he didn't have five hundred pounds to throw about, either, not with trade the way it was. Free trade, I assume he meant. The boatbuilding side is healthy enough. We need shipping to guard our shores from Napoleon.'

'So what happened in the end?' James said.

'The finger ought to point at Laurence Wheelwright,' Mr Silcox said. 'He's got money now – he went away for a while and the Lord only knows what he's been up to, but he's come back to Minehead, saying he'd had a second legacy last year, from his father, who had a saving disposition, according to Laurence. Both his parents are dead now. He's taken the lease of a shop in Minehead and turned himself into a ship's chandler. You know – ropes, paint, sailcloth, lanterns, all the rest of it, bar masts. They're the Duggans' province and Josiah wouldn't want Laurence Wheelwright, of all people, trespassing on his ground. Laurence has had the good sense not to. *He* could have afforded that five hundred, easily. Only Daniel Hopton holds to his story that Joseph never left the barn roof that afternoon. I wonder about that, you know.'

'In what way?' I asked.

Mr Silcox frowned uneasily. 'It's maybe not fair to specu-late. Anyway, if it was Laurence, he's at least paid for his crime in a sense! But I have wondered if he might have a hold of some sort over Daniel. You see, where they were, wasn't so far from where Maisie worked, only a quarter of a mile or so. Laurence wouldn't have had to be away from the barn for very long if he wanted to accost her as she set out to see her parents. They could have quarrelled and . . . well, you can imagine. He had far more chance of seeing her than Philip had.'

'But he couldn't have got her all the way to Codsend,' I protested. 'And in daylight, too!'

'Who said anything about daylight?' said James. 'There's a nice patch of woodland near the Avill smallholding, with a good tangled thicket in it. He could have left the body there and fetched it away to Codsend during the night. Wasn't that talked about at the time? He'd only have to slip out quietly. Where did he sleep?'

'He was a foreman,' said Mr Silcox. 'All this was said at Maisie's inquest. He slept over the stables like the other hands but he'd fixed himself a bit of privacy and *because* he was foreman, no one said anything. He'd screened off a little place at one end of the stable loft. He could have come and gone pretty freely and no one the wiser.'

'What came out of the enquiry?' James asked.

'It seems it was agreed in the end that it was most unlikely that Josiah was responsible for the money,' said Mr Silcox. 'That's what the Cutlers told me. Philip's apparently safe and well and happy where he is. I dare say Josiah would like it if the boy's name were cleared, but to fling away five hundred pounds! As one of the magistrates apparently said, it makes no sense. No. It was reckoned that whether it was Laurence or some other of Maisie's lovers – she was flirtatious and maybe she was seeing a lad or two, that no one knows about – this was conscience money from the murderer himself. Five hundred pounds! You'd need a very powerful reason for handing over an amount that size!'

'And then?' James persisted.

'Well, the final outcome was that from now on, the matter's closed. Maisie's murderer, whoever he is, clearly has a conscience; let him carry his guilt as a burden to the grave and let her parents have money to comfort their old age, even if they don't have Maisie. Odd how these ancient customs reappear,' said Mr Silcox peacefully, blowing more smoke rings.

'And what old customs would those be?' James enquired.

'Oh, back before the Norman Conquest,' said Mr Silcox, 'the Anglo-Saxons didn't execute murderers; they fined them. The fines varied according to the status of the victim and whether it was a man or a woman. They were called Weregild – it meant Man's Gold. Or Man's Value; you could translate it that way. Murderers had to compensate the victim's dependants. That's a law that's long gone, yet here it is, reappearing a thousand or so years later, as if some old instinct's been awoken. Interesting.'

'I call it outrageous,' said James.

I looked at him, startled by the hard tone of his voice, and saw that his eyes were as cold and as hard as blue marbles. They looked like that when he was very angry.

'This is 1806,' said James fiercely. 'It's not the days before that old Conquest. From all I've heard about Josiah Duggan, I shouldn't think that money came from him, any more than anyone else does, but Laurence Wheelwright's another matter. He's been let off, to my mind. I reckon that Daniel Hopton ought to be had up and questioned hard about what really happened that afternoon. Hammer the questions home hard enough and long enough and maybe he'd have a different tale to tell!'

I had lived with James long enough to know that and I knew he had a harsh side, but it had not shown itself with this much force before. It made me uncomfortable.

He said now: 'Did the Cutlers come all the way from Dunster on a borrowed horse just to tell 'ee all this?'

'No,' said Mr Silcox. 'They wanted advice. They'd been told they could keep the money but they wanted to know my opinion about that. They weren't sure if they should, not knowing where it came from, and considering the likely reason for it. Ernie said it felt as if they'd sold their daughter. I thought they should rather have gone to their own vicar, at St George's, there in Dunster but they said no, they'd always thought my advice was good and here they were, in need of it and please would I advise them.'

'And did you?' James enquired.

'Yes, I did. I told them to keep the money. Giving it away for some charitable purpose might be a pretty gesture, but it wouldn't bring Maisie back and they're not wealthy folk. Ernie won't be able to work in the castle grounds for ever; he's got a bad back now. They will be rich now and safe from poverty in their old age. Maisie was their only one, you know. Lilian's grieved over that, but that's the way it is, sometimes. So they've no young people to help them in their old age.'

James remarked: 'Well, Philip Duggan's clear, by the sound of it. I fancy you're right about that.'

I was careful to show no emotion. Presently, I withdrew to the kitchen. Dinner would be ready soon.

I kept my face calm but my mind was in turmoil like the sea in a gale. Philip was innocent. That seemed proved, now. If it had been proved at once, at the time, yes, I would now be married to Ralph. We had been robbed.

It was confusing because of course, if we had married, neither William nor Rose would exist and that was an awful thought. I could hardly imagine a world without them. But I supposed there would have been other children, just as dear. Children that I *was* without, would never know . . . it was too muddling.

I couldn't go on thinking along those lines. I could only think of Ralph, and what we might have had and could never have now.

It was like a ravine opening up at my feet. I did not dare look into it, for fear of falling.

Return of the Past

Our ponies, aged though they were, were as yet not showing their years. In May, James went to Minehead in search of a new and better plough, taking our two-pony wagon to fetch it home in. He came back not only with the plough but with news.

'Josiah Duggan is dead,' he said, as he came into the kitchen and sat down.

'Mr Duggan?' I was surprised. Josiah had always seemed to me to be full of health and vitality. 'What . . . what happened?'

'Keen for news of 'un, are 'ee?' There it was again, that jealous edge that James always showed when the Duggans were mentioned, in any context.

Mildly, I said: 'Well, he was once a friend of my family. What happened?'

'He didn't drown, or get himself hanged,' said James, a remark that was so surprising that I couldn't stop myself from saying: 'Smuggling isn't a hanging offence now even if it still went on!'

'I allus reckoned it ought to be,' said James. 'Not much better than wrecking, in my view.'

'Wrecking?' I said. 'What's that? I've not heard the word before.'

'Something that wicked folk get up on parts of the Cornwall coast,' James informed me. 'Leading ships astray. Showing lights, as if they're lights of another ship ahead, so as to draw vessels on to the rocks. Then in the wreckers go, kill anyone as hasn't been drowned in the wreck, and grab the cargo.'

'I'm sure the Duggans never did *that*!' I said, appalled.

'Maybe, maybe not, but b'ain't the line just a bit fine, between bringin' in contraband and maybe fightin' Revenue men – there's always the chance someone'll get killed – and outright murder? Still, Josiah Duggan died in his bed, decently enough. Stricken with an apoplexy in his own parlour, carried to his bed, died next day. That's the word in Minehead. It's said that his missus has sent abroad for her sons to come home.'

'Well, naturally,' I said.

That, of course, was the reason for James' sharp tone. He didn't like the idea of Ralph coming back to England. As for me, I was once more standing on the edge of a ravine, into which I dared not look.

I didn't usually go to the October fair at Bampton. It was on the far side of the moor and a long way from Foxwell. In the main, it was a pony fair. The ponies were driven off the moor and the foals were looked at, branded if they were to go back on to the moor; otherwise, sold for use when grown in harness or for riding. Someone from Foxwell always went, though. We had foals of our own to sell and such things as new tools, seed, poultry and much else were for sale there. This time, I had several purchases in mind, and also we were going to choose the foals we wanted to keep and buy a pair of mature ponies. That would be interesting. In the October of 1806, I asked to accompany James.

He and Fred had taken part in the annual pony roundup and Fred, with Reggie, another of our farmhands, had taken them on to Bampton in advance and would stay there with them until the fair. The rounding-up was a major business involving the whole moor and covering a couple of days. While it was in progress, I had caught distant sounds and glimpses of galloping ponies, manes and tails wildly flying, tearing along the crest of the hill above us.

We didn't take the children. Mattie Webster was willing to look after them for us, so we left them with her, and set off the day before the fair, riding our elderly but still hardy Clover and Spots and taking our time, planning to spend two nights at a Bampton inn.

It was a beautiful day. Clear, cool sunshine came and went between the high and harmless clouds that a steady south-west wind was blowing across the sky. The cloud shadows flowed across the moorland hills and valleys, and made the land look as though it were moving, like the sea in a swell. A kestrel hovered for a while overhead, almost as though we were its intended prey, but then swooped, lethal as an unsheathed sword and yet with the same fierce beauty, towards some luckless vole or mouse somewhere away to our right, and all the time, like a twinkling in the sky, there were skylarks.

I enjoyed that journey. I was happy that day. It was neither too hot nor too cold and there were no flies. In summer, flies are the curse of Exmoor, especially where there's bracken. We stopped in the town of Dulverton, in the middle of the moor, for a midday dinner and came down into Bampton comfortably before suppertime, to find the place already humming, for the animals to be sold were already there, foals separated now from their dams. The air was full of frightened whinnying, the pens full of tossing manes and white-ringed eyes, the air smelling of horses and dust.

James had written to arrange a room for us at an inn, and the room was duly ready. We took supper, slept well, breakfasted heartily and went out next day into the uproar of a fair already well under way, raucous with the shouts of stallholders, and that persistent whinnying. Fred and Reggie, who had found themselves a room in another inn, met us by the pen where our own foals were.

I felt sorry for the ponies. The separated mares and foals cried for each other, rearing at the fences that enclosed them. The foals that were to be returned to the moor were being branded and this was not pretty to watch, although the foals on the whole seemed more furious than hurt, biting and kicking their human assailants whenever they got the chance. But I didn't like to see it and as Fred and Reggie were watching over our ponies, James, to please me, said we could shop at the stalls until the selling began. I wanted a new winter shawl and some knitting wool and James required a hat, while the stalls selling tools of various kinds drew James as magnets draw iron. We roamed about for some time before we went to inspect possible equine purchases.

When we returned to the pens, James immediately caught sight of a likely animal. 'Look at that one, Peggy, that mare colt over there. What a beauty!'

The foal in question was indeed striking, because for one thing, although she had the pale, mealy nose of the Exmoor pony, her head was not quite the right shape and she was bright chestnut with white socks, a colouring never seen in true-bred Exmoor ponies.

'Not pure Exmoor,' James was saying. 'She'd never stand a winter on the moor, but with us, she'd have a nice warm stable.'

'There's another one,' I said, pointing to a colt on the other side of the pen. 'Darker, but he's certainly chestnut.'

'By the look of it,' James said, 'someone's turned a chestnut Arab stallion out on the moor for the summer. That mare colt has an Arabian head.'

'I'm surprised you never caught sight of 'un,' said a voice behind us. We swung round and found ourselves face to face with Stephen Duggan. I barely recognized him. He was leaning on a stick and looked very lined. His hair was hidden by a big cap but his eyebrows were now white. He had got rid of his beard and the stubble on his imperfectly shaven chin was white as well, and his grin was as unlovely ever.

'I had him out on the moor for four months last year,' he was saying. 'Arab stallion, name of Emperor. Bit of an experiment I've been longing to try since I don't know when. Sold 'un at the year's end, got an offer of more than I paid for 'un so I took it. Those two are the only foals of his that took his colouring. I'm sellin' all his colts, though; it's right enough that they're not bred for winter on these hills. I hope to get good prices. There are things to see to on the farm. I reckoned there weren't much point takin' a lot of trouble with it when I didn't know who'd have it after I'm gone, but that's over now. Ralph's home so I've left my tenancy to him and I thought I'd best spruce the place up a bit. Philip's staying out in Antigua, seems he's settled and don't want to come back. Ralph can farm the place hisself or let it on, but it'll be in Duggan hands just the same. And he'll have Duggans to come after him, with luck, because . . . Oh, there they are! *Ralph! Here!*'

I had realized that by now Ralph might well be back in Minehead, but I hadn't expected to encounter him at Bampton. Yet here he was, walking towards us through the crowd and he was not alone. At his side, smiling, *glowing*, was Harriet Baker. I knew her at once. They came up to us, and before

Ralph introduced her, I saw who she now was. On the third finger of her left hand gleamed a golden wedding ring.

Time had made no difference; I could not look at Ralph, could not behold his dark, smiling eyes or the shape of his dear face, and not feel the world reel beneath my feet. But I must make no sign. A commonplace exchange was taking place.

'So 'ee came back.' That was James. 'You got tired of growing sugar or cotton or summat in a nice warm climate?' The undercurrent of aggression was unmistakeable.

'I was supposed to stay there for five years,' Ralph said. 'And so I had when my father died. I'd been thinking things over, in two minds whether to stay on with Philip, but as soon as my mother's letter came, that settled it. I knew I must come back. Besides, Philip didn't need me any more; Cousin George did help us to buy a small plantation of our own and it's doing well, so I persuaded Phil to buy me out, and found a passage home. I've been home for three months now, and more than that, I've got married! This is my wife, Harriet! Harriet, this is James and Peggy Bright, from Foxwell Farm, not so far from my great-uncle's place.'

'I remember Peggy!' said Harriet, smiling. 'We met years ago, when Peggy was staying in Minehead.'

She was a tactful woman, this radiant Harriet. Her smile was joyous, her chestnut hair gleamed; her chestnut eyes shone. She had met me when I was staying with Ralph's family; she and her brother had come to dine and Ralph had been there. She had known that I was then engaged to Ralph. She had sense enough not to mention that now and her eyes searched mine, wondering if I still remembered, if I were now contented. I made myself smile back, to tell her that I was indeed content. 'You look well!' she said.

'I am very well, thank you.' It wasn't so very difficult to return her smile because Harriet was the sort of person it is impossible to dislike. 'I remember you, too,' I said. 'But it was a long time ago. I'm Mrs Bright now and I have two children!' The world was spinning round me.

I saw Ralph's eyes change. It was momentary, but it was there. I, his Peggy, his love, had two children, by another man. James Bright, standing at my side, had had what I had once pledged myself to give to Ralph. But Ralph had pledged himself to me, as well. Neither of us had kept that pledge. Ralph had married Harriet, and I had stood at James' side before the altar at St Salwyn's and taken certain vows.

For life.

Stephen Duggan began to talk about his experiment with the Exmoor–Arab cross. Ralph and I exchanged one long, intense look. In it, we made each other know that nothing had changed, nothing at all. We were still part of each other, for ever. And then we looked away.

It was such a brief exchange of glances, but James saw it and understood. I saw his gaze shift from one of us to the other, and I saw his blue eyes grow chilly. Then he turned to attend to what Stephen Duggan was saying about crossbred horses and after that he exchanged a few commonplace, amiable sentences with Harriet. He also purchased Stephen Duggan's two crossbred foals. But then, he drew us away. We went on to buy the mature ponies we needed, a pair of purebred Exmoors, both past four years old, but James said little to me. He had gone very quiet. We returned to the inn and went up to our room to change our clothes before dinner. As soon as he had closed the door behind us, he rounded on me, taking me by surprise, so that I sat down suddenly on the side of the bed and stared at him, hardly recognizing James, my husband, in this red-faced man whose eyes had once more become like blue marbles, hard and bulging.

'I saw you and Ralph Duggan looking at each other. Don't you try denyin' it, don't you dare. You looked at him and he looked at you and it was all there. But for that there business over Maisie Cutler, 'ee'd have married Duggan and not me, and you still wish it had been! Don't 'ee!'

'But I married *you*,' I said weakly. 'Years ago. Ralph Duggan's all in the past.'

'Is he? Didn't look like it today, did it, you two gawping at each other like a pair of mooncalves!'

'We didn't! That's not true!'

'I always knew you'd sooner it had been him, but after all these years, I reckoned 'ee'd got over it; put it behind 'ee. I reckoned by now, I'd have your heart, *Mrs Bright*. But I b'ain't got it! Have I? I *saw* that look 'ee gave him and the look he gave you! Don't lie to me! Your heart's still his!'

I shrank away from his furious face, feeling the tears just below the surface. 'I suppose that just for a moment, we both remembered the past, but that was just natural,' I said timidly. 'We can't change the past, or forget it completely.'

'Do 'ee have to throw it in my face the way you did?'

'I *didn't!*' I was really crying now. 'I did *not!* You're imagining things! You're not being fair. The past makes no difference now. You're my husband! And Harriet's married to Ralph! Harriet's nice. Ralph wouldn't want me now.'

'*Bah!* I know what I saw and believe me, I could have killed the both of 'ee, then and there!'

Anger came to my aid. Through my tears, I said: 'Poor Harriet! What did she ever do to you, that you would want to make her a widow!'

'Keep your voice down! Do 'ee want the whole inn to hear?'

'You began it! You attacked me! Oh, *James!*' I was still crying. 'Are we going to be at loggerheads over it for the rest of our lives?' I took a deep breath and wiped my eyes, and then added: 'I love you, James. I want to go on loving you. Only it's difficult to do that when you glare at me and say you'd like to kill me. When you say threatening things like that, I just feel frightened and I don't know what to do. I want things to be ordinary again.'

Some of the rage was dying out of his face. My flash of indignation had apparently done some good. 'Can't we change and have supper?' I asked. 'And just be ourselves again?'

He sat down heavily on the bed beside me. 'Yes. We can. But we're not goin' to supper yet. I'm goin' to remind 'ee who you belong to.'

James had always been a kind and considerate lover. That evening, however, he was neither. That evening, his embrace was not loving but imprisoning, his entry an act of conquest, his search for satisfaction a furious pounding as though he were trying to conquer an enemy. We were both exhausted when it was over. There was none of the usual pleasant afterglow, only weariness and, on my side, something dangerously near to hatred; on his, probably, guilt.

I had told him I loved him. It had never really been true. There had been affection, friendship, warm, pleasant feelings like that but the bonding I had once had – still had – with Ralph; the huge need, the desire not just to be with him but to give myself away to him; these were absent and could not be created by an act of will.

But from now on, I must be careful. From now on, my life and Ralph's must be totally separate and if, by accident, we should encounter each other, we must give no sign of that which still lay unspoken between us.

What we felt must stay hidden always, lifelong, for eternity.

Eternity suddenly seemed to be a very long time indeed.

Storm

Time slipped past. We didn't quarrel again. We talked as we always had concerning things on the farm, and the children. The next winter was appalling. We were snowed in for six weeks and although we had ample supplies of grain and preserves, bacon and home-cured ham and salted beef, we had never depended completely on these salted meats in any previous winter. We had treated ourselves, now and then, to freshly killed chicken or sacrificed a sheep, and since James followed the hounds and went to Exford now and then to drink with the huntsmen, we were presented with the occasional haunch of venison.

But with the snow piling up against our windows, and ten-foot-deep drifts in places, there was no hunting and as we didn't know how long the snow would last, we preferred not to kill our own stock. We could feed them, since we had good stores of fodder, hay and turnips and the like, and despite the infuriating depredations of the deer when they got into our cornfields in summer, that winter, we tried to put out food for them when they came down from the moor in search of it. Neither of us could bear to see them gnawing at tree bark, or trying to paw a way through the snow for a few mouthfuls of sour winter grass. The wild ponies did best and somehow most of them survived.

In the summer of 1807, I was very ill with a miscarriage. Mattie Webster was a blessing, for she understood these things and skilfully took charge of me. She was a blessing again, early in 1809 when I had my son John. I had produced William and Rose quite easily, within a few hours, but with John, I strove and suffered for two agonizing nights and two dreadful days and was near the end of my strength when at last he emerged into the world.

'There shouldn't be another child,' said the Exford physician Mattie had sent for in desperation on the second day. 'It would be dangerous.' He gave James a stern look, and then took him out of the room for some private talk.

When it was all over, James said: 'The doctor had a few words with me. Well, three's enough; they're all healthy, and I don't want them losing their mother. As for us, well, he had a word or two about that.'

Thereafter, James claimed his marital rights only rarely and when he did so, he withdrew before he could plant his seed. I didn't mind. I had no desire to conceive again and I didn't mind the long gaps between our uneasy unions. I had never found much satisfaction in James' arms, anyway.

As a couple, we did well enough, I suppose. There was, always, an area of silence between us, things that must never be mentioned, but as long as we were careful about that, all was more or less well. There was no excitement but there was affection – yes, there *was* affection – and we had much to share and talk about.

The farm continued to prosper. We enlarged our herd of Red Devon cattle and our flock of sheep and acquired a shepherd called Zachariah Searle, a tall, lean, dour but very competent individual, who came of a line of shepherds so long that according to Mr Silcox, who still dined with us sometimes and sometimes brought Edmund Baker with him, they'd been looking after sheep on Exmoor since before the Norman Conquest.

Rose, growing rapidly now, was becoming prettier than ever. When she was seven, we sent her with William to what was now Edmund Baker's school in Exford. She learned to read and write and if she was not a particularly gifted pupil, William was very sharp and also attentive, so Edmund told us with approval. James was remote with Edmund at first, but Edmund was tactful, talking freely about our children's studies, but never mentioning Harriet – or Ralph. Gradually, to my relief, James relaxed.

The long-drawn-out conflict with France and the ambitions of Napoleon Bonaparte continued. We heard a rumour of an attempted French landing somewhere in Wales, but that was nowhere near us. The beacons on Dunkery and Selworthy remained unlit and at last, in the June of 1815, came the Battle of Waterloo – it was William's thirteenth birthday, in fact – and the end of Napoleon's hopes.

'Peace from now on,' James said, when we learned of it, through Edmund Baker. A messenger had come from Minehead to tell the vicar, who happened to be at the school at the time, giving a lesson on religion. Edmund promptly gave his pupils the rest of the day off, and set out on a round of as many moorland farms as he could reach, to spread the glad news further. The vicar went back to his church to ring the bells so that all Exford would know that something momentous had occurred.

Edmund Baker, who before continuing his news-bearing ride, had stopped to drink tea and eat a slice of cheesecake in our kitchen, said: 'It may not be as peaceful as all that. Mr Silcox never gambles but he says that if he did, he'd lay money on folk starting up with smuggling again, now that it won't help pay for French soldiers to invade us.'

'Oh, surely not,' James said. 'The government's come down hard on smugglers these last ten years or more. We've got a Riding Officer patrolling the coastline nowadays and a Waterguard at sea, patrolling in the Channel. I saw one of their rowing galleys, the other day when I was in Porlock. That's where it's kept, so I hear, it was just pulling out of the harbour. I doubt if any of that'll be withdrawn; it's worked too well. And the *Shark*'s still at sea, too.'

'There's a new one now,' said Edmund, gathering up cheese-cake crumbs and eyeing the parent cake so wistfully that I automatically reached for the cake knife and cut him another slice. 'This one's called the *Harpy*. A dreadful name, in my opinion; I suspect that whoever named her isn't quite in sympathy with her purpose.'

As a rule James never mentioned Ralph if he could help it but now he said: 'Is your brother-in-law, Ralph Duggan, likely to start free trading again? Or has he repented of the past? Did he build the *Harpy*?'

'No, he didn't,' said Edmund, and added: 'I've wondered if he might still be interested in smuggling but I hope not. He's got the Hathertons, Luke and Roger, father and son, both working at the boatyard now, though, and they're a bad

influence, I'd say. But he'd be taking a terrible risk. He and
Harriet have four children now, and what would become of
them if Ralph was taken? She doesn't say very much, but I
think Harriet worries.'

I busied myself with refreshing the teapot, and avoided James'
eye. Edmund, tactful again, moved from the fraught subject of
Ralph to the less fraught topic of Stephen Duggan and remarked
that he had heard somewhere or other that Stephen Duggan
had made further experiments with crossbreeding ponies.

'Ah. We've done quite well with two of his Exmoor–Arab
crosses,' James said.

They had been good purchases. We had named the chestnut
mare colt Goldfinch and called her darker half-brother Copper.
They were good-tempered and when the time came were
easily broken both to saddle and harness. They were strong
enough for a long day out round the farm, and good-looking
into the bargain. Only Goldfinch had ever given us any trouble,
and that was to do with shoeing.

Sweet-natured though she usually was, we had a terrible
time with her the first time we took her to Exford to be shod.
She reared, squealed, kicked Ezra Kent, who was still the Exford
smith, and bit his twelve-year-old son who was working with
his father to learn the trade. Later, she came to realize that the
smith would not harm her, but she was always nervy when
we took her there which, unfortunately, was rather often. Like
many horses with white socks, she had hooves with pale horn,
which tends to be soft, and in her case, it seemed softer than
was desirable. Her shoes frequently came adrift. She would
then go instantly lame on the exposed foot, as though the
uneven walk that resulted really hurt her. James maintained
that this was actually a form of sulking about having shoes
inflicted on her at all, though he did add that that if so, it
showed what an intelligent animal she was.

The conversation drifted back to Ralph after a while, because
Stephen Duggan was in poor health, and there had apparently
been much talk of what would happen to Standing Stone when
he finally went.

'Harriet did say to me once that she would like to see
Ralph sell the boatyard and move to the farm,' Edmund said.

'Ralph knows something about cultivation now – he learned it in Antigua.'

I held up the teapot, in a gesture that enquired *who wants another cup?* James' eyes were on me and once again, they looked like hard blue marble.

'If Ralph Duggan has the good sense to keep his hands clean until Stephen Duggan passes away,' he remarked, 'maybe he will move into Standing Stone. That would take him further away from temptation, I suppose.' His expression dared me to say I was glad.

Edmund held his cup out and I filled it, pretending to have noticed nothing, but if James were wondering how it would be when Ralph and Harriet were at Standing Stone, only a short distance away from us, so was I.

We were not yet old. I was only in my mid-thirties; Ralph much the same age. To have him so close would be wonderful, a joy. I would surely see him sometimes!

It would be dangerous.

That night, I found out how dangerous, for James made love to me, except that it wasn't love. It was as it had been after the fair at Bampton, so many years ago. It was an act of conquest. He claimed – almost *pro*claimed – his rights over me, his rights of possession.

Ralph was not mentioned. We did not quarrel. James made himself clear without words. I continued to pretend that I had noticed nothing untoward.

But I remembered James saying, at Bampton, that he had wanted to kill us both, and I remembered that sudden harshness of his, long ago, when whoever had murdered Maisie had bought himself free of the law. There was a demon in James that must never be aroused.

I hoped that Stephen Duggan would cling to life for a good while yet.

In the autumn of 1815, James said: 'Now that William is thirteen, it's time he finished with book-learning and spent his time on the farm with me. He can read and write and he adds up better than I do, and he can spout dates in history the way I never could and that's enough. None of that'll tell him when the wheat's ripe for cutting. And he agrees. Says he feels like a man now, and it's time.'

I nodded. Only the week before, William had told me that he thought he should leave off going to Edmund Baker's school. 'But we'd better tell Mr Baker, hadn't we?' I said. 'We know him well – it might look rude just to stop sending William there, or even just to send a note.'

James was agreeable to that, and on a clear early November morning, we harnessed Goldfinch to the cart, and set off for Exford.

It was a very clear day indeed. Exmoor's hillcrests and the folds in the land are nearly all smooth; where the land falls away into river valleys, it looks as though it has been partly liquid at some point and was poured over the edge like treacle being poured from a spoon. In weather of such clarity, we could see details miles away. As we left Foxwell, I saw that the standing stone on Stephen Duggan's land, though tiny with distance, was plainly visible, and the colours of the dark heather patches and the stretches of golden-brown bracken on the slopes below it were as separate as a small cloud drifting from the west was separate from the blue sky in which it sailed. I said to James: 'I can make out the very shape of the standing stone today. It tapers a little at the top. I wonder what it was for?'

'Does it matter? Some pagan thing,' said James, not interested. He looked about him and added: 'This weather won't last. Never does when it's this clear.' He looked up at the little cloud. 'That's the first of them. It'll be pouring by tonight.'

'I hope we get home before that,' I said.

It was a Saturday, when Edmund's school was closed. We took Goldfinch to the back of the house, where we found the groom who was one half of the domestic staff, giving a bucket of water to a strange horse, a big, raw-boned dapple grey, quite different from the quiet dun gelding that Edmund rode. Mr Silcox had given up the saddle because he said that riding tired him. When he went visiting, he used a trap. We left Goldfinch to be unharnessed and rubbed down and made our way to the front of the house, which meant passing the schoolroom.

It had once been the drawing room of the house which

Edmund Baker and Arthur Silcox now shared. Mr Silcox had put in three rows of desks with lift-up lids, with benches behind them, and it was he who had bought the numerous textbooks and the blackboard and the globe that I remembered so well. In his day, ink had been provided but pupils had to bring their own notebooks and pens. Edmund had gone a step further, buying notebooks and pens in quantity, at a discount, from a supplier he knew in Minehead. He had also added to what he called 'our little library'.

As we passed the schoolroom windows, I stopped to look through them and smile as the memories came back. I wondered if my children would remember their schooldays so kindly. William now wanted to leave them behind yet of all my children, he was the one most like me, at least in temperament. He took after James in looks, but he seemed to think in the same way that I did. Lately, as he grew up, there had been times when we both began to talk of the same thing at the same moment.

We found Edmund and Mr Silcox in the parlour that their dignified housekeeper Alice Meddick — the groom was her husband — kept so carefully polished, but they were not on their own. A third man was there, someone we didn't know, a quietly dressed, unobtrusive kind of man, though if that big dapple grey was his, there must, I thought at once, be more to him than met the eye. That was a horse that would need handling.

Though it was mid-morning and a long way from teatime, the three of them had been sharing a tea-tray. The stranger rose when Mrs Meddick showed us in, and said: 'I'll be off, then, since friends are calling on you. My thanks for the tea. I'll collect my horse myself, don't see me out.'

'There's no need to rush away, Ben,' said Mr Silcox. 'Please sit down again. Alice, bring us some more tea and bring some cakes too. Ben, I'd like you to meet James and Peggy Bright, old acquaintances, and parents of two of my pupils. Their third one will no doubt join them soon.' He smiled at us. 'This is Mr Benjamin Hartley, Riding Officer for the Revenue. He was one of my pupils too in bygone days. He'll be much on the alert now that the war's over.'

'True enough,' said Mr Hartley. He had a slow, low-toned Somerset voice but there was a sharpness in his gaze that didn't match with that. 'There's a deal of folk sayin' that now Boney's out of business and English ships can get into French ports in the night without the risk of being sunk if they're seen, there's no harm in running contraband from France. And the same with French vessels sneakin' into our coves and harbours, too. The Waterguard started workin' extra hours a good three months ago. Because it's actually happening. Contraband has been getting ashore again.'

'Do I hear a note of warning?' James asked easily, as we sat down. 'No need. I've never bought contraband. Don't hold with 'un.' He caught my eye. 'Sorry, Peggy. I know your father got his baccy and brandy that way. But he's gone now and we've no interest, one way or another.'

'I've never agreed with smuggling,' Edmund said, 'and nor has Arthur here. We'd be sorry to see it start up again. Even sorrier if anyone we knew were involved in any way.'

'That,' said Mr Hartley, 'is one of the hardest things about my work. This spider's web of friendships and relations, spreading all along the coast and inland. Even folk who wouldn't buy contraband know where they could get it if they wanted to, and they keep quiet because one of the smugglers is their third cousin twice removed, or their Auntie Mary is married to him, or they were at school with him when they were young.'

He sounded exasperated but then saw me looking at him and said, more kindly: 'Not that I'd ever ask a woman to tell on her menfolk. That wouldn't be right. Women mostly keep out of these things and so they should. I can't imagine you drinking contraband brandy, let alone smoking the baccy your father bought when he was alive, Mrs Bright.'

'Quite,' I agreed, keeping my face straight. The mental picture of me smoking tobacco made me want to laugh.

'It must indeed be difficult for you,' Mr Silcox said to Hartley.

Hartley shrugged. 'Well, there you are. I can't even trust all my own colleagues. I know quite well that some of them are hand in glove with smugglers. They claim to be ardent upholders of the law, and they'll be anxious to report a rumour about a landing at Watchet, but all the time, it's a ploy to draw the Waterguard that way, because the landing's to be at Porlock! I can't *prove* that they misled me on purpose. Bah!' The exasperation was back in his voice.

'I believe the Waterguard fleet has proved a success,' said James.

'Aye, that's so. We have one based at Porlock. A good strong rowing crew can do better than a sailing ship sometimes – they don't have to tack against a headwind.'

'Let us not talk about it,' said Edmund pacifically, as Alice came in again with a heavy tray of tea things plus a pile of scones, a dish of plum jam and another of clotted cream. 'Let's enjoy the refreshments. And the sunshine.' He twisted in his seat to look out of the window into the garden. 'It's warm for November, but a little too clear for my taste. Rain's on the way, I fancy.'

'It'll do no harm, this time of year,' said James. 'It's to be expected.'

'As long as it isn't a bad storm,' said Mr Hartley. 'That's never welcome, on land or sea. I could swear, today, that to the south-west I could see a little hump in the sea that might be the island of Lundy.'

'Oh, that's impossible,' protested Mr Silcox. 'You can't see Lundy from this far up the coast.'

'Ah, well, maybe I imagined it,' said Mr Hartley, slicing a scone in half and piling it lavishly with jam and cream. 'I've had Lundy on my mind a lot. It was used a good deal by smugglers up to the start of the war. We put a stop to it then. A family called Hunt have it now and all through the war, Sir Aubrey kept trying to get the government to use it as a base for troops – and pay him for the privilege, of course. But that's over now and he's likely enough to be thinking of some other way to make a profit. He's got Irish lands and he has a lot of Irish folk living on Lundy with him and they're a wild lot by all accounts. I keep my ears open. I overhear more than folk tell me . . .'

'He sits in taverns, looking harmless,' said Edmund. 'And sometimes, no one realizes he's there at all.'

'Maybe,' said Hartley. 'But I've learned, never mind how, that now it's started up again, the smugglers are using Lundy

as a halfway house with French ships unloading there and
leaving things for our smugglers to pick up, or having a rendezvous with our miscreants in Lundy Roads. Well, I'm not in a
fuss about it today. I'd say that the weather's going to turn very
treacherous and no one will be running contraband in a storm.'

There were murmurs of agreement, and we all drank some
more tea and then Silcox turned to James to ask what had
brought us here on this Saturday. James began to explain about
William's wish to leave school. I ate a scone with plum jam
and cream, and wondered anxiously about Ralph.

Would he – was he – now thinking of resuming the trade he
had once shared with his father? I could only hope not.

Mr Hartley took his leave shortly after that. Mr Silcox and
Edmund persuaded us to stay for the midday meal but we ate
it rather quickly, because the bright morning sky had begun
to dim, and James remarked again that it was uncommonly
warm and close for November.

'Not natural weather,' he said, shaking his head. 'I reckon
that Mr Hartley is right; there's trouble coming.' I noticed
suddenly that although the basic tow colour of his hair was
always bleached after the summer, it now had a few genuine
white hairs in it. His health was sound and after all, he was
not yet forty; it seemed too soon for them. I experienced a
sudden wave of tenderness for him. He was an honest man
and he had been, by most standards, a good husband, and for
fourteen years, we had worked as a team to look after Foxwell
and rear our children, the children he had given me.

I shouldn't still be hankering after Ralph. The way my insides
had melted whenever I as much as heard his name was wrong.
It was time to put all that behind me and try appreciating
James for a change.

I looked towards the window and as I did so, a gust of wind
shook the house and the sun finally went in.

'We should be on our way home,' I said.

The drive back to Foxwell usually took about an hour. This
time it took less because the sky to the west suddenly began
to look so ominous that we were anxious to get ourselves and
Goldfinch under cover. We kept her to a brisk trot wherever

possible, letting the cart bounce as it would over the ruts and tussocks of the rough track. The wind, which to begin with came only in occasional gusts, started to strengthen and the gusts came closer together.

'Gale's on its way,' said James. 'Pity anyone who's at sea in this weather. They'll be running for shelter. Whatever's coming, it's coming from the Atlantic. Reckon I've just seen a flicker of lightning over there towards the sea.'

Our waiflike maidservant Annie had blossomed during her time with us into a quite a pretty lass and also a trustworthy one. We had left her in charge of Rose and John and she came running out to meet us when we came creaking and clattering into the farmyard.

'I'm that glad to see 'ee back. Nasty feel in the air. Heard thunder in the distance, I have. I've shut up the hens and taken the dogs indoors 'cept for Racer. He's out still, with Reggie. The cats are indoors. Any livin' thing'll need shelter from what's on its way. Mr Searle said just after you'd gone that he didn't like the look of the weather. He's brought the sheep down to the shippon.'

'What about the cows?'

'Reggie's gone for them. That's why he needed Racer. He got the bull into his stall first.'

Fred Webster had appeared and was unharnessing Goldfinch. 'Don't care for the look of the weather,' he said. 'Let's get the horses under cover quick.'

He and James saw to that, but by the time they had finished and followed me into the house, the sky was darkening alarmingly.

We heard lowing and trampling, and our Red Devons appeared, followed by Reggie, who was using Racer, the biggest of our three hounds, to herd them. They were obeying the man and the dog because they were used to doing that but they were also snorting and disturbed by the threatening weather, the increasingly noisy wind, and the change to their routine. The whole atmosphere felt tense.

The light was vanishing fast. Nightfall was far away, but this was just like night. It was beginning to be frightening. Fred hurried off home. William came in from the fields where he had been working and we all gathered in the kitchen. There was firelight there but it wasn't enough and Annie set about lighting lamps and candles. The wind howled in the chimney and shook the window frames, and now and then came flickers of lightning.

Then, making us all jump, came a huge blue flash that seemed to fill the room, accompanied by a colossal crash of thunder, as though tons of rock were falling out of the sky. A second flash followed almost at once and showed us each other's white, scared faces. Rose and little John began to cry.

'There, there,' said Annie in a trembling voice as she picked John up. I went to Rose and pulled her against me. 'It's all right. It's only a storm. Nothing to be afraid of.' I hope she couldn't sense how scared I was myself.

The animals were certainly scared. Racer had joined his brother Tufty and his mother Russet and the cats by the fire where they made a furry heap, but now Stripey, our big tabby, sprang up spitting and fled for shelter under James' basket chair while Racer was growling ominously. William picked up Whiskers, who was female and small, and shivering.

Thunder roared again. There was another flash, another howl of wind, and then the rain came, hammering the ground and clattering against the windows, flung by the wind. It was as though some monstrous entity were trying to force a way in. Whiskers yowled, digging her claws into William's arm so that he let her go. She bolted into a corner of the room. Racer got up and barked and his brother Tufty joined him. Their elderly mother, Russet, whined.

And then, out in the farmyard, there was a slithering crash, a rattling noise and a cracking of timbers, and frightened lowing from our cows. Rose screamed. Still holding her against me, I made for the window, to behold, by the lightning that was now almost continual, a sea of tossing horns and gleaming wet bovine backs, filling up the farmyard.

'James! Something's happened to the byre! The cows are out!'

They were indeed and not merely out of their byre. Even as I watched from the window, they found the gate of the farmyard, which, as the lightning showed me, had been torn open by the wind, and they were vanishing through it, jostling, stampeding, as if the storm were somehow sucking them out of the yard, to vanish into the murk.

'*James!*' I wailed.

He was there, beside me, looking out on the same scene as I was. In fourteen years, James had never sworn in front of me. Now, he said: 'Oh, my God!' and dashed to the back door. But when he opened it, the gale threw the rain inside as though it were hurling the contents of a pail at him, and he reeled back, drenched.

'We can't go out in that!' William shouted. He had to shout, because the thunder was roaring again and Rose was sobbing in wild alarm.

James came back and stood by the window again, banging his fists on the sill. 'I know! Not till the storm stops! God knows where they'll get to, what harm'll come to them . . .!'

I tried to be sensible. 'We'll go after them in the morning,' I said. 'This can't last long!'

'Every bog on the moor'll overflow; every stream'll be in spate. We'll lose some of those cows, Peggy. Bound to. Now, hush, Rose. We're all here and we're safe, at least; no need for all this to-do. Peggy, you and Annie get these young ones to bed.'

I gave him a shaky smile and he hugged Rose and me together, somehow getting his arms round both of us. He and I were closer then than we had ever been, I think. Closer then than we would ever be again.

Rockfall

There was no chance of rounding up the cattle that night. The storm raged almost until dawn and we barely slept. But as soon as the uproar had abated, James and I roused ourselves to dress in haste and go out to assess the damage.

The stable, which was a good solid structure, had withstood the elements very well, but the cattle byre was more exposed and the door had been blown open, breaking its hinges. Hence the escape of the cows. The bull, who was kept in a separate building, was still safely there.

Some of the cows were now wandering back, looking bedraggled, lowing to be let in and milked. We attended to them, and counted heads.

'There's still nigh on a dozen out there somewhere,' James said. 'William and I had best go out on horseback and look for 'un. Fred and Reggie can start repairing the byre door. We've got some spare hinges somewhere.'

I looked at the sky. It was cloudy but no longer threatening. The wind now was only a light breeze. An unexpected restlessness seized me. I wanted to be out on the moors, with a horse's mane tossing in front of me; not confined to a hot and steamy kitchen. Annie and Mattie could deal perfectly well with the midday meal, without me. 'I'll help the search,' I said. 'I'll take Lady.' Lady was one of the mature mares I had bought on that memorable day at Bampton. We had done well to buy her and the other mare, Brownie, for Clover and Spots had both died the following year. Lady and Brownie were steady, broad-backed ponies and could keep going all day long. 'I'll put my leather leggings on,' I said.

Many farm women didn't ride but those that did, as I did, usually rode astride. To do that in bundled-up skirts, however, meant calves badly pinched by the stirrup leathers, unless one had protection. Leggings were essential. 'I think I can manage a few hours on Lady,' I said. 'It might help, having three of us.'

William, crossing the farmyard to join us, said: 'I fancy we've lost two cows for good. Over there – look. Red lumps lying on the ground.'

'Your eyesight's better than mine,' said James. 'But you may be right. There's been animals killed by lightning on that there hillside before now. Iron in the ground, so I've heard. We'll get over there. All right, Peggy, take Lady and go towards the coast. William and me'll spread our net inland and hope to heaven that the lightning didn't get more than two!'

Foxwell was about three miles from the coast in a straight line, but who knew how far cattle might stampede when panic-stricken. It would mean crossing moorland and then going through a belt of trees called Culbone Wood. It was far more likely that our cattle had bolted in the opposite direction, since the gate they had fled through faced inland. But one never knew, so I pressed on.

Heather doesn't take footprints so I had no way of tracking our strays. I did come across a sheep caught by a gorse bush and silently thanked James for his good advice about carrying a knife. I released the animal, which cantered off, bleating, in thanks or relief or resentment; who knows what sheep feel? I continued towards the wood. I didn't really expect to find any of our cattle there but I didn't turn back. I had set out to search for them and I might as well do it thoroughly, or that is what I told myself. Now, looking back across the years, and remembering another time, much later, when once again I took a decision, suddenly and for no very good reason, because some deep instinct said *do it*, I am not so sure. Both times I felt as though I had in some way been summoned. I can't put it more plainly than that.

At any rate, I did ride on, threading my way through the trees, to emerge at last on a narrow strip of open land, where scanty grass grew on thin soil over the hard rock of the cliffs. The Bristol Channel was before me, grey and restless after the storm, with white horses here and there, but navigable again, for I could see two ships in the distance. The Welsh coast was dim and misty, the dangerous clarity gone.

Then a sound made me turn my head, and a little way off to my right I beheld a surprising sight. Something, probably lightning, must have startled two of our Red Devons into changing direction and fleeing this way after all. For there they were. They had found their way through the trees to the cliffs. One of them was calmly grazing, though the poor grass of the exposed clifftop could hardly have been very satisfactory. The other was being held by a man who seemed to have made a rough rope halter for the purpose, while a second man, sitting beside her on an upturned bucket, was milking her.

Beyond this surprising tableau, I could see several other men, close to the cliff edge, all staring downwards and apparently discussing something. I turned Lady towards them and realized as we approached that they were standing where a sloping pathway down the cliff began, the path that according to Ralph had been used by free traders until a landslide blocked it.

As I came within earshot, I heard one of the men remark: 'Still needs a bit of clearing but spades and shovels and a moon-light night, and there's the track, good as new, ready for a pack train.'

Another voice replied: 'Needn't even use a pack train. How about a good strong plough horse and a kind of trailer?'

Then the man holding the cow's halter saw me and called: 'We have company!' and they all became aware of me. They fell silent, heads turning.

I recognized some of the faces. Luke Hatherton, lean and bleached as ever. The fisherman I had met when I stayed with the Duggans, big, slow-moving Barney Oates with the grizzled beard. Roger Hatherton was there and the fellow holding the cow by the rope halter was surely Daniel Hopton. I hadn't seen him for years but the big ears and the dust-coloured tuft of hair sticking up above his forehead were unmistakeable.

And then I saw Ralph.

He knew me at the same moment and came striding towards me. 'Peggy! What in the world brought you here?'

'Whatever it was, it shouldn't have done!' Luke Hatherton came hurrying after him, his face as hard as rock. 'What're we goin' to do about this, now? She heard! I'd take my oath on it! We weren't whispering. Who'd have thought it, a woman turnin' up out of the blue just as we're . . .'

'Don't be daft, Luke,' said Ralph brusquely. 'It's *Peggy*. Peggy Bright. We can trust her, same as we can trust my Harriet.'

I was glad Ralph was there, for the rest of them made me nervous. I said: 'Our cows got out last night. We're out looking for them and that's two of them you've got there. What's Mr Hopton doing, milking one?'

'I'd intended to milk them both,' said Daniel. He put down his pail and came over to me. 'We fancied some refreshment and when these cows came wandering by, well, why not? We'd be doing them a favour as well as ourselves.' His voice had a harsh note that it hadn't had in the old days. He had changed, I thought, as he grew older.

'That milk belongs to Foxwell,' I said. 'I'll milk them when I get them home. What *is* all this?'

I slipped out of Lady's saddle, handed her reins to Daniel, who took them automatically, and walked forward. Ralph said sharply: 'Careful! Keep back from the cliff edge.'

Luke growled: 'Might be just as well if it crumbled,' and got a savage glance from Ralph.

But I had already stopped. From where I stood, I could see enough, for to my right, the cliff curved a little. The blocked path was blocked no longer but continued, as far as I could see, free of obstructions, down and down and out of sight.

'The boulder's gone!' I said. 'The one that's always been there – it's vanished!'

'Last night's rain seems to have brought down another landslide and it took the boulder into the sea with it. There's some rubble left on the path but that's all.'

'But what . . . I mean, why are you all . . .?' Then I understood. I looked at Ralph and blurted out: 'You're going to start smuggling again, aren't you? And using that path.' Then I wished I hadn't spoken, for the appalled and angry expressions on the faces of Ralph's companions were frightening.

'Christ!' muttered Barney Oates. 'Now we're on the rocks, good and proper!'

'Come with me.' Ralph took my arm. Luke said: 'Don't tell her any more, Duggan.'

'Leave this to me,' said Ralph over his shoulder. 'Come over here, Peggy. I tell you, Luke, we can trust her! Daniel, tether that mare to that outcrop there, well away from the cliff edge.'

He led me back towards the trees to where a fallen trunk made a seat. 'There's no point in hiding anything from you now,' he said. He spoke quite roughly and I looked at him, startled.

'You have wide scared eyes,' he said, more gently, his own eyes searching mine. 'Yes, you've seen what you've seen and you've a brain in your skull. The old path is clear again now except for the rubble and we'll soon get rid of that. The path goes right down to the shore and the cave I once pointed out to you. At low tide there's a landing place below it. That cave is where we hid Philip, as a matter of fact, till we could get him embarked for Antigua. One could always get there by sea – only while that great big boulder was in the way there was no getting anything up the cliff. There're rocks in the sea, of course, but there's a safe way in for something smallish, and that's still there, right enough.'

I remembered, with pain, sailing with Ralph in the old *Bucket*. I remembered the sweetness of his company. I remembered how it was to be young, and in love, with the promise ahead of years in which to go on being in love.

'But now you can use the cave,' I said. 'Well, James won't be one of your customers. Don't approach him, whatever you do. He's not like Father. And he's made friends with the Riding Officer, Benjamin Hartley. You'd better know.'

'Thank you. So – you won't tell James all about meeting me here and what you found me doing, and with whom?'

His voice was without emotion, but his eyes, eyes that had once been so full of love, love for me, seemed to be burning holes in me. I stared back, however, knowing that though he had defended me to his associates, he did doubt me at heart. I resented it. 'Of course I shan't tell James, or anyone else! What do you take me for? I shall just say I found two of our cows. I'll take them home.'

Ralph drew in a long breath. 'Thank God. I believed we could trust you. I thought so. I hoped so! But it's been years . . . people change . . . James disapproves and you've been his wife for all that time . . .'

'I haven't changed,' I said, and yes, there was a double meaning there and we both knew it. 'I wish you wouldn't do this,' I told him, 'because it's so dangerous, more than it was before the war. The Revenue keep too vigilant a watch! You could get transported! I'd never do anything to harm you.' The idea made me shudder. 'Never,' I said. 'For your sake *and* for Harriet's.'

I meant that, in all honesty. If things had been otherwise, if Ralph and I had married, if Harriet could have married someone else, she and I might have been friends. We had been robbed of that just as Ralph and I had been robbed of each other.

I said: 'How did you know, about the boulder going over the edge? What happened?'

'Yesterday,' said Ralph, 'I and my friends, that you see here, were wondering if the cave could be used sometimes for temporary storage, especially now that the Revenue's so suspicious and so vigilant and other landing places aren't safe. The Revenue keeps an eye on shipping; the officers often guess when consignments are likely, and then most of the regular landing places are watched. But we could dump barrels in the cave, Luke Hatherton said. They wouldn't be watching that. Then we could bring the things properly ashore somewhere else, sometime when the Revenue aren't expecting a landing. So me and Hopton landed yesterday to take a look, see if the cave and the landing were still the same. We didn't know how long we'd take and we'd seen the Waterguard hanging about so we didn't leave our ship anchored nearby . . .'

'Is she still the old *Bucket*?' I asked suddenly, overcome by nostalgia.

'No, the *Bucket* started leaking badly years ago. I've a better ship now, much bigger, called the *Moonlight*. Carries extra sail, for speed. Can't bring her in close because of the rocks, she's too big, but we got into the gig while we were still well out and Luke Hatherton sailed on. Said he'd be back to fetch us in a couple of hours, assuming the coast was clear. But while he was gone, the weather changed and we knew that Luke probably couldn't get back for us. Well, we're always prepared for that sort of thing. We had food and cider with us and a few rugs. We slept in the cave last night, or tried to.'

'It must have been frightening,' I said.

'It was bloody dangerous!' said Ralph forcefully and without apology. 'The sea can't normally get into that cave – it's well above the high-water mark. It used to be quite a business sometimes, hauling heavy barrels up to the cave mouth. But last night nothing was normal and the tide came surging up with great big waves half as high as a house and they smashed right in. Luckily, the cave goes well back and slopes upwards. We huddled there just out of reach of the water. And then,' said Ralph, 'there was a noise like the end of the world that frightened us half to death. It wasn't till later, when the light began to come and the sea dropped, that we saw. We went to the cave mouth and looked round and we saw that that old boulder was gone off the path. In fact, we could see it sticking out of the sea, away to the left.'

'*Ralph!*' I found myself trembling, horrified to think how near death he and all his companions must have been.

He grinned. 'So *now*,' he said cheerfully, 'we have a cave with a safe approach *and* an outlet to the land above, only the Customs men don't know about it. They know the cave's there, of course, but they've long assumed that it is useless as a landing place. It'll take time before they realize what's happened. And meanwhile . . . well, we all came along together this morning and took a look and we liked what we saw.'

There was laughter in his voice, the ring of adventurousness that had always filled me with love and joy. I had missed this so much. Ralph had always had this side to him, this eager reaching out to exploit new things. He had stimulated my mind as well as my senses. James was honest and decent and attentive to his land but he rarely spoke of anything not connected with the farm or our family or, sometimes, local people or events. Part of me, an untamed, unwomanly part, an inner wildness that had once sent me out in the night to get rid of Philip's tell-tale pony, had gone hungry for many, many years.

Ralph was still talking. 'Anyhow, we mean to make good use of our cave. As you are now aware.'

'Yes,' I said seriously. 'You *can* trust me but I still wish I didn't know. What does Harriet think about all this?'

'She knows I'm hoping to start free trading again. She doesn't like it but she knows she can't stop me, and she won't betray me. Harriet's a good woman.'

'Your freedom, maybe your life; they're in her hands,' I said slowly. 'And now, perhaps, in mine.'

'They were in your hands from the moment you rode up to us,' said Ralph. 'It's as well I was there to defend you. You know, back in the days when we were engaged, my father said I wasn't to tell you any details about our . . . side business until we were married. I would have been open with you from the start. I wanted to give you my trust as a second betrothal ring.'

'How very romantic.' Luke Hatherton had come up to us quietly, from the side, and because we were looking into each other's faces as we talked, we hadn't seen him. We turned sharply, realizing that he had probably overheard a good deal. 'If she's to be privy to our secrets,' he said, 'she'd better take our oath. How about it?'

'What oath is this?' I asked. Ralph looked uncomfortable.

'It's an oath everyone used to take who joined our little band of free traders,' said Luke, answering for him. 'We've revived it.'

'Harriet hasn't taken it,' said Ralph.

'She's your wife. Mrs Bright isn't.'

'What does it involve?' I asked.

They told me, and I flinched inwardly, for it was a heavy commitment, even for someone who wasn't going to take any active part in the business.

But although Ralph himself demurred, I agreed, and it was mainly for his sake. In trusting me, he had risked the trust that his confederates had in him. I wanted to secure it for him.

And that was how I came to stand there on the clifftop, with my right hand – I felt somewhat absurdly – raised in the air. 'We don't carry Bibles around with us,' Luke said, acidly humorous. 'Now, Mrs Peggy Bright – is Peggy your right name? It's mostly a pet name for Margaret.'

'I was christened Margaret,' I told him.

'All right. Mrs Margaret Bright, repeat after me. I, Margaret Bright . . .'

'I, Margaret Bright . . .'

'Do solemnly swear loyalty to all in our band of traders . . .'

I repeated it.

'I swear never to betray any of them to the law, nor to risk their safety by careless talk, in my cups or otherwise . . .'

I repeated this, too, noticing as I did so that Luke had given Ralph a fierce glance. Clearly he considered that in talking freely to me, Ralph had been guilty of carelessness.

'I also swear that if I learn of danger to any of us, I will warn those in peril if I possibly can.'

This was a frightening one but I had gone too far to draw back. I said the words, as steadily as I could.

'And if I fail in any point and harm comes to any of us because of it, may God strike me dead.'

I said that too.

'And so say we all.' The men around me spoke the words together. Then it was over and even Luke looked happier. I sat on the grass and drank cider with them, before I mounted Lady once again. Daniel had taken the halter off the cow he had been milking, and I set about chivvying the two Red Devons towards the path through the wood, helped by Ralph, on foot.

At the moment of parting, we were among the trees, out of sight of the others. I leant down to shake Ralph's hand in farewell, but Lady, being an Exmoor pony, was under thirteen hands. Ralph rose on his toes, bringing himself within easy reach, and kissed me goodbye. The warm heady taste of him, as familiar as the taste of bread and as intoxicating as strong wine, was still with me when I reached Foxwell, herding my recaptured cows ahead of me.

Perilous Knowledge

'Two cows killed by lightning,' said James, as he sat in the basket chair in the kitchen, pulling off his muddy boots. He had been out all day. 'And four calves aborted. Could've been worse. We needn't waste the cows we've lost. We can eat fresh beef and salt some too. Might sell one carcass whole. John in bed?'

'Yes, earlier than usual. He needs sleep,' I said. 'None of us got much last night and he's only six. I got a little rest after I came home. I was fairly worn out myself.'

'I saw Fred just now. He says the two you brought back were found right out on the cliff beyond Culbone Wood. It's a wonder they didn't go straight off the cliff in all that darkness and wind. What made 'ee push on so far?'

I was stirring the stockpot, while Annie chopped ham to go into a chicken and ham pie and Rose rolled pastry. I peered into the depths of the pot, as if concerned that something might have stuck to the bottom. I had wondered myself why I had ridden on through Culbone Wood, even though I thought the cows weren't likely to have plunged on under the trees. They would already have come far enough to tire them and wear out their panic.

Since I now knew that they *had* gone on into the wood, I supposed that they had wanted to hide from the rain and thunder. But at the time, I hadn't considered that. And yet, I had ridden on, telling myself that I might as well be thorough.

I remembered that feeling of being summoned. Had some part of me known that on the other side of the trees, I would find Ralph?

'I just don't know,' I said casually, as I resumed my stirring. 'That pie won't take long to cook; you must be hungry after being out all day. I think I went on because I'd already come so far that I thought I might as well press on, and make a job of it. It's as well I did. How far did you have to go to find the rest?'

'Right on to Standing Stone land. We met Stephen Duggan's foreman, out lookin' for *his* stock,' James said, and then broke off as William arrived at the kitchen door, also muddy and looking exhausted. 'Ponies are rubbed down and fed. Fred and Reggie have got that door back on hinges, I see. Dad and I had a midday meal at Standing Stone. The foreman asked us back and we went, didn't we, Dad? Mr Duggan seemed quite pleased to have our company.'

'Has he lost much stock?' I asked.

'Some sheep and three cows that he knew of by the time we left,' James said. 'Said he never remembered a storm like that in all his life. His Three-Corner Field is awash – his duck pond overflowed and a stream spated and water poured into the field from two directions and dumped all manner of rubbish there; alder branches and stones and mud. We found two of his cows there, drowned. The ducks were all right! That's something, Mr Duggan said.'

'We got some gossip from Duggan, too,' said James.

'Oh?' I said, reaching into a cupboard for a jug. The bubbling stock would make a good rich gravy to pour over the pie. I set about pricking some big potatoes to go into the oven alongside the pie dish.

'He's mighty lame now; and no strength in his legs; poor old man can hardly get out of his favourite chair without someone to give 'un a heave,' said James. 'And he's worried about more than cows and sheep and Three-Corner Field. He's bothered about his great-nephew, that he wants to leave Standing Stone to. Says he's afraid, now Boney's defeated, that Ralph'll start smuggling again. He wishes Ralph would bring his family to live at the farm and get away from that boatyard. The Hathertons could run that for him and run it well. Too much temptation, he said, Ralph being near the harbour and having boats to play with.'

'Seems the boatyard made a near fortune during the war,' William remarked. Though born tiny, he had nevertheless grown up strong, yet he was still only thirteen and it had been a hard day for him, after such a terrible night.

'Yes, Duggan said that too,' James commented. 'Said Ralph doesn't need to go free-trading for money. Just that he likes taking risks, it seems. Gurt fool if you ask me, though it won't worry me overmuch if he gets caught and transported to Van Diemen's Land or the West Indies as a convict.'

'Where're they?' asked Rose, looking up from her pastry.

'Hasn't Mr Baker shown you yet on the globe?' William asked, teasing her.

'He hasn't shown my class every place in the world, not yet,' retorted Rose. 'There's a lot of world, he says.'

'The West Indies are islands before you get to the New World proper,' I informed her. 'And Van Diemen's Land is an island off Australia. Convicts are sent to either of them. Good, Rose, you've got the pastry lid on to the pie. Give it here. I'll push it into the oven.'

'Transportation – yes, that's what will happen to a good many men if smuggling starts up again,' said James. 'I've heard that from Benjamin Hartley. The government's not going to stand for it. Stephen Duggan knows that, too. That's why he's worried. Said he'd have to make hisself responsible for Harriet and the children if Ralph got caught and sent halfway round the world. Seems to me that Ralph Duggan could be asking for trouble. Me, I wouldn't care if he gets it. Edmund Baker and Uncle Stephen'll see the family right.'

The malice in his voice was unmistakeable. At that moment, I was at the oven and had my back to him. This was fortunate, because he couldn't see that my hands were shaking. My mouth still remembered the taste of Ralph's kiss that morning, and in my mind, my guilty mind, I could see the top of the track that now led all the way down to the cave, and had encour- aged Ralph in dangerous ideas, to which I was privy. Which I had sworn to protect.

I felt as though my perilous knowledge must be written in fiery letters across my forehead. I was slow to turn round.

'Do you not like him because he was once engaged to Mother?' William asked, quite casually, as though he were enquiring whether it was likely to rain again tomorrow. James sat up straight and stared at him, and his eyes, once more, had that blue-marble look.

'What do 'ee know about that, son? Who told 'ee that?'

'I've known since I was nine,' said William, surprised.

'Mr Duggan – Mr Stephen Duggan, I mean – he told me. I've dropped in on him, now and then.'

'Have you indeed? And not a word to me or your mother – or did you know of this, Peggy?'

'No, I didn't,' I said tersely. 'William, it seems to me you've been getting independent a bit soon in life.'

'I'd second that,' said James. 'And 'ee hearkens to Stephen Duggan's gossip and never let on what 'ee told 'ee?'

'Mr Duggan said, maybe he shouldn't have told me and then he said to me, don't let on that you know. So I didn't,' said William simply. 'Only, I'm older now and I've thought sometimes, well, why shouldn't I know? There's nothing wrong about it, surely? But it does sound as if you don't like Mr Ralph Duggan much. I wondered if that was why, that's all.'

'No, I don't like him,' James said. 'And I'd sooner not have to listen to his name being bandied round. What are we having to follow the pie?'

Christmas passed and the March of 1816 brought the day that changed everything, so that afterwards, none of our lives were ever the same again. It began though as just another ordinary, busy day. The day before, James had gone to Exford with two hams in a satchel, to have a drink in the White Horse with a huntsman and had returned with a parcel of good venison occupying the satchel instead. James liked such barter transactions and we often did well from them. I had decided that we would have the venison in a casserole for supper. The men would appreciate it, for they had a hard task ahead, clearing a drainage ditch of leaves from the alders that had grown up beside it.

'Might as well deepen it a bit, too,' James said when he set out with William. The two of them and Fred would be busy with spades for hours.

It was grey, chilly weather but dry. They came back to the house for a midday meal – that was substantial too, finishing up a rabbit pie – and then, across the table, without warning, James remarked: 'I heard a bit of news in Exford yesterday, Peggy. Didn't mention it to 'ee straightaway; maybe it won't be welcome news. But it'll get around anyhow. I had that drink in the inn with Marshall, the huntsman, like I said I would, but someone else come in while we were there. Benjamin Hartley.'

'The Riding Officer?' I said.

'Aye, the same. Ralph Duggan's had his day, by the sound of it.' He grinned. 'If he don't end up in Van Diemen's Land, he'll be lucky. The Revenue men are on to him. Seems he's found a landing place under the cliffs that he thinks is secret, but it b'ain't. It's some cave or other, with a fairly safe way up the cliff, so Hartley says. Seems he's heard that Duggan and his friends are planning a landing there tonight but the *Harpy* or one of the Waterguard rowing galleys'll be standing by to catch them red-handed, so to speak. She'll land a squad of officers the moment the first barrels start being heaved ashore.'

'I see,' I said. I added: 'I wish you hadn't told me.'

'You'd hear, sooner or later. Thought it might be kinder to prepare 'ee. I know there's a kindness in 'ee for the fellow, even after so long.'

The words appeared to be thoughtful, a husband warning his wife that news was coming that might hurt her. Only, he wanted me to be hurt. Yes, the malice was there, as strong as ever.

'I'm sorry,' I said carefully. 'I mean I'm sorry that Ralph Duggan has been so foolish as to start free-trading again and put himself at such a risk. *Anyone* would be sorry for someone being sent away in a convict ship! And what about poor Harriet, and their children!'

'Better off without 'un. I've said it afore, Stephen and Edmund, they'll look after Harriet,' said James easily. He set about eating, in haste. 'Come on, Fred, William. We've a good bit to do yet, with that there ditch.'

They went back to their work, leaving me to clear up the kitchen with Annie and await the return of Rose and John from school. I washed dishes in apparent calm, while my thoughts whirled round in my brain in panic-stricken fashion.

I ought to warn Ralph. Love for him and fear for him told me that and besides, I had made a promise. Out there on the cliffs, I had sworn an oath.

If I learn of danger to any of us, I will warn those in peril if I possibly can.

Only, how could I do any such thing? Walk out of the house, take a pony and ride off to Minehead now, at once? What excuse could I possibly give for doing such a thing? James would see through any invented tales.

Nor could I send a messenger. I couldn't send any of the men off the farm without James hearing of it. I could ask one of Fred's older children to go, but Minehead was a long way off and children shouldn't be involved in this kind of thing and Mattie certainly wouldn't like it. Also, she was expecting her ninth child any minute and shouldn't be upset.

No. The responsibility rested with me. And the risk.

Could Ralph, could Luke Hatherton, expect me to throw my entire marriage into jeopardy, for love of Ralph, or fear for him, or to keep my vow? If James found out, he would not forgive me; I knew it. Part of me pitied him. If I had never seen Ralph, I could have loved James properly and I knew well enough that in his fashion, he did indeed love me. But that wouldn't save me if he ever thought I had betrayed him. Besides, I would be breaking the law. I had done that once already and I hadn't worried then about being caught but I worried now. I was older and shrank from such dangers.

The truth was that I was afraid. I admitted it. In gnawing misery, I did the usual tasks of the afternoon, and I was there, in the kitchen, preparing my casserole, when, later, Rose and John came home, using the trap, since Rose was now old enough to drive Lady. James and William came back together only a few moments later.

James, remarking that it was growing colder, went out again to bring Goldfinch and Copper into the stable for the night. There was nothing unusual about that. We left the horses out when we weren't using them, but although the Exmoors throve well outdoors even on winter nights, Copper and Goldfinch, with their Arab blood, were more susceptible to cold.

James returned looking exasperated. 'Goldfinch has cast a shoe *again* and oh my, she's lookin' so pathetic, hobbling as if she's got nails in her off fore, when she hasn't a nail left in that hoof at all! And it would happen at this hour! I can't leave her like that. Anyhow, I don't want to waste any time tomorrow. Lambing's started now and I've got to see Searle . . .' His voice trailed irritably off.

'Fred could take her into Exford,' said William. 'Shall I run to his cottage and ask him?'

James shook his head. 'He won't want to leave Mattie. It could mean staying overnight at the inn. He'll have to lead the mare dead slow; it'll take him an hour at least to get her there, maybe more, and it'll be black dark by the time she's shod. Mattie's near her time and she's not been well. And *you* b'ain't goin'! Can't have 'ee stayin' in inns alone at your age, and I don't want 'ee ridin' in the dark either. I'll have to go. I'll ride Copper and lead the mare. Save my feet, after the day I've had. Damned animal; *her* feet are never anything but trouble. I'll stop the night and eat in the inn. You make that casserole just the same, though, Peggy. Keep my share and heat it for me tomorrow.'

'Yes, of course,' I said.

He would be away all night. *All night.* I could slip out as soon as everyone was abed. I need not go to Minehead. I could go straight to the cliff and the cave and hope to find Ralph there and warn him before the landing took place. I might not get there in time but at least I would have tried.

While I was thinking this out, I was continuing to do this and that in the kitchen, remarking that if James meant to stay at the inn in Exford, he must take his nightwear and shaving gear with him, and a clean shirt, too. My face and voice were as calm as I could make them. Terror was like a fire in my guts.

If anything went wrong. If I was caught, creeping out. If James found out . . .

If Ralph was taken . . .

I thought of Ralph. Not lasciviously. I was remembering all I had heard about convict ships, about men chained in the hold, about the slavery – for it was slavery in all but name – that awaited them at the end of the journey to the West Indies or the Antipodes, about the many who never reached the end of it, but died on the way, of disease, malnutrition, or in shipwrecks.

Not Ralph. Oh, please God, don't let that happen to Ralph.

I also thought of Harriet, who had never done me any harm and whose heart would surely break. I was trembling inside but I knew that I must act. I went to bed early, saying that I felt a little unwell. It was an understatement. The state of fear I was in made me feel very unwell indeed.

But I *wasn't* going to betray James in any way. I was simply going to try to protect someone who had once been very important to me from a terrible fate. I was going to discourage someone from breaking the law (well, for tonight, anyway). Since when was it a crime to dissuade someone from committing one? I surely wasn't going to do anything that was really wrong.

Only neither James nor the law would think so. I changed into night things and went to bed. And yet, all the time, I was listening to the sounds of the house, the voices saying goodnight, the slam of bolts as William took over the task of locking up for the night; the feet on the stairs as people retired. Annie put her head in to see if I needed anything and I pretended to be asleep. I heard her go away. I heard bedroom doors closing. Two of them. John and William shared a room; as did Annie and Rose.

I waited, shivering under my blankets. And then I got up and lit a candle, and dressed. My heart was thundering like Ezra Kent's mighty hammer. But I must warn Ralph if I could, and that was that, no matter what came of it.

I put on socks and leggings and a thick skirt, and a patched old jacket that James no longer used but which still had warmth in it. I put my usual knife in the pocket and made sure I had my keyring on the belt of my skirt so that on return, if I found I had been locked out, I could get back in, quietly. I blew out the candle and then set out in socks, carrying my boots, and in the dark, I made my way downstairs.

It wasn't actually full dark because the sky, which had been overcast earlier, had cleared and there was a half-moon, which shone in through windows here and there, letting me see my way well enough. The dogs in their baskets raised their heads but didn't bark, just thumped their tails in amiable greeting as a familiar human being tiptoed past.

I put on my boots, undid the back door, stepped out, closed

the door noiselessly behind me. I made for the tack room, collected a saddle, a bridle and a halter with a lengthy rope, and then went to the paddock where the Exmoors had been left out. Lady had been to Exford and back that day, but Brownie had spent it in the field. I would take Brownie. I was thankful that she hadn't been in the stable. There was no risk of being heard as I led her out into the yard.

I saddled her, mounted, and set off.

I went on being afraid. It felt as though I had swallowed a lump of ice and it was sitting in my stomach and refusing to melt. Across the moorland I went, pausing on a hillcrest, looking to the distance where the sea was a silvery streak. Then I pressed on, downhill and into the woods. The darkness under the trees wasn't too intense because the trees were not yet in leaf and the moonlight found its way in. It was very cold. My teeth showed a tendency to chatter, and not just with fear.

In the middle of the wood, there was a small clearing, an open patch of grass, pale in the moonlight. I halted. Anxious thoughts had come into my head. I could only guess just when the landing would take place. At high tide, most likely, but I didn't know the state of the tides. What had I overheard the smugglers say? Something about dragging goods up the cliff path on some sort of trailer, presumably to meet a pack train of ponies at the top. Mr Hartley had said something to James about the *Harpy* but it was likely enough that Revenue men would come overland as well and wait at the top of the cliff, where they could see the ship arrive with its contraband cargo, and they might catch the pony train.

Perhaps there would be a pincer movement, from sea and land both at once. If any of them were going to come to the clifftop, then I was about to ride straight into their arms.

I dismounted. I took off Brownie's saddle and exchanged her bridle for the halter, which I had carried slung round my shoulders. I tethered her to a tree. The long rope would let her graze or lie down if she wanted; I hoped she would come to no harm. Saddle and bridle I stowed in the fork of another tree. Then, treading as softly as possible, I went on, on foot.

At the edge of the wood, I stopped, wary as a wild deer, wondering whether it was safe to emerge into the open. I listened. There were no human or animal sounds at all, only a fretful wind and the murmur of the sea below. Cautiously, I moved forward.

No one was there. I stopped, rubbing a hand across a tired forehead. I had hoped to find some of the smugglers, perhaps with the ponies, at the head of the path. Had I come in vain? Wasted my efforts, taken a serious risk for nothing?

But there might of course be someone down in the cave.

I had come too far to turn back without making sure. If I couldn't deliver my warning then I couldn't, but I had to try to the bitter end. I went to the cliff edge and found the start of the path.

The path was a good ten or twelve feet wide and basically rock, with only a thin covering of soil and grass. The west wind was steady but not violent. It was safe enough.

It didn't feel safe, though. The drop on my left was sheer, and it was a long way down to that wrinkled moonlit sea and the vicious rock fangs that jutted from it, with white spray spurting over them. That edge seemed to draw me, as though the emptiness below wanted me to fill it. Wanted to swallow me whole. The night seemed huge and dangerous. It was a monster that could consume me at a gulp and notice it. I felt small and lost and giddy and terrified.

But having started, I went on, not walking so much as creeping, keeping close to the other steep face, the one that rose on my right, sweating with fear, feeling my legs tremble.

I did it for Ralph, not for my oath. Not because I yearned to make love to him, either. No such idea had as much as touched my mind. I wanted to save him from those convict ships. Even those who would condemn me would, I felt sure, have done as much for a loved one. Well, wouldn't they?

It seemed a very long way down. But at last I was there, stepping down on to a tiny patch of beach and there was the sea, only yards away, seething over a reef of rocks. I couldn't tell what the tide was doing. I crossed the little stretch of sand and then stumbled as the ground beneath my feet turned to shingle. I landed on all fours amid big rounded stones and then, scrambling to my feet, I saw a slope of shingle just above me, and there was the cave mouth above that. Then someone was there, coming out of it, staring downwards, demanding angrily: 'Who's there? Who is it?'

I stood up straight. One knee felt as if it had been skinned but I didn't care, for surely I had recognized the voice and at least this was no Revenue officer. 'It's Peggy Bright! I came to warn you! Don't land anything tonight! Is that Daniel Hopton?'

'Peggy Bright? But what . . .?' He was scrambling down. He came close to me, peering into my face in the moonlight. 'What's that? Come to warn us? What are you on about?'

'You *are* Daniel, aren't you? Daniel Hopton? Don't land a cargo tonight! The Revenue are on to you! My husband heard it from Benjamin Hartley. You know, the Riding Officer!'

'What?'

Exasperated and still shaking after my creep down that horrible cliff path, I snapped: 'Benjamin Hartley told my husband they know about it — isn't that enough? They saw men being interested in the cave, I suppose, or saw someone clearing rubble off that path or . . . oh, never mind that.' Why was Daniel Hopton so slow of wit? 'The point is that you're all in danger. Where's Mr Duggan — Ralph Duggan?'

'On 'un's way back from Lundy Roads, that's where he be! Oh, dear heaven, what a tangle!'

Evading the Law

'*Lundy Roads!*' I gasped rather than said it. 'But that's hours away! If he went out there tonight . . .'

'No, he went this mornin',' said Hopton. 'Went off at nine in the *Moonlight*.'

'And when is Mr Duggan due back? There *is* to be a landing tonight?'

'Aye. He was to meet a French vessel in Lundy Roads soon as it got dark, transfer the goods and start for here. Some Frenchies are still scared of coming near the English mainland,' said Hopton. 'Revenue'll put a shot through their rigging as soon as look at 'em, if they find one hangin' round here, and board 'em and grab any cargo they think's contraband. So Mr Ralph had to go out to Lundy.'

'Does Sir Aubrey Hunt know?' I asked, bemused.

'Dunno. He hasn't interfered. Been bribed, maybe, or just don't realize. There's always ships anchoring in the Roads, Lundy keeps them sheltered from the Atlantic winds and they can wait for the tide if they're heading for Barnstaple or whatnot. Sandbanks outside Barnstaple – some bigger ships can only cross at high tide. Mr Duggan, likely enough, just waited in the Roads till dusk.' Hopton shrugged.

'Where will the *Moonlight* be now?'

'Well on her way here. Got a following wind.'

'If the landing takes place, you'll all be caught. I could only get here to warn you because my husband's away tonight. The Revenue'll be here any minute – either by sea, or else they'll send a squad to get you at the clifftop. I don't know the details. Mr Hartley mentioned the *Harpy*. But they'll be here, by land or sea or both, and they'll pounce.'

'There'll be nothing for them to pounce on up top,' said Hopton. 'We're getting the goods up in two stages. Getting them here from Lundy's a long job and so is getting them up the cliff, though we should make a fair job with it, with a horse and a wheeled trailer the Hathertons knocked together for us. Still, we reckoned it were best to land them one night and take them up the cliff the next. So no one's bringing a horse and trailer to the clifftop tonight.'

'Thank heaven for that,' I said. 'But whether the Revenue come by land or sea, they'll surely look into the cave. They mustn't find anything or anyone here.'

'Quiet!' Hopton suddenly held up a hand. He caught my shoulder and spun me round. 'Look!'

He was pointing upwards. I stared and then saw. At the top of the cliff, something moved against the stars, and then I saw the glimmer of a lantern. 'That'll be the Revenue!' I said and realized as I spoke that I could not now get up the cliff and back to Brownie. I was afraid of the climb back but I had known that I must face it and so I would have done – but for this. Now I was trapped.

In a whisper, I said: 'How can we warn Mr Duggan? Why were you left here?'

'The goods need to be landed in stages, by gig. I'm here to light a lantern to help guide the boat in. I come here in my own little gig.' He pointed again, this time to the far edge of the tiny cove, and I saw that a small boat was lying close in, her bows just out of the water. 'That's my little *Seabird*,' Hopton said.

'We'll have to go out and meet the *Moonlight*,' I said. 'Warn them not to make the landing.'

'We? You mean you're comin'?'

'I'll have to. I can't go back up, not with the Revenue men waiting at the top! How I'll get back to my horse, or get home, I don't know but for the moment, we've got to warn *Moonlight*.'

The journey out in *Seabird* was nearly as alarming as the cliff path.

The fact was, firstly, that although Daniel Hopton was presumably a competent sailor, since he had sailed here on his own, he was in a dither. 'It's all these bloody rocks. The passageway in is good and deep but it b'ain't straight and it *is* narrow. All right in daylight; pick your moment when the tide's not full up and a man can *see* they damned rocks to either side, but in the dark and havin' to manage the oars . . .'

We inched along. Daniel rowed, warily, constantly looking over his shoulder. The gig had a sail, though it couldn't be used in these conditions. I took charge of the tiller and kept a lookout, and found that even though the moon was only half full, I could generally make out the rocks, most of which were just clear of the water at this point. I could call warnings.

'*Straighten her, Daniel!* . . . No, too much to port . . . *Ware rocks!* . . .' A rock like a black fang was sticking out of the water, so near that I was sure I could touch it if I stretched. '*Careful! Shift to starboard . . .!*'

Daniel was swearing softly, whether at me or himself or the *Seabird*, I couldn't tell and didn't ask. Fortunately, it wasn't very far and at last we moved into open water. Daniel continued to row for some way and then, after changing course for a while, said: 'We can anchor here; it's shallow enough. Nice handy sandbank. We can signal the *Moonlight* from here. No point trying to sail further out to meet her. We'd have to tack; we might miss her.'

When we were anchored, he fetched out a tinderbox and lantern from somewhere, lit the wick and then set the lantern down near his feet. 'We'll signal with that when she comes,' he said.

As yet, there was nothing to be seen. And so, nothing to do but wait.

I sat shivering inside my warm clothes. Much of it was the cold of dread, of course. I was far from home, and worrying badly because I could not begin to imagine how I would get back to collect Brownie and be home at Foxwell before James reappeared, or anyone else noticed that I – and Brownie – were missing. I had done something to my life that was irrevocable and probably catastrophic.

I could do nothing about it. There we sat, rocking on the swell, listening to the sigh of the sea, watching the half-moon travel slowly across the huge, starlit sky and catch the wave tips with its silver light. Constantly, we scanned the water for signs of other vessels. I was looking for the Waterguard or the *Harpy* as much as for *Moonlight*. I could see no trace of any of them, though I knew that against the background of the moving water, a rowing galley, with no sails to show against the sky or in the moonlight, would be hard to see at any distance, and so would the *Harpy* if she was standing off with sails lowered. *Moonlight* should be easier, for she would come under sail. But as yet, there was only an empty sea.

In the dimness, Daniel Hopton said: 'Mrs Bright . . .'

'Yes, Mr Hopton?'

'There's something I want to tell 'ee. I think 'ee've a right to know, though it can't make any difference to anyone now. You'll likely want to push me overside when I tell 'ee, but better not. Unless you want to handle the *Seabird* alone.'

'Hardly. What's all this, Mr Hopton?'

'*Someone* ought to know. Mr Ralph ought to only I can't get up the nerve to tell 'un, even though I did it for him as much as anyone.'

'Mr Hopton, what on earth – or on sea – are you talking about?'

'It's funny,' said Daniel ruminatively. 'Don't think I'd ever have got to the point, only it's kind of queer out here, on the sea, in the moonlight. Nothing's real, like. It's as if we're out of the world. It's easier to *say* things. As though they somehow won't get heard in the everyday.'

'What is it that you want to say, Mr Hopton?'

'That Laurence Wheelwright. Someone paid for Maisie Cutler and the case was shelved, but folk are still wondering, was it him, and if it was, how did he manage when he didn't leave the barn roof? I swore on oath that he never. But he did. For a while. So I think it was him. He made me swear I'd never tell. He said, he knew I was mixed up in smuggling.'

'How did he know that?' I asked.

'Oh, half a dozen ways, I think. He said he'd seen me down at the quay one day, with Mr Hatherton and Mr Josiah Duggan, and Maisie'd told him if he wanted cheap baccy, to ask me about it. You know how it is. More people know about it than don't, hereabouts.'

Unexpectedly, Daniel spat over the side. Then he said: 'Laurence said to me that if I ever told anyone he hadn't stayed all the time on that there barn roof, he'd split. He'd have me, and the Duggans and the Hathertons and all the rest, in gaol in five minutes, he said. So I said what he wanted. I protected us all – Mr Ralph and his father as well. But I know your engagement was broken, and there's them that say you and Mr Ralph didn't want that. I'm sorry.'

I was silent, thinking of what might have been, and should have been, but for that one lie. But if Laurence Wheelwright had carried out his threat, it would have come to the same thing. I would have lost Ralph.

I said: 'It's all right.'

Time couldn't be unravelled; I knew that. For a moment, I had felt a thrust of pain, strong enough to make my stomach muscles clench, but it was fading now. After all, like everyone else, I had long felt sure that Laurence Wheelwright was guilty. I had long suspected that Daniel Hopton, for whatever reason, had perjured himself. He had now told me why. That was all.

'You'll tell Mr Ralph?' Daniel asked nervously.

'Do you want him to know?'

'I dunno. But Philip got blamed for Maisie. Best not, perhaps. Don't know why I told you but there's something about this empty sea and the moon . . .'

'The sea's not so empty,' I said. 'Look. Is that *Moonlight*?' Daniel got cautiously to his feet, to stare where I was pointing. I said: 'I won't tell Ralph Duggan unless somehow need arises. Philip is all right. He's in Antigua, doing well. *Is* she the *Moonlight*?'

'Aye. I reckon.'

I was on my feet too. The mass of shadow approaching from the south-west was gathering shape.

'But I can't see her sails,' I said.

'Black sails, for this work,' said Daniel, snatching out the lantern from between his feet and holding it high, using a shutter to make what was evidently a coded signal. I could see the vessel's figurehead now and had realized that above it, a deeper darkness against the night sky, blanking out the stars, was actually a sail. She changed course and came alongside. Daniel shouted: 'Moonlight *ahoy!* Seabird *here! Daniel Hopton! Danger!*'

There was an answering shout that I couldn't make out and then the moon showed us a man leaning over the rail above us and then Ralph's voice said: 'What is it? What's wrong, Dan?'

'Ralph! It's Peggy here! The Revenue are on to you – I came to warn you! There're Revenue men on the clifftop now!'

'*Peggy!* How did you get here?'

Calling, I had moved position to be heard more clearly and I had made the dinghy lurch. Daniel pulled me down and started to call explanations of his own. I stayed seated this time but broke in now and then, with extra details, ending: 'It's as likely as not that the Waterguard are about! You've got to get away from here! You mustn't go through with the landing!'

'Have I got it right, Peggy? You've left a horse in Culbone Woods and can't get back to it?'

'Yes. I had to come down the cliff. There was no one at the top to warn. I just hoped I'd find someone at the bottom! I found Daniel!'

'Wait.'

He withdrew but we could hear him snapping out orders and a voice – I thought it sounded like Luke Hatherton's – replied. Then he was back, tossing a rope ladder over the side. 'I'm coming down!'

A moment later, he had joined us in the gig and was calling up to someone to pull the rope ladder in. He sat down and said: 'Get that sail up, Dan. We've got to get Mrs Bright back to land. Porlock's nearest. *Moonlight*'s going to make off towards Steepholm. Hurry!'

It was done, at remarkable speed. Then the *Moonlight* was moving away, her dark sails once more set, black against the stars until distance swallowed them. Ralph was getting the *Seabird*'s anchor up, while Daniel raised her sail. I noticed that this too was dark and would not be easily visible.

I lent a hand. I could remember, in the past, helping to get up the sails in the *Bucket*. The business seemed oddly familiar, as though, back then, over fifteen years ago, some part of me had separated from the rest and stayed there. Only part of me, I thought, had journeyed on to marry James and live with him at Foxwell. The rest had remained unchanged, waiting, until need, Ralph's need, summoned it out of the past.

When we were under way, Daniel took the tiller. In a low voice, Ralph said: 'I've only understood about half of what Hopton shouted up to me. Now, you tell me all over again, just what happened and how did you come to be here tonight?'

I told him, as quickly and simply as I could. 'You shouldn't have done it!' he said, horrified. 'What will James say to this if you don't get back home in time? Oh, Peggy! I wouldn't have had you take such a risk for the world! And I'm grateful that you did. I'm lost for words. You should have turned back from the clifftop!'

'I had to do my best. I *had* to. Where are we going now?'

'Porlock, like I said. Daniel can put us ashore and take this dinghy back to Minehead harbour, where he keeps it. We'll have to walk back to where you left your horse. It'll be a long, steep walk, my love, and we have to keep away from the cliff, though I fancy by the time we get near the danger point, the Revenue men will have given up. It'll be close on dawn by then. Perhaps you may yet get home in time. I hope so. Why did you do it, Peggy? Risk so much for me?'

There was a pause. Then I said: 'You know why. Don't you?'

'It still like that, is it? Still the same?'

'I wanted to wait. Only, you were so far away and maybe you'd never come back at all – Philip hasn't. And the years would go by and what would there be for me? People kept saying things like that. My parents. James. So, in the end . . .'

'I know. Don't think I'm blaming you.'

'I have the children. I wouldn't be without them. It's all so complicated.'

'I wouldn't be without mine, either. Charlie's nearly nine now; he's going to grow up the dead spit of me. Joan's five, and she favours her mother – and Peggy, Harriet's a dear soul. I can't regret marrying her. And we've got our twins, too. Ann and Phyllis. There's no going back.'

'Of course not. But I couldn't let you be taken – imprisoned – transported. I couldn't!' I added: 'I was terrified, coming down that cliff path. I felt as though the drop over the edge was pulling me towards it! But I had to go on, because I was even more terrified for you.'

'Really?' Ralph was surprised. 'But it's a very good path – wide enough for a big horse!'

'It didn't feel like that,' I said in heartfelt tones.

'My poor, gallant Peggy! I can only thank you. And see you safe back to your horse and pray that you get away with this escapade.'

'I hope you get away with it as well. What if the Waterguard see the *Moonlight* and follow her?'

'She'll be hard to see, under those black sails,' said Ralph, and suddenly laughed. 'But if they do, and chase her, she'll have the speed of them with this wind. She'll be away up the channel and slipping out of sight behind Steepholm Island and by the time they get there, there'll be no sign of her. Then the dawn'll break and in the distance they'll maybe catch sight of a ship with red sails seemingly making back from Cardiff, and if they chase her and get close enough to see her name, they'll find she's a Danish vessel, carrying a Danish flag.'

'Oh, *Ralph!*'

And like him, I was laughing.

No Awaking

We landed at Porlock unseen and unchallenged. Daniel Hopton pushed off, leaving us together on the shingle amid a powerful smell of seaweed. The moon by now was low in the west but there was just enough light to see the rounded stones under our feet. Ralph took my hand to guide me.

It was a long, long walk, most of it uphill, and I remember little about it except that tiredness kept overwhelming me, so that all I could do was keep putting one foot before the other. Without Ralph, I couldn't have done it, because I didn't know this area well, even by daylight. He, though, seemed able to see his way and to be familiar with it.

Until at last, Ralph said: 'Dawn's near. I don't want this to cause trouble for you at home. Peggy . . .'

'Yes?'

'Thank you for saving me – and all the rest of us – tonight. But we mustn't meet again. You know why.'

'Yes, of course. There's James and our children; there's Harriet and yours. It's all right.'

I stumbled, and he held me up. 'You're so weary and no wonder. Let's talk as we go – it'll help to keep you awake.'

'I don't know what to talk about. I don't think I want to talk about that cliff path!'

'I can believe it. Wild weather and the way the sea gnaws the cliffs – this coastline's always changing. There are traces of drowned forests here and there, and all that flat meadow and marsh between Dunster Castle and the sea – all that used to be seabed. The castle was on a promontory when the Normans built it, and Dunster was a port instead of being nearly two miles inland.'

'Tell me more.'

He kept on talking, and was as interesting as ever, only my feet were dragging and as we entered the eaves of Culbone Woods, I stumbled again. 'Careful!' said Ralph.

'Sorry. I think I must rest for a moment,' I said.

'Over here,' he said. 'There's a sort of bank.'

We sat down. Once more, the cold was finding its way through my clothing. I started to shiver. Ralph still had an arm round me. It tightened, a band of warmth and security, drawing me into his shoulder, so that I turned my head and pressed my face into his coat.

I do not know how to explain or describe what happened next. I know I was pressing against him for warmth. I sensed the strength of his hard body; I inhaled the scent of him: salt, leather, something that I can only call maleness. Then he turned to me and kissed me and the kiss went on and on and he held me close with one arm while with the other he fumbled at his clothing. I began to loosen mine. Something, which felt like a power from outside us, had seized hold of us and would not be denied. It had been there, calling to us, shouting to us, ever since the day we first saw each other in the parlour on the day of my father's funeral.

The moon had set and there was no sign yet of daybreak. What was between us flowered and triumphed in the secrecy of a forest darkness. We knew each other in more than the biblical sense, for this was a knowing of contour and texture, an awareness of scent and taste as well as the simple act of penetration. Afterwards, we lay for a while still clasped together, unwilling to abandon this, the union for which we had ravened for so long. Indeed, I fell asleep in Ralph's arms, until he roused me, gently, whispering: 'Peggy, you must get home. You must!'

By the time we pulled ourselves to our feet and were going on in search of Brownie, the day was fully broken.

We found Brownie placidly grazing, though she seemed pleased to see us and had probably felt lonely, left tethered all alone in a strange place for so long. I fetched her saddlery from its hiding place.

'Will you have to walk all the way home?' I asked, thankful that I wouldn't. He laughed.

'No, I need only get back to Porlock. I have friends there. I can take a few hours' rest with one of them. Is that Brownie's tack? I'll saddle her for you.'

When he had done so, he helped me to mount and then I leant down to him and he kissed me goodbye. Neither of us said: this is our last goodbye, but we knew that it was, and what our tongues did not say, our eyes and lips said for us.

And then I went home. I remember nothing of the ride because I was so tired and so preoccupied with my own thoughts and feelings. I knew I should be ashamed, horrified at myself, at what I had done to James. I had betrayed him, unforgivably, once by creeping out of the house to break the law by carrying a warning to smugglers (though how it could be a crime to tell someone not to commit one still eluded me), and then again and more dreadfully by taking one of the smugglers as my lover. But all the time I was glowing with the joy of having known Ralph, exulting in it like a cat stretching in a patch of sunlight, and I could not be sorry.

But, wondering what would greet me at Foxwell, I was afraid.

I left Brownie in the paddock and walked quietly towards the house, carrying her saddle and bridle. I expected to find people about in the farmyard but there was no one, although smoke was rising from the chimney in the usual way. I put the tack away and made for the kitchen. It was, as ever, warm and welcoming, the fire lit, used breakfast dishes on the table. At first I thought that no one was there. Then, from his basket chair by the hearth, startling me, James suddenly arose.

'So,' he said. 'You fell into the trap.'

I was too taken aback to answer. He was staring at me, with that blue-marble look in his eyes again. 'I thought you might,' he said.

I found my tongue. 'What trap? What do you mean?'

'Don't try lying. I went to Exford right enough but I didn't stay there. Goldfinch hadn't cast a shoe, my dear. That were my little pretence. When I were talking with Hartley, I got an idea. I told you what Hartley had said to me, on purpose, maid. I wanted to see what you'd do. Now I know. I've allus wanted to know what you'd do if Ralph had any need of you. Will she stand by me, I used to ask myself, or go whoring after him?

I was home again just after midnight, Peggy my love, and where were 'ee?'

It seemed impossible to answer.

'Out on the cliffs, looking for Ralph Duggan,' said James. 'Gone to warn him, if you could find him. That's if you needed to search. How often have you and he met, with me not knowing? I've been wondering that all night. Did you manage to warn him?'

Attacked, I decided to fight back. I thrust the memory of that strange, ecstatic, union under the trees of Culbone and retorted: 'Yes! Why shouldn't I? I nearly married him. Why shouldn't I want to save him from being arrested and transported? And why shouldn't I worry about Harriet? You *can't* want to see her husband taken from her!'

'Harriet b'ain't the point. She'll be right enough. *You* left your home to warn a smuggler. Did 'ee manage it? Did it take all night? What else did 'ee get up to?'

'You don't think that! You can't!' I hoped my voice didn't waver as I told the lie.

'I think you did. I can almost smell him on 'ee. There's a different look to 'ee, a queer sort of shine. You gave yourself to 'un, I know it, you that's had so little to give me, this long time past, and when 'ee does oblige, I have to cut things short in case there's another babby. Did Ralph Duggan take care the way I do?'

'James! How dare you?'

The words rang hollow and he knew it. His eyes were almost bulging from their sockets.

'I dare!' It was a shout. 'It's allus been the same; he's allus been there, in between us, all through the years. I've tried and tried but 'ee've never been properly mine. Stood at my side in church, didn't 'ee, and made promises? But all the time wishin' you were makin' them to *him*, and he's never been out of your heart.'

'No! Not true!'

Yes, it is true but I couldn't help it. I tried, I have tried. I've tried as hard as I can but there's a cold, hard place in you and it held me away from you . . . in God's name, I tried.

'I'm tired of it all,' said James. 'Tired of you. Tired of him.

Too weary of the whole thing even to clout 'ee, though most men would and they'd be right. Don't want to swing for 'ee, either. Or for him. Neither of you are worth it.'

'*James!*'

'You'll have to go. Now. Out of Foxwell. Go away and leave me be. Turn round and go out of that there door, and don't come back, ever.'

'But . . .'

'Do it!'

'James, we've been married for fourteen years! We've loved each other. I still love you.' That was true too, in a way. It wasn't the instantaneous oneness that held me and Ralph together, but it was still a kind of love, woven from working together, having children together, sharing, from time to time, some perfectly happy moments. 'I don't believe you've stopped loving me. And we have children, James! What about them? William, Rose, John . . . John's only just turned seven . . .!'

'I don't know what love means any more. I've loved 'ee, yes, but *he's* allus been in the way. You'd not do what you've done for someone you didn't care for more than you care for me or the children! What if the Revenue men had caught *you*? You went to Ralph Duggan tonight and stayed with 'un till dawn and I can guess what the two of you were about so don't pretend. You'll *go*! I can't bear to have 'ee near me, not any more. William can stop here with me; he's big enough. Rose and John – the Websters'll take care of 'un, with Annie to help. But *you* . . .!'

The door to the kitchen burst open and William rushed in, red-faced and furious. 'I was listening! I heard it all, I did! That's Mother there and you're trying to send her away and you can't, you can't! We want her. Mother, don't go, stop here!'

'I told you and all the rest to get out of this kitchen and stay out till I said otherwise!' James shouted. 'When I saw her comin' from the paddock with a saddle over her arm, I told 'ee, and your brother and sister and the maids, to go upstairs and mind your own business! What do you mean, you were listening? Had an ear to the door, did 'ee?'

'Yes, I did, and you're not sending Mother away, no, you're not . . .!'

'Oh yes, I am!' James had rounded on him. I cried out: 'No! James!' because two or three times over the years James had beaten our son, and although William was shooting up and strong for his age but still no match for a man like James, heavily muscled, his strength honed by years of physical toil. One swipe of James' powerful right hand, and William was on the floor. He started to get up but James knocked him down again. Once more, though there were tears in his eyes and I knew his head must be ringing, William started to struggle to his feet, and this time I seized a chair and leapt to his defence, fending James off with it, jabbing its legs at him.

We stood there, glaring at each other, momentarily frozen into a tableau of rage. Then James heaved the chair aside, wrenching it out of my hands and reached for my throat. I screamed and kicked out at him and caught his left shin. William, staggering up, sobbing but valiant and charged his father, head down, butting like a young bull.

And then the room was suddenly full of people, for the uproar had brought Annie and John and Rose, who came rushing in, followed by the two other maids we had lately acquired, Lucy and Phoebe. The latter two shrank into a corner, their eyes wide with horror and their hands over their mouths, but Annie bravely rushed at James, shrieking: 'Stop it! *Stop it!*' John, small as he was, actually snatched up a frying pan and banged it down on James' head.

Then he and Rose backed together into the corner with the maids and started to howl in unison. Phoebe and Lucy tried to comfort them. John had not been strong enough to do much harm with the frying pan and now James swung round and grabbed it from him. And then stood still. We all stood still, gasping. William was wiping his eyes furiously, his face crimsoned where James had twice struck it. I knew that tears were streaming down my face. Annie was pop-eyed with fury and horror.

'James!' I said. He glared at me. He was still clutching the frying pan, which added a touch of the ridiculous to the scene. 'I'll go,' I said. 'For now. I'll go to Fred and Mattie. I have indeed been out all night. I need breakfast and a sleep . . .'

'You'll leave Foxwell now! Fred and Mattie won't want 'ee, any more than I do, and least of all today, with Mattie lyin' in! Had a son, she did, last night; sent one of her brood to tell us this mornin'. They won't want to shelter the likes of you just now. You get right out of Foxwell! Go out on to the moor and die, or jump off one o' they cliffs where 'ee've spent the night with thy lover . . .!'

'Don't talk to Mother like that!' shouted William.

'If Fred and Mattie, or any other that works for me, even Searle, that thinks himself a prince just because his forebears have herded sheep here since the Fall, if any of them lifts a finger to help 'ee, they'll be out of work and off my land before they can recite their own names! I mean it! You go! *Now!*'

William, fists clenched, burst out in a new protest. 'Mother can't go! We need her. I *know* she's done nothing wrong!'

'Nothing worse than be unfaithful, and take a warning to a gang of smugglers!' said James.

'My grandfather used to buy his drink and tobacco from them. Half the county does,' said William. 'Half the county would say it was right to warn them. And my mother has *not* been unfaithful. I *know!*'

'I don't! How do I even know you're my son?'

'Try looking at William and then look in the mirror!' I shouted. 'William's not to be hurt any more! Don't you dare raise your hand to him again! And how you can threaten to harm the Websters, to turn them out when Mattie's just given birth . . . well you'd miss them soon enough but you're too eaten up with rage even to have any sense, let alone humanity! You disgust me, James! No wonder I couldn't love you properly, you with your cold, hard heart! Just let me leave in good order, that's all I ask. Annie, can I have some eggs and bacon? I really do need something.'

'*No! Get out!*' James screamed.

'All *right.*' There was nothing else to do. William tried to burst out again but I shook my head at him, vigorously enough to hush him. 'Very well,' I said. 'You will let me collect my clothes, I trust. I'll put them in a hamper and I would also like to take a pony, to get me and the hamper to Exford . . .'

'Travellin' like a lady, after what 'ee've done? You'll *walk* to Exford, you whore, and don't worry about any hamper; you don't set a foot further into the house than you already have. I'll not give 'ee thy clothes, nor any money! Ha! Where'll 'ee be, with not a penny piece to thy name? Go out and earn your bread doin' what 'ee did last night!'

'James, be reasonable!'

'*Reasonable!*'

'You can't throw me out without food or a rest or a change of clothes! Let me have those and then I'll pack and William can drive me into Exford and leave me there. I . . . I'll decide later where to go.' Was all this really happening? I was sick and trembling, my whole world dissolving about me. 'Let us,' I pleaded, 'try to behave like decent folk . . .'

'You'm not decent folk! Now will 'ee *go* afore I lose my senses and kill 'ee here and now, yes, in front of thy children. Maybe I'm sure of William but I hope the rest be mine!'

'*James!*' But there was murder in his face.

'I'll go,' I said.

I did. I turned my back on James, on our children, on Foxwell. I walked out of the kitchen and away round the corner of the barn.

Not a penny piece, James had said. Well, he was wrong about that.

Out of sight of the house, I leant against the barn wall and waited. No one came after me. Over the years I had from time to time checked that the loose stone was still loose enough to be pulled out quickly. Indeed, I had occasionally added a coin or two to the store inside. Now, in haste, I pulled the stone out again, and seized my secret hoard, and Ralph's engagement ring. It would all be heavy to carry but I must manage. I had replaced the original drawstring bag with a new one, and it was in good order. I could carry it on my arm, during the long walk that I must take to Exford.

I spared a moment to kneel and then, low-voiced but aloud, I thanked God for my father's forethought and his connivance with that wicked, good-hearted, free trader Josiah Duggan, for the secret gift of money, which now would keep me from facing the world as a pauper.

Then, shaking off my exhaustion as best I might, I started on the trudge to Exford, marvelling a little as I went because everything looked so completely normal, so ordinary; surely if I turned round and walked back home I would find everything as it used to be and the morning's drama just a dream.

Only, I knew that it was not, and as I plodded along, I wept.

Once in Exford, I went to the White Horse. They knew me there, and though they showed surprise because I was alone, they let me have a room. I went to it and lay down on the bed, too tired to think, too tired to be frightened. There were muddled thoughts in my head, which for the moment I couldn't set in order. But when I woke, I found that in the night they had clarified. What it amounted to was that *I must be careful.*

I had money. A good deal of it, in fact. But I also had a completely uncertain future. Trying to see ahead was like trying to see through a dense moorland mist. The time might come when I could need resources even more than I needed them now. Also, when it came to using the money, I must be cautious for another reason.

I must go away but I didn't want to go too far. I didn't want to leave my own home county of Somerset. I didn't want to find myself making a new start in some other part of the country, where people wouldn't speak with the local accent I was used to, where there was no one even vaguely connected with anyone I had ever known. Had I ever wildly believed I wanted to voyage to Antigua? I couldn't now imagine even *thinking* of such a thing. Besides, to go far away would separate me too completely from my children. Perhaps I might regain contact with them one day, and if at any time they had need of me and tried to find me, I wanted that to be possible. I must leave my immediate surroundings but I must not go too far – and that could mean that James might from time to time get news of me. He might wonder how I was supporting myself.

If James knew I had money, well, he was still my husband, and as such he had the legal right to seize it. Furthermore, I thought he was capable of doing so.

With a shock – and it was a shock, and it filled me with

outrage – I realised that I dare not spend that money, except in an emergency. I would be wiser to live, if I could, without using it. The law, the damned law, would keep me from benefitting from it.

Hadn't I once said to my mother that there were agencies in places like Minehead and Taunton that would help people to find work? Minehead was where Ralph and Harriet lived and I must not go there. I must not turn to Ralph, because of Harriet. I clung to that. I had made love with Harriet's husband, harming her, even though she might never know it. But Taunton – yes, Taunton would do. I did briefly think of going to Mr Silcox but that would also mean telling Edmund Baker what had happened and he was Harriet's brother. No, that was no solution. Taunton it would have to be.

The White Horse sometimes hired out traps for people wishing to make journeys, and would provide a lad to drive it. Next day, I hired a trap and went to Minehead. There would be no harm in passing through it. From there, I knew, I could get a stage coach to Taunton.

I would have to tell any agency something about myself and it couldn't be the truth. I must pretend to be . . . what? A widow, left without a home, perhaps. I began to invent a story to account for myself.

I have never felt more alone. Nothing seemed real. I felt as if I were in a dream from which I would soon wake up. But there would be no waking.

I longed for home but Foxwell was lost to me.

Probably for ever.

The Exile

I was in a daze, of course. Things had happened too swiftly. One moment I was Mrs James Bright of Foxwell Farm, secure, with husband, home and children; then, literally overnight, I was cast upon the world like driftwood on the sea. In the stage coach to Taunton, I dozed a little and then woke, thinking it had all been a bad dream, only – where was I now, and why? And then I woke fully, to the creak of the coach and the smell of the leather seat and the decidedly unwashed farmer beside me and the sound of the horses' hooves, and I knew that my horrible situation was no mere dream, but reality.

I had bought some clothes in Exford. There was a dressmaker there who always had some ready-made dresses and pelisses in average sizes, ready-made in stock, and some underwear items as well. I also wanted some white cloth that I could cut up for my personal needs. I bought a hamper too and I was now provided with luggage. Once more, I silently thanked my father for his gift of money, and the help that Josiah Duggan had given him. James had tried to fling me out to beg my bread but I had no need to beg. Legally, of course, all my money belonged to James. Well, how absurd, to have money and not dare use it. James would never know my hoard existed.

In Taunton, I found a hostelry that would take me, and next morning, I found an agency. Miss Jane Connor, who ran it, was tall, angular and intimidating, but efficient. She could suggest a suitable position. It was in the home of a Taunton lawyer who had a wife and several children. The rate of pay was good. Regular attendance at the parish church was expected and everyone employed by the Waters family at the Grey House must be a true Christian. There were morning prayers every day, at seven o'clock, and more prayers in the evening and everyone had to be present.

I said I was agreeable. Like most farm wives, I was used to early rising. I didn't mention my farm background, though. I said my name was Mrs Margaret Woodman and my story was that I was the widow of a Dorset shopkeeper. He had sold tools, including farm tools. He had died three months ago, leaving me homeless, since my imaginary husband had rented his shop and the living quarters above it and now the landlord wanted to put a new tenant in. I had relatives but they were a long way off, in . . . er . . . Salisbury, I said hastily. I didn't wish to seek their charity. I preferred to seek respectable employment. I had come to Taunton because I had lived there before my marriage, returning, as it were, to my home district.

I was sent to the Grey House to be interviewed by Mrs Waters. She was a plump and well-spoken lady but her dark hair was austerely dressed and her blue eyes were uncomfortably like James' eyes. I noticed, too, that the maidservant who answered the door was not only respectful towards her mistress, but rather too much so. Mrs Waters did not at any point smile at her or at me. She told me to stand in front of her, while she looked me up and down.

'Can you do everything required to run a household well? Cook and clean? Do laundry? I expect my housekeepers to work, not merely supervise. Can you make preserves and read and write well enough to label them?'

'Yes, Mrs Waters. I am fully literate.'

'Have you children? Do you not have a family?'

I thought of William and Rose and John, thrust their memory away and said steadily: 'God did not see fit to grant us that blessing, Mrs Waters.'

'I have three children,' said Mrs Waters. 'My son Thomas, who is now twelve, is at Blundell's school, here in Taunton. He boards, however, so you will see him only occasionally. My daughters are aged thirteen and ten, and are educated at home. They have a governess. When the governess has her time off, I hope you will be able to look after them, even though you have not had offspring of your own. You will not be required to teach, just to amuse them, take them for walks – except in inclement weather, naturally – and the like. It won't encroach very much upon your time.'

'I am quite willing to do that, Mrs Waters,' I said.

'If you come here, you will address me as madam at all

times. I take it that you are of honest reputation and a regular communicant at the altar of our Lord?'

James and I had usually attended church, unless the farm work were too heavy. I said: 'Yes, Mrs . . . madam.'

'You must understand that I do not allow my women servants to have followers – at least they may not bring them here. They have their times off and may do as they wish elsewhere, provided I hear of no impropriety. I recognize their right to marry, naturally. I will also recognize yours, since you are still comparatively young. But there is to be no hint of scandal. Anyone who incurs the slightest breath of that is instantly dismissed. You understand?'

'Yes, madam.'

Dear heaven. She looks like a plump kitten and she talks like a headmaster.

She said: 'You may have a month's trial. We will see how you acquit yourself.'

Life with the Waters family was dreadful. Oh, not on the surface. For instance, I was given a room to myself, and if it was plain, it was also comfortable. My dressing table had one lockable drawer and here I hid my bag of money and Ralph's ring. I wondered if James was missing me now, and surely my children were crying for me. Perhaps, one day, he would soften and I could go home. One day.

The schoolroom, just across the passage, would not usually be my concern, but as I was to relieve the governess on occasion, it was shown to me. It had an ink-stained table, a cupboard holding supplies of paper, pens and ink, a set of bookshelves laden with educational works and, ominously, a birch. I looked at it with dislike and a determination never to touch it. I made no comment, though. I already knew that in this house, one trod carefully and watched one's tongue.

There was no butler at the Grey House. The other servants were a cook, a kitchen maid and two other maids, one of them the girl who had opened the front door when I arrived. There were two gardeners-cum-handymen and two grooms for the horses, but they were outside staff and I rarely had to speak to them, except to order the grooms to harness or saddle horses when required. All the staff, indoor and out, were extremely correct in their manners and conscientious in their work. Again, a little too much so.

Mr Waters was a large, quiet, serious man, who spoke to me only rarely. He was perfectly courteous but something about him worried me. Perhaps it was the lack of expression in his light brown eyes. He presided at the household prayers, which took place in the drawing room every morning and evening. The evening ones, after supper, were particularly wearisome because there was a rule that no one should sit down. By then, many people were tired, but there we had to stand in attitudes of respect, the whole household, grooms and gardeners included, while Mr Waters stood commandingly before us, his back to a sofa upholstered in dark red velvet and his heels precisely placed at the edge of the square Turkish carpet with its pattern of red and blue, and recited interminable prayers, some of which contained digs at his family and servants and business clients.

He regularly asked the Lord to look with favour on his servant and then to grant him various blessings such as dutiful daughters who conned their lessons as they ought or trustworthy clients who would not try to deceive him as so and so had – he named names – and would pay their bills on time. He referred to himself as a servant but he addressed the Almighty in an astonishingly familiar way, as though the Almighty were *his* personal servant instead.

When this tiresome process ended, we were all supposed to say *Amen*. The one who said it with most fervour was Miss Ariadne Worth, the governess.

Before I was introduced to her, I had imagined her as a wispy and downtrodden creature, anxious to please her exacting employers and practically curtseying whenever she encountered them. I was wrong. Ariadne Worth was one of the most terrifying women I have ever come across. She was at least five feet ten inches tall and sometimes looked taller because she held herself so very straight; as though her spine was an iron rod. She always wore black dresses and she had a nose so sharp that it looked capable of being used as a pick or a chisel. Her mouth was set as though she had just been sucking a lemon and her eyes, which were of no particular colour, stared straight through one. She too, was perfectly courteous towards me, and her speaking voice was cultured. Mrs Waters, making a rare jest, said after she had presented me that Miss Worth was rightly named, for she was of very great worth. 'Highly educated and properly firm with her pupils. I feel safe when I entrust my daughters to her. Not that they are brilliant pupils, I fear. My son is doing well at Blundell's, but my girls are not clever.'

Probably too frightened to think straight, I said to myself.

'Not that it matters particularly,' said Mrs Waters. 'Girls need not be intellectuals. They are both good with the needle, and they can sketch and play the piano. However, my husband feels that they should have informed minds and some knowledge of English literature and the French language, and there, I fear, neither of them show much aptitude, though Maria, the younger one, will I think turn out to be brighter than Augusta. Augusta has a bad memory. However, that is hardly your concern. I must finish showing you round the house and explain where we buy our foodstuffs . . .'

When, presently, I met Augusta and Maria, they resembled two pink and white dolls, prettily dressed, their light brown hair tightly braided. They had their father's eyes, but theirs were not expressionless. They seemed, always, to have a pleading look. During my first three weeks in the house I had to watch over them several times and when I took them for walks, I found it difficult, even in an open park, to get them to run about and be playful. They were clearly used to walking sedately and taking great care not to soil their clothes or gloves in any way.

The housekeeper's work was not that onerous, simply because all the staff knew their tasks and did them well. The Grey House was well furnished and thoroughly polished, with bowls of flowers in the hall and the downstairs rooms. I did not like my employers but I had a sound roof over my head, enough to eat – the servants' meals were plain but ample – and enough to do to keep me from brooding too much.

Though I did brood, of course. God help me, I think I cried myself to sleep every night, longing for home, for my children, even yearning to get up at five to milk cows, even wishing for James' unexciting embraces. We had not made love for weeks before that fatal night and the parting in the morning, but we usually put our arms round each other for a few moments before falling asleep.

But there was no going back. So I wept, silently, under my bedcovers, and each morning rose to carry out my duties, and fit in, because the Grey House was my only refuge. Twice during those first weeks, when passing the schoolroom, I caught the sound of a swishing birch and heard one of the girls wailing, but I closed my ears. My heart ached, but there was nothing I could do.

I had been at the Grey House for over three weeks when there came what I still, even now that I am old and looking back across the years, remember as That Terrible Evening.

From the start of the evening prayers, there was a tension. I saw Miss Worth once or twice give sharp looks at Augusta and I saw that the girl's shoulders were hunched a little, as though she was trying to make herself smaller. In the course of his prayers, Mr Waters implored the Almighty to grant him the favour of a truly dutiful and obedient elder daughter, at which Augusta seemed to hunch a little more. I was near enough to see that her right hand, clenched on a fold of her skirt, was trembling.

At the end, Mr Waters did not dismiss us all as usual. He said: 'The servants may leave but not my family. Miss Worth will remain and Mrs Woodman, since you occasionally take charge of my daughters, I think you should remain as well.'

The rest of the servants filed out. Their faces showed very little, but I heard the kitchen maid whisper to the cook that it was too cruel, and heard the cook whisper back that it was none of their business.

As the door closed behind the last of them, Mr Waters said: 'Step forward, please, Augusta.'

She did so. He beckoned her right up to him and then caught her shoulder, turning her so that we could see her face. Inside myself, I recoiled in shock. In my whole life, I have only seen one other face as terror-stricken as that, and that was the face of a man confronting death. Augusta was so white that I thought she was about to faint.

She didn't, however. Her father, still gripping her shoulder, said: 'You have one last chance, Augusta. If you can recite, without any mistake, the speech from Shakespeare's work *Henry V* that you were given to learn yesterday and bidden to recite in the schoolroom this morning, you will be forgiven. For I hear that when asked to repeat it to Miss Worth during your lessons, you were unable to do so. How often has she had to complain to me that you will not apply yourself; that you *will* not try hard enough to acquire the skill of learning by heart. Now!'

In a trembling voice, Augusta began: 'He that hath no stomach for this fight, let him depart. His passport shall be made and mon . . . no, crowns . . . crowns for convoy p . . . put into his purse.' She saw Miss Worth frowning over her stumbles and visibly shrank, but ploughed on, with stammerings and hesitations, for some way before she reached '. . . then will he s . . . strip his sleeve and sh . . . show his scars and . . .'

She broke down. 'I can't . . . I can't . . . it's too long and I can't . . . I can't remember . . . Oh, Miss Worth, I *begged* you not to tell Papa . . . I knew he would be so angry. I did try, I did, I did! Papa, please . . .'

She burst into tears. Mr Waters let go of her shoulder. 'Miss Worth,' he said. 'You know what to do.'

Miss Worth stepped forward. From a reticule that she had concealed beneath her bodice, she drew out what appeared to be some short thongs, and advanced upon Augusta. Augusta did not resist, or say anything more, but her eyes were the eyes of an animal being led to slaughter and aware of it. She went obediently with Miss Worth and lay down on her face on the dark red sofa. Miss Worth used the thongs to tie her wrists and ankles to the legs of the sofa.

Meanwhile, from a drawer in a polished corner cabinet, Mr Waters was taking out what I at once recognized as a set of leather strips, bound together at one end. They looked like lengths from a cut-up belt, for the free end of one of the strips was tongue-shaped. Mercifully, the buckles had been removed. But what was left was bad enough.

With my stomach gradually clenching into nausea, I watched

– along with Mrs Waters and the ten-year-old Maria, who was now silently crying – as Miss Worth removed Augusta's lower clothing. Augusta did cry out in protest then. 'Papa, please don't, please don't . . . I'll try harder; let me have another chance, I'll have it perfect tomorrow, I promise, I promise . . .!'

And then, anything more that she meant to say, was lost in the sound of the leather strips swishing through the air, and the tortured scream that followed.

I don't know how long it went on. Between her screams, Augusta implored him for mercy, in vain. Mrs Waters remained still and silent throughout. Maria was silent too, though the tears ran down her face. Miss Worth stood upright, a pillar of rectitude, her hands folded at her waist, her face like stone. It seemed interminable. At last, Mr Waters desisted. And then he walked round to face the wailing, writhing wreck he had made of his own daughter, pushed the leather strips against her mouth and ordered her to kiss the rod.

I stood rooted for one moment more and then I turned and fled from the room, away along the passage to the green baize door that divided the kitchen and the servants' quarters from the main house. I burst through it. The cook and the maids were all there, sitting or standing, but silent. I brushed past them to the back door, threw it open, and went outside, in order to lean one hand against the kitchen wall, and be sick.

Dear God. Philip Duggan has now been proved innocent, but because I helped him to escape while he was a suspect, I would probably, in the eyes of the law, still be accounted a lawbreaker. And I would certainly be condemned as such for warning Ralph of the Revenue's plans. Even though I had but warned a group of lawbreakers not to proceed with their crime!

But the horrible Mr Waters can viciously torment a terrified girl of thirteen, his own daughter, because she found it hard to memorize a long speech from Shakespeare, and no one would utter a word of protest. He is paterfamilias of his house and he is within his rights to bring up his children according to his own ideas. What kind of insane world am I living in?

At last, I straightened up, swallowing. I returned to the kitchen, where the others stared at me but did not speak. I collected a glass of water, and went upstairs to my room, where, before long, Mrs Waters came to find me.

'I was shocked, Mrs Woodman, by your behaviour this evening. It was not for you to criticize the way your employers discipline their children, by rushing out of the room without leave, when you had been bidden to stay.'

'I was unable to stay, madam. I left the room in order to be sick.'

'How *dare* you?'

'I couldn't help it,' I said. I found that I was quite unable to be apologetic. I was frightened but something reckless in me, perhaps the same recklessness that had sent me out into a dark night to warn Ralph of his danger, insisted on speaking the truth. '*I* was shocked. To treat a young girl – a child – in such a way just because she has difficulty in memorizing Shakespearean speeches!'

'Has difficulty? She could do it if she applied herself. She is lazy and must learn better ways, that's all. When she has had time to recover, she will be set once more to memorize that speech. She will do it, I assure you.'

'She'll probably be too terrified to memorize anything,' I said.

'This is insufferable. Mrs Woodman, I have valued your services; which I admit have been excellent. I had quite decided to keep you on, but neither I nor my husband can tolerate the way you have acted and now spoken this evening. You may have a day, one day, tomorrow, in which to find a place to stay. We are Christian folk; we will not turn you out into the night with nowhere to go. The day after that, you must leave. Do I make myself clear?'

'Entirely clear,' I said.

There was no need to say any more, no need to tell her that my bout of sickness hadn't been entirely due to horror at the scene I had witnessed. It was over three weeks since I had been cast out of Foxwell. Ten days ago, I should have needed some of the linen squares I had made ready. The need had not arisen, and I had been sick, as unobtrusively as possible, three times before this.

I had told Mrs Waters that the mythical Mr Woodman had

died three months before my arrival at the Grey House. The Waters family would throw me out soon enough, whatever I said or did. Even if they had been prepared to keep me on if I produced a posthumous baby, they would quickly have realized that it couldn't be my husband's.

And indeed it was not. James and I had not been together for at least twelve weeks before he cast me off. This child would be the son or daughter of Ralph Duggan.

The Only Hope

I left the next day. My wages would provide for my stagecoach fare; I left my father's hoard untouched. I had needed to use a little of it earlier for travel and clothes and the like, but I knew I must keep the rest hidden. It made me angry, but I was afraid of James and the law.

One of the maids brought me some breakfast. Then I packed my hamper, which was mercifully not too heavy, and shifted it downstairs. In the hallway, I met Mrs Walters.

'May I say goodbye to the children?' I asked. 'I have grown fond of them.'

'As you have made abundantly clear,' said Mrs Waters coldly.

'Mrs Waters, did you really approve of what was done to Augusta last night?' I said.

Her cold eyes flashed, like ice in bright sunlight. 'You have no right to ask me such a question!'

'I know, but I do wonder.'

'I obey my husband, as I promised to do when we were married. His decisions must therefore be right in my eyes.'

So, at heart, she didn't approve. Perhaps one day he would go too far and she would turn on him. Meanwhile . . .

'Please let me say goodbye to the girls.'

'You may not see Augusta. Maria . . . well, here she is. You may take your leave of her, as long as I stand by.'

Did she think I was going to preach rebellion to a scared ten-year-old child? 'I am leaving the household, Maria,' I said. 'Your mother will explain. I have much enjoyed knowing you and I wish you happiness with all my heart. Do please tell Augusta the same.'

She looked bewildered. I kissed her forehead and that was that. I never saw the Waters girls again. I have always hoped, and even prayed, that eventually they grew up to find kind husbands who would give them the love their parents had denied them. But I shall never know.

I left the house, coping with my hamper as best I could. Fortunately, it wasn't far to the inn where I could board a coach. It pulled into the yard of the Wellington inn in Minehead during the afternoon. I was able to bespeak a small private parlour and I ordered myself a good meal. It was always like this when I was expecting. When I didn't feel sick, I felt ravenous. After that, I picked up the hamper and once more prepared to set off, but the innkeeper, seeing that its weight was a worry to me, said: 'Where be you bound, missus? That there's a bit of a load for a lady.'

'I'm going to the hiring stables round the corner. I must hire a trap to take me to Exford. I hope they can supply one.'

'Lord love 'ee, we've stabling here and a couple of traps for hire if wanted. You set back down now in this liddle parlour and I'll get Bruce, that's one of my grooms, nice sensible lad, he is, to harness up a trap for 'ee, and he'll get 'ee to Exford easy enough before the afternoon's out. There'll be a charge, o' course . . .'

'Of course,' I said reassuringly.

If I were to hold by my decision to protect my secret store of money, both to safeguard it from James and to be prepared for future disaster, then I would have to apply to friends for help. This time, I would have to go to Mr Silcox. It would mean that Edmund, and, presumably, Harriet, would learn what had happened that night in the forest, but I needed assistance badly and could think of no other way to obtain it. Besides, the coming child was Ralph's and Ralph was entitled to know. The child was entitled to have a father, too.

By early evening, I was dismounting from the trap in front of Mr Silcox's door and saying goodbye to Bruce. He was a cheerful, pink-faced youth who had enlivened the journey with anecdotes about his work at the Wellington, and I suspected that like most youths, he had a healthy appetite. I therefore gave him a healthy tip so that he could if he wished eat at the White Horse before starting for home.

I did, though, ask him to wait until I had been admitted to the house. 'If they're all out, I'll go to the inn myself and you can take me.' I really wanted transport for the hamper. It seemed to have grown heavier as the day wore on.

However, there was no difficulty. Alice Meddick opened the door to me, looked surprised, but at once held it back for me to enter.

'They both be in the parlour,' she said. 'School's well over for today. They'm takin' tea.'

I waved to Bruce, and he nodded and drove off. 'Let me put my hamper down in the hall, please, Alice,' I said. 'I haven't come to stay, of course. I shall go to the inn; perhaps your husband would be kind enough to carry the hamper across the green for me. But I do need a word with Mr Silcox.'

Alice duly announced me and I stepped into the parlour, where Mr Silcox and Edmund, who had been seated opposite each other at a tea table, at once came to their feet.

'Peggy!' they said in unison.

'I am sorry to intrude on you without warning,' I said. 'But I need to speak with you both. It is important.'

They knew, of course, that James had thrown me out. I had not thought of this before, but probably Rose and John had continued at the school and would have told them that I was gone, though I hoped that they had only spoken of warning smugglers, and not realized that there was more to it than that.

Meanwhile, I watched Mr Silcox and Mr Baker recover from their surprise. Mr Silcox pulled up another chair and asked Alice to bring more tea and cakes and then we all sat down and they stared at me. I began on my story. I approached the heart of the matter very slowly and also very fearfully but I knew that approach it I must. I was here because I was carrying Ralph's child. I could not avoid admitting it.

I left that to the end, though. First I talked of warning the smugglers, of going to Taunton, of being employed by Mrs Waters and how my employment ended, with the shocking scene that I had witnessed. At that point, Edmund interrupted.

'The man was within his rights, you know. As a father and the head of his household, he is entitled to discipline his children. They may well thank him for it in time to come.'

'I can't imagine anyone giving thanks for what I saw happen

to poor Augusta!' I said angrily. 'But I have not come here to talk of that. I spoke my mind to Mrs Waters afterwards and was dismissed, but she would soon have dismissed me anyway. There is something more.' I took a deep breath. The moment had come.

'I am with child and it is Ralph's. It happened when he brought me back that night, after I had warned him. We were once engaged,' I said defensively. 'We have never stopped caring . . . I am not trying to make excuses. I am just repeating a fact. And I have come to you because, yes, I need help and advice, but also because Ralph has a right to know. And his child has a right to be recognized by its father.'

They looked as though I were addressing them in Chinese. Then, after a lengthy pause, Mr Silcox said: 'Are you asking us to inform Mr Ralph Duggan? But why should you think the child you are carrying isn't James' baby?'

'Because since I was very ill with John, James and I . . . have not had much to do with each other. It cannot be his. I am unwilling to approach Mr Duggan myself. That would mean . . . intruding on him and Harriet. But yes, I want him to know. He ought to know.'

'You hope he will make himself responsible for you and the child?' asked Edmund. 'You say it is his child. Are you sure?'

The veiled insult sent the blood rushing to my face, and caused my whole body to clench, as if to defend itself from a blow.

'I am sure,' I said. I tried to speak coldly, but my voice trembled all the same.

I remembered then, the words that had spoken themselves in my mind when − was it only yesterday? − I had stood in the kitchen yard at the Grey House and leant on the wall after my bout of nausea. A version of those words, edited for my present audience, now spoke themselves aloud.

'I have something to say in answer to what you have just − hinted,' I said, addressing myself to both of them, but mostly to Edmund. 'Yes, in the eyes of the law, I have done wrong, for warning Ralph of the Revenue's plans. Ralph and I love each other and always have. We were dragged apart by our elders almost on the eve of our marriage! I suppose they

thought they were doing right but they were not. It didn't
change our feelings. We went on loving each other and that
was what brought us together, that once, the night I went out
to warn Ralph that he was in danger. Never, never, would I
. . . look elsewhere.'

I fixed my gaze firmly on Edmund Baker. 'You almost
suggested, just now, that I might have done. That was an insult,
Mr Baker, which I will not accept. Between Ralph and me,
nothing has ever changed. Forced apart, we lived life as best
we could, marrying . . . doing our best with that . . . but we
should have married each other. And now, because at last what
was between us dragged us together, just once, I fear – from
the look on your face, Mr Baker – that I am to be condemned,
cast out as an outrageous sinner. But Mr Waters of Taunton
can torment a terrified girl of thirteen, his own daughter,
because she finds it hard to memorize long Shakespearean
speeches, and who will condemn him? You defended him!'

Neither of them spoke. I said: 'I came to you to tell you
of my condition because, yes, I hoped you would inform Mr
Duggan, so that I don't have to do it myself. I am in your
hands.'

'You admit to breaking the law and also your marriage vows.
We can hardly connive at such things . . .' began Edmund and
was then silenced by a glare from Mr Silcox.

'I trust, Edmund, that you aren't proposing to tell the
Revenue that this young woman, who is with child, is in
league with the smugglers!' Mr Silcox spoke coldly. 'She could
end up in prison or transported. In her condition, that could
be fatal. Is that what you want? Anyway, the child's father does
have a right to know. I shall go myself to Minehead tomorrow
and see Mr Duggan. Peggy, you will stay at the inn here. I
have no doubt that some arrangement can be made, without
upsetting Mrs Duggan too much, or at all. Perhaps she need
not even know, if I can speak to Ralph privately.'

'Wait,' said Edmund. 'I am shocked, scandalized, by what
Peggy has told us' – his eyes were hard as he looked at me
– 'but I see that your mind is made up, Arthur. However,
you need not go to Minehead tomorrow. I will go. Ralph

Duggan is my brother-in-law. I will try to speak to him alone, as you recommend.'

Alice's husband, the groom, Mr Meddick, did carry my hamper across to the White Horse for me, and there, once more, I bespoke a room. I stayed in the inn all the next day. All the time, my mind was trying to follow Edmund Baker to Minehead. Would he find Ralph at home? What would Ralph say? Would Ralph . . . perhaps . . . come to see me? Oh Ralph, please come. I have but to think of you and my bones turn to water. No, not water. To something much warmer and much rarer. To molten gold. Ralph. *Ralph.*

At the end of the afternoon, when I was sitting disconsolately in the inn parlour, thinking and longing and worrying, Mr Meddick came to fetch me. 'You're wanted at the house, Mrs Bright.'

He walked across the green with me, talking amiably about people I knew in Exford. He was just his ordinary, slightly bow-legged and slightly wizened self. Probably, neither he nor Alice knew anything of my purpose here. When Alice opened the door, he touched his cap and left me for the stables, while I went inside. Mr Silcox came from the study which he and Edmund shared. 'Ah. There you are, Peggy. Go into the parlour. Someone is waiting for you there.'

I went into the parlour, and Harriet Duggan, who was standing by the window, turned to face me.

It was several years since I had seen her, but she hadn't changed much. Her chestnut hair had faded a little but she had the same regular features and grave expression; the same beautiful chestnut eyes. Her smile would probably still be beautiful too, but she was not smiling now. She was well-dressed, in a high-waisted yellow gown patterned with dark blue dots, and lying on the wide windowsill beside her were a fashionable bonnet and an elegantly beaded reticule. The plain pelisse and workaday shawl in which I had travelled and was still wearing looked shabby in such company. I also noticed that at her feet was a basket. I wondered what it contained.

I didn't know what to say, and waited for her to speak first. 'Peggy,' she said. And then stopped.

I said: 'Harriet.' And also stopped. Then I felt that this was absurd and added: 'Shall we sit down? I take it that you have a . . . a message for me.'

Harriet nodded and we did sit down, on opposite sides of the room. Between us was the table where I had taken tea the day before, and on it lay a box of polished wood, with a brass lock. It was about eighteen inches long, perhaps a foot from front to back, and roughly six inches high.

But Harriet was not looking at it. Her eyes were on me. Not for several seconds did she speak. Then she said: 'I am grateful to you, Peggy. I know what you did to save my husband and his friends from arrest and — very likely — a passage as convicts to the other side of the globe. I *am* grateful. With half of me. The other half would like to hate you but can't quite manage it.'

'Please,' I said. 'Please don't hate me. Even though . . .'

Some things, in some circumstances, just refuse to be put into words. I stopped trying.

'I know all about it. Edmund spoke to Ralph in private but there are no secrets between Ralph and me. I know what happened between you and Ralph that night and I knew it before Edmund came to see us today. Ralph himself told me, the morning after it happened. It isn't that. The half of me that hates you does so because, all through our life together, you have always been there, like a shadow in the corner of the room. I was and am, second best. Not that Ralph has ever said an unkind word to me, or done an unkind thing. But still, you were and are there, custodian of his heart. When you live close to someone, as husbands and wives live close to each other, you know these things. You must be well aware of that.'

I was well aware of it. What had James said?

It's allus been the same; he's allus been there, in between us, all through the years. I've tried and tried but 'ee've never been properly mine. Stood at my side in church, didn't 'ee, and made promises? But all the time wishin' you were makin' them to him, and he's never been out of your heart.

'I'm sorry,' I said. 'It isn't a thing . . . that one can choose about. We did betray you, Harriet. Once. Only that once.'

'I accept that. And you risked your marriage and in a way, your neck, to protect Ralph. He told me you were terrified on the cliff path.'

'I was,' I said.

'And now you've been thrown out of your home, on to your own resources, and thrown out of your employment. Edmund told Ralph everything. I wasn't there at first but when Ralph started to shout, I rushed into the room and then . . .'

She stopped, and her eyes were angry. Nervously, I said: 'Yes?'

'Ralph . . . was raging. Well, I knew about his . . . little adventure with you, but neither of us knew that you had been cast off by James; we had heard nothing of you since – that night. I said, *What is it, what is it?* And he told me and then I had to cling to his elbow and Edmund actually had to get in his way, physically – stand with his back to a closed door and refuse to move – because Ralph wanted to rush straight out of the house, saddle up his horse, ride to Foxwell and half-kill James. Or maybe just kill him! Somehow we got him to see sense . . .'

She paused and then said: 'I think I really did hate you then. I kept wondering whether Ralph would ever be so angry on my behalf!'

'Harriet, I . . .'

'And then I wondered whether I would ever have taken the kind of risks for him, that you took, when you went out at night to warn him. I hope I would but I can't be sure. Oh dear heaven!'

Suddenly it burst out of her. 'If only he would give up the free trading, as he calls it! I loathe it. I'm frightened all the time, and I think it's so wrong, anyway! But mostly I worry about him, so much that sometimes I feel ill. You did save him, and I thank you, and in the end, he and Edmund and I sat down at the dining table and discussed what ought to be done to help you – without breaking Mr Bright's neck. Ralph is determined that you must not be left in penury, homeless, because of him, least of all with his child on the way. He was delighted to hear about the child! That made me hate you too, but unborn babes must be protected.'

She had opened her reticule and taken out a key. She held it out to me and pushed the polished box nearer to me.

'This opens the box,' she said. 'Inside, you will find the deeds of Standing Stone farm. From now on, it belongs to you.'

'What?'

'There are tenants there now; Great-Uncle Stephen died four months ago.'

'Did he? I didn't know.'

'Yes. It was sudden. Ralph could have taken it over but he didn't want to and he knew people who would like to rent it. He has the freehold of Standing Stone; his great-uncle apparently bought it from the Acland family and so Ralph is now the true owner of the place. He has let it. The new tenants are to pay rent to him, except that in future, the rents will be passed on to you.'

At last, a trace of smile lit the chestnut eyes. 'Legally, of course, what is yours is Mr Bright's. Everything a wife owns is actually the property of her husband. But by doing it this way, Ralph thinks we can make sure that Mr Bright never finds out. I too am now privy to something that is on the wrong side of the law! All of us are, even my virtuous brother. I understand that you have some funds but Ralph thinks you should conceal them, as your husband could claim them. So Ralph has sent you some money – in this box – to rent a home with. He suggests you stay in Taunton because you have already got to know the town a little. My brother will tell us your new address when you are settled.'

'Thank you.'

Harriet's eyes were shrewd. 'Are you wondering why Ralph didn't come himself?'

'I . . . no.'

'I expect you are. He wanted to. I said no, I would come instead. The rents of Standing Stone will be delivered by messenger, and for the same reason. You know what that is.'

'You would rather he and I didn't meet.'

'Quite. And now,' said Harriet, beginning to gather up her

belongings, 'I must be away. I came in our trap, driving myself. I must return to Minehead.'

We both stood up. Doubtfully, I held out my right hand, and after a moment, she took it. We shook hands.

I said: 'I too wish that he would give up his dangerous . . . interests. For your sake as well as his. I mean that.'

'Thank you,' said Harriet.

A Pale Horse in the Shafts

I came out of my cottage on the outskirts of Taunton on a fine morning in early spring, and drew in a long breath of fresh air. It was good to feel well again, after two weeks of being very ill indeed, followed by a further week of gradual recovery. My legs were now only a little trembly; my head and chest were clear. Half my neighbours had fallen ill with the influenza epidemic and two had died. I was glad to be among the survivors. It was a vicious type of influenza, that year of Our Lord, 1827.

To strengthen my legs further, I began to pace about in the garden, and as I paced, I thought about my years in Claypit Cottage.

I had lived there now for eleven years. It was a pleasant place, taking its name from the claypit that was now worked out but had once been in an adjacent field. It wasn't large. Downstairs it had a modest parlour and a tiny dining room, and an equally tiny kitchen. The stairs went up from the parlour, and overhead, there were two bedchambers, one leading out of the other, both with dormer windows sticking out of the thatched roof. But for me, it was enough. The rent from Standing Stone, together with a regular sum that Ralph sent me for the support of our little daughter, Charlotte, was adequate for paying the rent of the cottage with suffi-cient left over to feed and clothe us and I was content with that.

I was very content. I had agreeable neighbours, who knew me as widowed Mrs Woodman, left to bring up my posthumous daughter alone. They called on me and I called on them. There were little gatherings; I was invited to supper at one house, to join a birthday party at another; in return, I occasionally invited people to take dinner or supper with me. There was a little school for Charlotte, which she attended on weekday morn-ings. It was a pleasant way of life.

Well, most of the time. I can't say I missed James very much, but I missed Foxwell and above all, now and for ever, I missed my children. I was thankful to have Charlotte; she was not only a very sensible little girl, she also resembled Ralph strongly and I loved her all the more for that. But I longed for William and Rose and John, wondered constantly how they were faring, and still, often, I wept for them in the night.

Though during the last five years, I had at least had news of them. In the summer of 1822, William found me.

It was afternoon. I was in my kitchen and I saw him from the window. I stared in disbelief and some alarm, thinking that he was James. Then I saw that this was a much younger man, and suddenly realized that it was William and with that, I rushed out to greet him.

'William! I knew you at once but . . . you're so big!'

He'd been a gangling lad when last I saw him. Now he was twenty, stocky and muscular, the very image, indeed, of James, except that his tow-coloured hair was thicker and there was an affectionate smile in his brown eyes.

'It happens,' he said, laughing. 'Lads do grow!' He dismounted from his pony, which I recognized as Copper, and tethered him to my front gatepost. 'I'd have come sooner but Dad never let me go anywhere and not say where I was going and if I ever said I wanted to see you, well, you can imagine. He'd beat me. Only lately, I've put on a few inches, sideways as well as upwards, and a lot more muscle, and the last time he tried to use a strap on me, I knocked him down. I said I was going to find you and it was my business, not his. Ma's my mother, I told him, and if I want to find her, I will.

'He tried to say he'd throw me out but I laughed at him. You'll have hard work to run Foxwell without me, I said. I do three men's work here as it is. And that's the truth! He always was a bit on the stingy side and now he's worse.'

'Oh, William! I don't like to think . . . I am so sorry. How is Rose? And John?'

'Well enough. They do as they're told and believe what they're told. Rose looked at me as if I was an army deserter when I said I was going to look for you. John went off by himself to think — that's a trick he has. When I was setting off, though, he came out of the house and said *good luck* so I think he's secretly pleased. He's missed you, I think, same as I have.'

'But how did you find me?'

'Oh, dear old Silcox. He's getting older now but he and Mr Baker are still there in Exford. I wondered if they by any chance knew where you were. I had an idea you might have gone to them for help. So I did the same thing. Ma, they told me about my little sister.'

He paused, awkwardly. 'Is she my full sister or my half-sister? They said half-sister. I'd like to know. You're my mother, whatever you've done, and my sister wasn't responsible anyhow. I talked to Mr Silcox and Mr Baker about it all. Mr Silcox said to me that a son should respect his mother and that it was true that my sister was blameless. Mr Baker was all stiff and disapproving, and he just said, "The Commandments tell us to respect our parents, and I also respect my elders and I've nothing to add to what Mr Silcox has said," and I said to him that the position I was in was a bit awkward; as things were, I couldn't very well respect both parents, but my father did have three men's work out of me and that ought to be respect enough! Now it was my mother's turn.'

'Oh, William!' I said, laughing.

'Mr Silcox told me where you were and I went home and thought it over. That was a week ago and . . . well, here I am. Aren't you going to ask me in?'

I said: 'I haven't answered your question about Charlotte – your sister. She is indeed your half-sister. Her father is Ralph Duggan. Your father was entitled to reject me, for I was unfaithful to him, though only once, under very extraordinary circumstances. I have not seen Mr Duggan since that night. I don't want to say any more, or make excuses. It *was* only once. Only – it resulted in Charlotte. Your father will never forgive me and most people would agree with him. But oh, William . . . I am so very glad to see you!'

'I want to meet Charlotte. If she's my sister – well, I'm her brother. We ought to know each other.'

Dear William. He must have been so puzzled, so bewildered, caught between his natural love for his mother and the storm of condemnation from his father, along with all the moral upbringing he had had. I am grateful, have always been grateful for the existence of William. Which means, of course, that I have in a way to be grateful to James, who fathered him! I often think: how complicated it all is.

Adopting a practical tone, I said: 'You'd better look after Copper and then come inside. I've a neighbour with a spare stall. Did you come from Foxwell today?'

'Started at dawn. Copper's tough.'

We got Copper settled and then William came in and was introduced to Charlotte. After that, he came every few months or so. On the next occasion, he arrived in the company of a small, pretty girl with soft light brown hair and light blue, sparkling eyes, and I heard that this was Susie Harding from Exford where her father had a hardware shop, except that she wasn't Susie Harding now; she was Susie Bright, because she and William had just got married. A year later, I was able to congratulate William on the birth of a son, Harry.

I heard that Fred and Mattie had changed very little. Their eldest son Dickie was foreman at Standing Stone and had a wife and family of his own. Neither William nor the Websters had any idea that this news had much significance for me. My ownership of Standing Stone was a secret that I would not risk sharing. But I was glad to know that it was in charge of a man with such a knowledgeable father.

I heard that Annie had married, a cowman on another farm. She had had two children, who were now in the care of her married sister in Porlock, and Annie had run away from her husband, who had mistreated her, and returned to Foxwell. Phoebe and Lucy had both married and left but nowadays Annie had a new maid called Jenny to work with her – the eldest of ten children in an enormous farming family near Molland, apparently. She was a lively little thing, William said, thin, dark but as active as could be. And naturally, I heard news of Rose and John.

Rose, at nineteen, had married a Mr Henry Hannaford, who had a farm near South Molton, on the other side of the moor. James had put aside his stinginess for once, and given her a big wedding, and 'away she went,' said William.

He added sadly: 'I think the big wedding was because she's what Dad calls a dutiful daughter. I did try to persuade him, and her, to invite you but neither of them would have it, and nor would Mr Hannaford. Properly prim and upright, he is; Methodist. Only tea in his kitchen, never cider, and he talks like a preacher even when he's got mud over the top of his boots.'

I heard later that Rose had had a daughter, a grandchild that I might never see. Never *have* seen, to this day. John, at sixteen, had rebelled against the overworked life at Foxwell and his father's slave-driving, and run off to sea.

Now, on this spring morning, with my legs still weak from the influenza, I paused in my pacing round the garden and wondered if I would ever see my younger children again. The ache was always there. Well, thank heaven for Charlotte.

I resumed my pacing. I didn't recover from illness as well as had done in the past. I was now well into my forties and sickness struck harder. I had been lucky to have a kind neighbour who had already had and got over the influenza, and came in to look after me when I was ill.

I was still prowling round my front garden when a trap drew up at my gate. I didn't recognize the grey horse in the shafts, but a moment later, I realized that the man who was driving it was William.

Charlotte came out of the house, calling his name, and he jumped down. 'Welcome!' I said as he came up to us. And then: 'But what is the matter?' One glance had shown me that his face was pale beneath its weathering, and his blue eyes were full of anxiety.

'It's Dad,' he said breathlessly. 'I think he's dying.'

We took him indoors and Charlotte made tea while I sat him down and got him to explain.

'It's this here flu that's going round, knocking folk down like skittles. Both the Websters are in their beds and their second boy, Ned, was laid up for ten days. Ned works for us now – looks after the horses mostly. We were hard put to it to keep the place in order without him but we managed, and then I got it and then Dad. I've recovered easy enough but Dad! He's desperate sick!'

His eyes filled with tears. 'Choking for breath, he is. Can hardly speak; just glared at me when I said I'd fetch you, but he's your husband still; you've a right to be there if so you want to be. I said I'd bring you and he needn't argue, the old devil, not that he can, as things are.'

'*William!* Who's looking after him? Susie?'

'No, Annie. She had it too, same time as I did; she's still shaky on her feet but she's coping. Susie can't, she's lyin' in; she's just had another boy but it was a long business; Susie's no stronger than the babe! She's lost two since the first one; I never told you. It upset her that much! Well, she's carried this one all the way and pray God all goes well now. We're keeping infection away from her all we can. Jenny has had it but she's better now and she's caring for Susie. Folk don't seem to get it twice, so she won't pass it on. We've sent Harry to stay with Annie's sister along with Annie's children, to keep him safe. Fine, strapping lad he is now, nearly four. We want him to stay hearty.' He hesitated, suddenly nervous. 'Only, if you come, I hope you won't get it too!'

'I've just got over it. I'm protected, like Jenny. You started out this morning?'

'Aye, I did. A good seven hours, it's taken me. It's been hard on Caesar – that's the grey in the shafts. Just bought him; wanted something a bit bigger than a pony. I brought the trap so that Charlotte can come, and the luggage too – you'll need clothes and things. Caesar must have a rest and a feed; it's a long way home and we must get back today if we can.' A wry look crossed his face. 'I'm remembering some of the things Mr Silcox used to tell us about – the four horseman of the Apocalypse . . . did he tell you about them when you were at school?'

'Yes, but what . . .?'

'A pale rider on a pale horse and his name was Death,' said William sadly. 'I have a pale horse in the shafts. Very suitable!

But we need to hurry . . . if we want to be in time. If you'll come, that is. I haven't even asked you properly yet!"

'Of course.' James *was* my husband, for all our long estrangement. And Foxwell was my home.

Bitter Reunion

The ride back to Foxwell was strange. During my years at Claypit Cottage I had never returned to the moor, and it should have been a joy to me. Indeed, it was so in part, despite the circumstances. I did find delight in jogging through the river valleys, where the trees grew out of the steep sides at such astonishing angles and met overhead, and the new young foliage cast a green, dappled light over the track. Though one also had to pluck leafy switches to brush the flies away, so that it was still more welcome to emerge on to the open moor and see the smooth moulded backs of the hills all round, behold the wide sky overhead, hear the twinkling music of the skylarks, feel the wind and see the heather and the moor grass, purplish at this time of year, though it would turn to pale gold later.

But my enjoyment was tempered for I kept thinking of James, suffering the illness which I had just had myself. I remembered all too well the pain of that vicious sore throat and how I had lost my voice entirely for three days. But I had not died and James, apparently, was likely to do so. His suffering must be far greater than mine.

I was sorry for him. I thought about that, while William talked to Charlotte about the farm. They were friends, as brother and sister ought to be. That was a happy thing. But I didn't think James would welcome Charlotte to Foxwell. I feared that even if he was sick to the point of death he would still hate me and would resent my daughter, and show it. Even though I might be able to help him. I still had some of the local physician's remedies, for I hadn't needed them all. I had brought them with me, hoping that I might at least be able to ease James' pain.

For our refreshment on the journey, we had brought flasks of water and cider, and assembled some bread and cheese and mostly we ate and drank on the move, though we did make a couple of short stops at inns, to let Caesar drink and take a brief rest. It was a long way and the sky had dimmed and the first stars were showing before we came in sight of Foxwell. However, there was still enough light to see the shape of the farmhouse as we drove into the yard and the familiarity of it came to me like a shattering blow. It looked so exactly as it always had. I could not believe I had been away so long.

Would I now be able to remain? I hadn't even asked William what the maids and the Websters would think of my reappearance.

William pulled up. Caesar stopped thankfully, his head hanging low. A brisk young man, like a rejuvenated version of Fred Webster, came to his head. 'Poor old fellow. Now don't 'ee worry; there be fresh straw waitin' for 'ee and a warm bran mash in a jiffy. Glad to see 'ee back, Master William, and the missus with 'ee.' The rest of the household were going to accept me, it seemed. 'Mr Bright, Annie says he'm holdin' on but it do be a bad business. Come you down, now. This the missus' little girl? Pretty wee thing, you be, maid. Best get inside, all of 'ee. Leave Caesar and the hampers to me.'

I picked up a small bag that had travelled between my feet. 'I have some medicines here,' I said.

I climbed out of the trap, and knew as I put my feet on the ground that I was not as strong as I had thought, for my legs were shaking again. But this was no time to concern myself with such things. I was in the house ahead of the others, stepping tremulously in at the kitchen door, to be confronted at once with Annie, older, heavier, and with a look of misery on the face that had once been so waiflike and was now so broad.

'Annie! How is he? How is James?'

'It's you, missus! I hardly knew 'ee – so many years! The master's still with us, missus, still fighting back. But Mrs Bright, you do be exhausted, I can see it. And this liddle maid'll be your daughter. She do look wore out, too. Best sit down a minute. I've water on the boil, I'll have a cup of tea for 'ee in two seconds . . .'

Dear Annie! But I shook my head. 'No, Annie. I mean, thank you, and presently I'd love some tea and please make some for William and Charlotte here. William, please look after Charlotte. I must see James. Which room is he in?'

'Same one as ever, missus, same one as ever.'

I was already halfway out of the door and making for the stairs, my bag in my hand. I made straight for my husband's room, which had once been mine too, thrusting the door open and entering without ceremony. I then stopped short, because James had company and I had startled her. The flaxen-haired young woman who was in the act of pouring water from a jug into a glass spilt some of it in her surprise. And then stared at me with hard blue eyes. Marble-blue eyes. She was glaring at me.

I took her in, slowly, startled in my turn at the changes wrought by the years. Then: 'Good day, Rose,' I said. 'How are you?' She was my daughter and I wanted to add *my dear* but the hard blue stare wouldn't let me.

'You shouldn't be here!' Rose snapped. 'Annie sent Ned Webster to fetch me this mornin'; it were all gettin' impossible, she said, doin' the work of the house and seeing to Susie. She told me William had gone to get you so I supposed you'd come but you *shouldn't* have come. You shouldn't ever be showin' your face here again. Father said it when he could still talk.'

I moved over to the bed. James was propped up on a pillow, presumably to ease his breathing, for he crackled and bubbled with every breath he took. His face, dewed with sweat, seemed already to have the waxy look of death. The room was warm, perhaps too much so. There was a fire in the grate and the window was tightly closed. James' eyes, so like those of Rose, stared at me inimically. He tried to speak, but could only manage a husky growl, which plainly hurt him.

'Go away!' said Rose furiously. 'I'm here now. He doesn't want *you.*'

'I may be able to help him,' I said coolly. I put my bag down on the end of the bed and opened it. 'What has been done for him?' I asked Rose. 'Has a doctor seen him?'

'Ned Webster went to Porlock for one, three days back, they tell me,' said Rose, grudgingly. 'But he couldn't bring 'un here. Doctor said he were run off his feet. He'd got a dozen folk in his care in Porlock, couldn't take time to come out here. Said keep 'un warm, give 'un plenty of water, say our prayers. Mattie Webster makes a horehound brew for coughs; she's always got some handy and Ned says it's doin' her and Fred good; gettin' better, they are. We've given him that as well. But it hasn't helped.'

'I've had the illness,' I said. 'I didn't use all my medicines and I've brought some with me.' I pulled two bottles out of my bag. About half of the contents had been used from each. 'This one, with the white medicine in it, is for bringing fever down,' I said, placing it on the bedside table. 'This one, with the dark brown medicine,' I held up the second, 'is to help breathing. Rose, go down to the kitchen and boil a kettle of water. Bring it up here, and bring a pudding basin and a little spoon. No, two little spoons. And a couple of towels. And hurry.'

'What's all this?' Rose was sullen.

'I told you. Medicines. They helped me and they may help him. And let's prop him up a bit more. That'll ease his breathing too.'

'Can't you leave him alone? Would you like to be heaved about when you're that ill?'

'If it made me more comfortable then yes I would! Please do as I ask!' I snapped. 'And fetch another pillow so that we can put two of them behind him. Yes, and an extra blanket. I'm going to open a window. There's not enough air in this room.'

'Doctor said keep 'un warm and you want to open a window and let in a draught . . .'

'That's why I said bring another blanket. *Will* you do as you're told?'

'You played my father false. How 'ee could dare show your face here . . .'

'None of that has any bearing on whether or not I can nurse a man with influenza. Now, get that blanket and the pillow and hurry! And then, please, the hot water, the spoons, the towel and the basin!'

Rose scowled furiously but I glared back and in the end she did as I wanted.

Opening the window let a cool airstream into the room. He tried to mouth something but his eyes still stared angrily and whatever he was trying to say, I preferred not to hear it. 'Don't try to talk,' I said gently.

There must have been water on the hob in the kitchen, for Rose was back with everything in a very short time. 'Give your father two spoonfuls of the white medicine while I get the inhalant ready,' I said. 'Thank you.'

I filled two-thirds of the basin with steaming water from the kettle, and put a spoonful of the dark medicine in it. It was thick and sticky but it had a pleasant, aromatic smell which now filled the room. I told Rose to steady her father while I held the basin under his nose and put a towel over his head to keep the steam in. I used the second towel to protect my hands because the basin was so hot to hold. 'We stay like this for five minutes,' I said.

James mumbled something as we positioned him with his head over the steam, but made no protest. Rose watched anxiously. James must have done his best to see that my character was well and truly blackened in her eyes and she was still unfriendly but she was cooperating. Probably she had seen that his needs had to come before her dislike of me and perhaps she was finding hope in my new treatment, since nothing had succeeded so far.

We waited in silence until five minutes had passed. Then I took away basin and towel, and set them aside. James promptly had a fit of coughing, which brought up some phlegm; all to the good, I said cheerfully. I turned to Rose. 'Can you find some warm chicken broth for him? It will give him strength,' I said.

It took four days. I despatched Ned Webster to Porlock again, this time with small samples of my two medicines, and although the doctor there still couldn't find time to ride out to us, he sent new supplies of both back with Ned. We gave two spoonfuls of the white one to James every few hours, and three times a day we made him inhale the aromatic steam. We kept him propped up during the day and recruited his strength with chicken broth, bread chopped small and soaked in hot milk and honey, and apples stewed soft. There were still some cooking apples left over from the last harvest.

It was a battle. One night, I was sure we were going to lose him. But somehow he held on until dawn and with the light, a trace of strength seemed to trickle back into him. His fever abated at last. And then the horrible crackling in his chest faded away and his voice came back.

'I s'pose I've got to be grateful and take 'ee back,' were the first words I heard him say, as I was straightening his bed on that fifth morning. 'Seein' as 'ee's likely saved my life for me.'

'I'll come back gladly,' I said. In a careful voice. His had been laden with resentment.

'Dare say 'ee would. So who's been keepin' 'ee, all these years? William let out to us as you was livin' in a nice cottage in Taunton. So who's been paying the rent? Other men, I take it. Brought a brat back with 'ee, so Rose says. Been sellin' thyself, have 'ee?'

I strangled a surge of fury and said quietly: 'No. I have an allowance from Charlotte's father . . .' James almost snarled but I went calmly on '. . . but I haven't seen him, or had anything to do with any man since that night. My daughter Charlotte is Ralph's, yes, the result of that one night. She's eleven now. She is a lovely child and not to be called a brat.'

'I'll call her what I want. William told me about her. So 'ee takes money from *him,* do 'ee! As for all this "only one night" stuff – expect me to believe 'ee, do 'ee?'

'It doesn't matter whether you believe me or not,' I said. 'I have a home, a life, to return to if need be.'

But I didn't want to leave Foxwell. Now that I was here, I knew I didn't want to go away again. Only I dare not plead. That would simply encourage to James to reject me again, even if he did owe his life to me. I said: 'I have lived honestly. I can't prove it, of course. But it is true.'

'Bah!' said James.

'It's time for your inhalation,' I said, and set about it.

Later, I sat in the parlour and wept. This was a bitter reunion if ever there was one, bitter with both James and Rose. She would not forgive me. She never has. While she was at Foxwell, she made it clear that she savagely resented my presence there and Charlotte she ignored altogether. She left Foxwell as soon as James was out of bed. I have never seen her since.

I had kept carefully away from my daughter-in-law Susie, fearing that I might carry infection to her from James' room. When I did feel it would be all right to visit her, she at least was pleased to see me, and I took great joy in cuddling my new grandson. She and William had decided to call him Michael, after Susie's father.

But time was passing. James was out of bed and almost himself again. No more had been said about my future, and I was afraid to raise the matter. I had missed the rhythms of the farm, the world of crops and animals, more than I knew, and I had missed the moors.

At the end of his first week of convalescence, James announced that he must start work again. He began going out on to the farm, first for an hour, then for two, then half a day, then all day, though I thought he was driving himself. I was myself perfectly well again by then but I remembered how weak I had felt at first and how long it lasted. I noticed that James still had a cough. He gave up the inhalations and refused to resume them. Another two weeks passed. I saw little either of him or William during those days, for the spring sowing and the lambing were under way.

It was as well that I saw James rarely, for when he was in the house, the atmosphere was unhealthy. James didn't repeat his first angry outburst. He was essentially a decent man and I suppose he knew he owed me something, and knew too that a little girl like Charlotte was not responsible for her own birth. What he did instead was to ignore Charlotte as Rose had done, and in my presence, be very quiet.

It was difficult for me and very bad for Charlotte. She had been aware of Rose's attitude and when James was once more on his feet and about the house, she noticed his as well.

Once she asked me: 'Mamma, why did my sister Rose not like me? And . . . the master' – she never worked out what she ought to call James – 'he doesn't, either. He walks past me as if I wasn't there. But what have I *done*?'

'Nothing, love,' I told her. 'It's all a bit too complicated for you, at your age. You'll understand better later on. It's a grown-up thing but I can tell you this; it's no fault of yours.'

But she felt it; I could see that. Sometimes she tried to

approach James, in simple ways, by saying good morning to him at breakfast, by making tea for him or if she heard him ask someone to find something for him, finding whatever it was herself. He never answered her greetings, never said thank you for any little services. Again and again she tried and again and again I saw her flinch from his obduracy.

After I had been at the farm for four weeks, I came to the painful conclusion that after all, I would have to return to Claypit. I could not let Charlotte be subjected to this much longer.

The day after I reached that unhappy decision, James came in from the fields earlier than usual. I was in the kitchen, helping Jenny to prepare the supper. Skinny, dark Jenny, who was only fifteen, was handy in both kitchen and dairy, though not as useful with the new baby as I hoped she would be. She said frankly that she had come from a household with a lot of children in it and it hadn't made her like them much. She was very helpful in other ways, though, and when James sat down in his basket chair, she went to pull his boots off for him. He sighed with relief and sat back and it struck me that he looked very tired. That he looked ill.

'James?' I said. 'Are you all right? The wind's cold today.'

'I b'ain't all right,' he said. 'I think I've got it back again. What I had afore.' His voice was husky. 'I bin feelin' funny since midday, and out there with the cows just now, it come over me all of a sudden, like. My legs don't belong to me. I'm going to bed. Likely I'll be on 'ee's hands again for a day or two.'

For a moment, I saw a gleam of the old James, the James I had lived with before the night I went to warn Ralph, the James I had known in the days when we called ourselves happy. 'If you've been thinking to go back to Taunton, I reckon it can't be yet awhile,' he said.

So once again, I must fight for him. Susie was up and about now, so I despatched her and the baby to stay with the Websters, who were also quite restored and free of infection, while William sensibly arranged for his elder boy, Harry, to join them there. 'We can't go on burdening Annie's sister with him and at least he'll be here at Foxwell if not in the house.'

This time Annie and I shared the task of nursing James. Ned Webster fetched further supplies of medicine from Porlock. We did all we could.

But the first bout of illness had weakened him and he was no longer young, and perhaps he was tired in more than physical ways, drained by the years of bitterness. He lost his voice again and his breath became more and more difficult, while his fever soared and nothing we did could make it drop. James seemed grateful for the care he was given. He even smiled at me once or twice.

I am glad that I was the one who was sitting with him when the last crisis came, awful though it was. It happened at midnight. He had a fit of coughing that wouldn't stop but grew worse and worse, until at last, he began to cough up blood, a little at first, and then a flood.

His eyes were terrified. I told him soothingly that this was a good thing and he would be better when it was over. He wanted to believe me. He clung to me with the very last of his strength and I held him fast. I was crying and covered in his blood and still holding him when his grasp slackened and he died.

The Sailor Comes Home

'You'll stay here now, won't you?' William said to me, when the funeral was over.

I still hesitated, wondering if Susie would really want her mother-in-law in the house, but Susie echoed him. The difficult birth had exhausted her, and from the first, we had had a rapport. Also, Harry had now come back home from the Websters, who were candidly glad to be relieved of him, for reasons that were all too clear. Susie, making excuses, said that he had been different before the epidemic broke out.

'All that upset when everyone seemed to be ill, and then being sent away to stay with strangers, and he's so little, even the Websters would seem like that; it's no wonder he's a bit nervy now.'

Susie was naturally bound to defend her son, but whatever the cause, Harry was now a handful. A noisier and frankly more disobedient four-year-old I had never met. 'I want 'ee to stay,' Susie said to me. 'And help with Harry.'

'Charlotte and I must go back to Taunton to get the rest of our things and vacate the cottage,' I said. 'But we won't be longer than we can help.'

We went back by coach from Minehead and in the event, we needed to stay only a week in Taunton. Then I hired a driver and a cart in which to transport the rest of our possessions. They didn't amount to much for the furniture belonged to the cottage. On the way, I posted a letter to Ralph and Harriet, thanking them for all that they had done for me. A reply reached me at Foxwell two days later. There was a stiff little letter from Harriet, saying that my Standing Stone rents and Charlotte's money would be sent to Foxwell in future, formally regretting the death of James and civilly pleased to hear that I and my family had all weathered the epidemic. I sighed a little. I could have liked Harriet so much, and in another world we could have been such good friends.

The actual moment of my return to Foxwell was stormy. The cart drove into the farmyard to find Fred Webster marching across it towards the kitchen door, dragging a bellowing Harry by the ear, while the hens in the yard squawked and darted about in wild agitation and within the kitchen a baby howled in a tantrum. Annie's voice, with an exasperated edge on it, was trying to quieten the child and I could hear Susie crying and between sobs, appealing for peace, in vain.

'For goodness' sake!' I said, scrambling down from the cart, and giving the driver a rueful look. 'We must give you something to eat and drink but I must calm this uproar first. Charlotte, go inside and go straight up to your room.'

'I'll see to the hoss,' said my driver placidly. 'Trough over there, I see.'

'I'll help.' Ned Webster had appeared from somewhere and my driver jumped down to meet him. I left them to it and hurried after Fred and Harry. Fred, over his shoulder, said: 'This young limb were chasing the hens. Laughed when I told 'un not to. If it isn't one thing it's another with this lad. Sets us all by the ears, he does. His dad's out on the farm or he'd give you what for, young Harry – and stop that yowling, you disobedient brat!'

Overhead, a window opened and Mattie appeared, shaking a duster into the air and then, catching sight of me, shouted: 'Thank the good Lord 'ee's back, missus! Maybe you can settle this here racket! Place is turning into bedlam these days!'

'And Jenny's no help,' said Fred, shaking Harry crossly, so that Harry's yells grew louder. 'Her don't like babbies, she says. Looked after missus when she had to and knows what to do on account of coming from a big family, but now she says she hates it, all babbies do is bellow and get wet at both ends and she don't want to know about Harry and as for Michael, she had enough of him while his ma was having him. Missus just ain't got the strength . . . be *quiet*, you little savage!'

'He won't be quiet while you keep yanking his ear about like that,' I said. 'Here, give him to me. Come here, Harry. You're not to chase the hens, Fred is quite right to be angry with you. Now, you come indoors . . .'

'Don't want to go in; want to play outside!'

'Your ideas of playing shouldn't involve the hens. Come along.' I got him into the kitchen by gripping his arm, though it took a surprising amount of strength and I could well understand why Fred had preferred to haul him along by the ear. Charlotte, still looking horrified, had done as she was told, and gone upstairs, out of the way. In the kitchen, baby Michael was howling with abandon while Annie stooped over him, trying to spoon milk into his mouth. Susie was weeping wearily in the basket chair. Jenny was peeling potatoes and trying to look as though she wasn't there.

'What on earth's going on?' I demanded. 'Sit down on that chair, Harry, and don't you dare move, and stop that yelling at once. Annie . . .'

'Missus b'ain't got no milk!' Annie mourned. 'This here's goat's milk; Websters be keepin' goats now, and their milk's all right for most babbies if their mothers can't feed 'un, but this little tyke Michael, he won't have it and . . .'

'Susie,' I said, 'take Michael into another room, or upstairs, somewhere quiet, anyway, and rock him – he might settle down then. Annie, warm some fresh goat's milk if you have some and we'll try it with some honey in it. Harry, *be quiet!*'

I said it so fiercely that he actually stopped bawling. Annie glared at him. 'He got the sulks when I said he'd had enough spoonfuls of my cake mixture. He's had four and he'll be sick if he has any more. He's the greediest child I ever did see. He run out of the kitchen in a pet, and then Missus came in carrying Michael and said she'd been tryin' again to feed 'un but her milk hadn't come back – failed, it did, days ago now – and that's why we've got goat's milk here, only little Mike, he'll hardly take it . . .'

It was a good thirty miles to Foxwell from Taunton, possibly more. I had been travelling all day. I ached. I wanted a cup of tea and a rest, before changing my clothes and starting to arrange my belongings in my room, the one I had once shared with James, probably. I had expected to ease myself into the household by degrees, taking days about it. I had *not* expected to find myself taking instant charge of a crisis as though I were a sheepdog rounding up a flock of recalcitrant sheep.

Susie crept out of the kitchen with Michael. His crying faded into the distance as she carried him upstairs. Annie stood looking with distaste at Harry. He was gulping miserably. His hair was tangled and his tears had made shiny streaks on his small face. He also looked pale. In fact, he was definitely tinged with green. The cake mixture, no doubt! Just in time, I snatched an empty bowl off the dresser and held it while he was sick. Jenny continued to peel potatoes with grim determination.

'It's a good thing I'm back,' I said resignedly.

William thought the same when he returned from the fields, and found the house moderately peaceful. 'I've been coming home every day to a whole lot of noise,' he said. 'Now you're here, perhaps life will be quieter.'

'I'll do my best,' I said.

In the succeeding weeks, I set about getting the household to run smoothly. I wasn't needed in the dairy since both Susie and Jenny were good at dairy work, and I was past the age for plodding round the fields to spread muck or join in the haymaking. Also, Foxwell now had a good cowman, Samuel Andrews by name, who along with his wife Marian could attend to the milking. What I took over was managing the children and seeing that the housework and cooking were done properly. I went to Exford and called on the vicar to ask if he knew of a suitable wet-nurse. He did: there was a Mrs Bridget Bond who had just lost a new baby and would be willing to stay at Foxwell for a while to feed Michael. I installed Bridget the same day.

The vicar also recommended a Sarah Jones, a childless widow, to help in the house. Sarah was about forty-five, a hefty, strapping woman who could scrub floors, carry buckets of water and beat rugs superbly.

Though she couldn't cook. We tried her at that but soon gave up. You could have shot rabbits dead with Sarah's bullet-hard potatoes while her pastry lay on the stomach like leaden weights and her cakes always sank in the middle. Her late husband had died of some mysterious internal complaint but William insisted (out of Sarah's hearing) that it must have been indigestion. However, her muscles and her tirelessness made up for everything. With Sarah to help us, life in the house became reasonably normal once more. Except, of course for Harry's too-frequent tantrums and outbursts of mischief, which his mother seemed unable to deal with.

Susie and I got along well. It wasn't Susie's fault that she was not strong, and not her fault that her attempts at child-bearing had damaged her in some way, so that it hurt her to move anything at all heavy or to stand for too long. She did what she could and was obviously grateful that she need not drive herself too hard. She took on the lighter tasks; feeding the poultry, sorting eggs, mending, and chopping vegetables. I didn't think that the upset of the epidemic was responsible for Harry's maddening behaviour. Mattie Webster told me that he had been much the same before that. 'Only 'un's growin' every day and as he grows, he gets cleverer at bein' a pest,' said Mattie.

The summer wore away. In August and September, the moor was at its most splendid, for the heather was out and the gorse was at its best and the hills were mantled royally in purple and gold, and the kings of the moor, the red stags, were now in full antler and beginning to roar their challenges. In Taunton, I had known that I had missed the moor and its changing seasons but only now was I fully realising just how much I had missed them. I was so very glad to be home – if only home were a little less prone to disruption from Harry.

His talent for mischief was alarming, for it was often dangerous, like the time he attempted to ride our Red Devon bull (but was fortunately thrown and landed in a gorse bush, which I considered served him right, though Susie wept over his scratches). It was beyond me to control him, just as it was beyond Susie. He needed constant supervision which we had no time to give him. I made up my mind and Susie was wise enough to listen to me. Harry must go to school as soon as he turned five.

Edmund Baker still ran the school in Exford and Charlotte was already studying with him. She had drooped for a while after our final return to Foxwell, and had been obviously homesick, but she was happier now that she was attending school, which got her away from the farm. She didn't like the highly physical farm life; she would rather read a book than weed the vegetable garden, any day, and she recoiled with loathing from spreading muck. Edmund sent us good reports of her work and once, confidentially, told me that she was a very intelligent child and would I consider letting her become a pupil teacher.

'It would be a future for her,' said Mr Baker. 'She's not a natural-born farm girl. She still misses Taunton,' he added. 'Did you know?'

'Yes, but I can do nothing about it,' I said. 'Your idea sounds practical, though, and yes, it would get her away from the farming world. Well, there's plenty of time to decide. I shall talk to her and see what she thinks.'

It was as well, I thought, that Mr Baker was so pleased with Charlotte, because he wasn't likely to be pleased with Harry.

The school was much as it always had been. Edmund and Mr Silcox – I always addressed my former schoolmaster as Mr Silcox, even though he had asked me to call him Arthur – were still sharing their home and though Mr Silcox was now not far short of eighty, he was remarkably brisk. He even took a class now and then, though for the most part, Edmund ran the little school with the help of one woman teacher, Miss Pearce. Miss Pearce was a spinster of about my age, a vicar's daughter, as Harriet had been.

She taught the youngest children of both sexes, instructing them in reading, writing and simple arithmetic, and took the older girls for needlework, for more advanced reading, handwriting and arithmetic.

When I met her, I thought she had a kind, tired face; as though she had known much disappointment but had managed not to become bitter. She had probably longed for marriage and her own children, and failed to achieve them. She was not ugly, but nor was she good-looking, which was probably the reason. Some men, I said to myself, could be singularly dim-witted. Instead of the pleasant, housewifely life for which I thought nature had intended her, she was going to be saddled with Harry next May. As a beginner, he would be in her class.

She and Edmund Baker eventually tamed Harry, though not without a tussle. We had news of the process from Mr

Silcox and Edmund when they visited us. Mr Silcox said that although he had always been opposed to caning the pupils, Harry had at first been so ill-behaved that he had given Edmund permission to do so if it really seemed necessary.

'And it has been, three or four times,' said Edmund Baker grimly.

Remembering the horrible Waters household, I felt troubled, but Edmund had nothing brutal in his nature and Harry didn't seem any the worse. Gradually, indeed, he began to improve. Edmund Baker's methods seemed to be doing more good than harm.

Edmund had not married but seemed happy about it. He was middle-aged himself by now and his long proximity to Mr Silcox had made him begin to look vaguely similar. Mr Silcox remarked on it himself, and told me that there was even speculation in the village that Edmund was his son. 'It amuses us,' he said. 'There's a nice tolerant streak in the people of the moor.'

I had noticed that myself. I had feared at first that I would be cold-shouldered. Everyone for miles must know why I had parted from James. But the years seemed to have eroded any bad feeling, even at Marsh, for William had kept them well informed and they knew I had come home to nurse James. Besides, it was likely that everyone for miles, including the inhabitants of Exford and Porlock, knew perfectly well that part of the quarrel between me and James was the fact that I had gone out at night to warn smugglers of a Revenue trap. At that time, at least half the population had been ready customers for cheap brandy and tobacco. No one had fallen out with James, but I had the impression that under the surface, there had been sympathy for me. The existence of Charlotte no doubt caused some tut-tutting, but even James' brother at Marsh Farm offered me no rudeness.

Free trading had more or less stopped, I learned. Ralph Duggan had withdrawn from it again, saying that it was no longer profitable. The Hathertons had persisted, and after only one year, they were caught. Both Luke and Roger had been sent as convicts to Australia. I was so very thankful that Ralph had backed out in time.

But I never saw Ralph, or tried to, and I rarely heard news

of him. Nor did I hear much news of Rose. She and her husband had cut themselves off from me. William saw them now and then, and two years after I had rejoined the Foxwell household, William returned from a visit to his sister in a state of high irritation and expressed himself forcefully.

'Henry Hannaford,' William said, 'is a pompous fool and a po-faced killjoy. Likes to stand in front of the fire on a cold day with un's feet apart, keeping all the warmth for hisself, while he lays down the law about everything under the sun to anyone else who chances to be in the room. Takes a grave view, he does, of these modern novels that are becoming so popular. Frivolous, he calls them, and morally unhealthy. He's ordered Rose not to read them. And he's so particular about observing Sundays. Their little daughters – Mary's just four and Ellie only two – they're not allowed to play with their toys on a Sunday! What do you think of that?'

'What does Rose think of it?' I asked.

'Rose does as she's told, not that she seems to mind!' said William with an outraged snort. I felt sorry for the daughters.

Since James was gone, there was no difficulty about receiving Charlotte's allowance from Ralph or the rent from Standing Stone. I wrote once more to Ralph, asking if he wished to continue the existing arrangements, or wanted to end them, since I was well provided for. A brief reply came which said that no, he didn't; I should have money for Charlotte until she was married, while Standing Stone was lawfully mine and so was its rent.

I told William about it all and he merely said: 'So you own Standing Stone! Well, splendid. Ralph Duggan is a good fellow, whatever the Revenue may think. But if Standing Stone belongs to you, shouldn't we start keeping an eye on it? We have a responsibility there now.'

In due course, therefore, I informed its tenants that I was now their landlord, and I went with William to inspect the place from time to time to make sure it was being farmed as it should. It was interesting, for I had scarcely ever been on its land before. On my first visit, I made a point of climbing the heathery moorland slope to look closely at the stone that gave the farm its name.

It was a strange thing, grey granite, about eight feet high, slanting a little, with moss on its east side, where it was sheltered from the prevailing west wind. It had an air of mystery about it, for no one knew who had put it there or why, though it was said to have been there for thousands of years. I liked it. I am glad that from the eastern windows of the farmhouse, it is easy to see. I can't climb the heathery moorland slope these days.

Back then, neither William nor I felt that the tenants, a couple called Darracott, were running the farm as well as they should. We found ourselves having to chivvy them sometimes. Their foreman, Dickie Webster, did his best to keep things running smoothly, but complained that Mr Darracott rarely listened to him and was forever countermanding Dickie's orders. 'I'm allus glad to see 'ee here,' he said to us. 'Sometimes, he does listen to *you*.'

In the course of those first two years, I had twice seen my younger son John, who would arrive without warning, whenever he could, though it didn't happen often. He was an able seaman on a ship called the *Eleanor Browne* – named after the owner's wife, apparently – and was for ever on the move, mostly round the coasts of Britain but sometimes sailing to foreign parts, going wherever a cargo was to be delivered. She would carry pine logs on one trip, ironware and coal on another, bales of cloth and raw wool on another, kegs of (legally imported) brandy and wine on the next. Her calls to her home port of Minehead were erratic.

John's visits were always immensely welcome. If he had ever had any hard feelings about me, they were gone now. He was independent, out in a world where people did far worse things than I had ever done. On his first visit home after my return, he had said to me, almost casually: 'I'm glad to see you back here, Ma,' and then never referred to my past again.

He was a good raconteur, was my John, and every time he appeared, he had tales to tell us. One of the things that amused him in his seagoing life was the contrast, he said, between his captain, Captain Summers, and his brother-in-law Captain Grover of the *Pretty Fairing*, whose home port, like that of the *Eleanor Browne*, was Minehead.

'They're better friends than most real brothers,' John said, 'but not a bit alike! Their wives are twin sisters but the husbands couldn't be less like twins if they'd planned it deliberately. Captain Summers is a burly, businesslike man, all for his work. I've never been in his cabin but I've passed it when the door is open and inside everything is plain as plain can be – narrow bed, table with charts and maps all over it, nothing ornamental. But Captain Grover, he's tall and . . . elegant, that's the only word for it.

'The men marvel at it, you know, and sometimes talk about what fine furnishings Captain Grover has in his cabin, and once when the *Eleanor* and the *Fairing* chanced to be in port together, I was sent over to the *Fairing* with a message and I saw Captain Grover and got a glimpse through *his* cabin door and all the tales I'd heard were true. Captain Grover's almost a dandy and he loves ornaments and novelties. His cabin has lots of pictures and a fine rug on the floor and ornaments on a shelf, stuck to it, I believe, so that they won't come loose in a storm. Those two men are so different they might have come from different nations and yet they're really attached to each other and when Captain Grover was ill, once, and Captain Summers heard of it, he was cast down for days until better news came when we got into the next port and there was a letter for him. Aren't people strange?'

That was John, and when in the January of 1830, after a stormy New Year's Day, a spell of calm though frosty winter weather set in and John walked into the farmyard, carrying his usual pack, and calling out: 'Anyone at home?' Susie and I, who had been chopping vegetables and beating eggs in the kitchen, both rushed eagerly out to greet him.

'John!' I cried. 'Are you ashore for long?'

'I can stop for a week. The *Eleanor* needs a few repairs. Had an argument with floating wreckage from another ship, after that awful weather at New Year. She's in Minehead harbour now, in the care of the Duggan shipyard. Lord, what a voyage we've had! Just as we were beating up past Cornwall, before the weather turned stormy, we nearly fell victim to wreckers . . .'

'*Wreckers!*'

'Aye,' said John, and his young face suddenly became grim. Susie said: 'This is going to be quite a tale, for sure. Let's get inside. Will 'ee take tea or cider or brandy, John?'

'I wouldn't say no to brandy,' John said as he picked up his pack and accompanied us into the kitchen. 'It *is* quite a tale and a miserable one. The *Pretty Fairing* – you've heard me speak of her – she's been lost with all hands and it wasn't the weather. Captain Grover's dead. There's been a deal of grief aboard the *Eleanor*, I can tell you.'

We settled him in the old comfortable basket chair, Susie brought out the brandy, and then we sat down too and waited. John took a couple of comforting gulps of his drink and said: 'We've had wild weather to deal with since then, but thinking about it just brings it back. Awful, it were!' He stared into space, as if seeing a vision invisible to us.

Then he said: 'Four months ago or so, the *Eleanor* and the *Fairing* were in the same port together – Marseilles it was. The *Eleanor* had picked up cargo there and we were bound for the Indies with it. Just before we were due to leave, Captain Grover had news from his wife that she had had their first baby, a son. So there was a party on the *Fairing* and all the *Eleanor*'s crew were invited. We all bought gifts; Captain Summers was ashore half a day, looking for just the right thing. When we went aboard the *Fairing* for the party, all the presents were set out on display.

'There was things for Mrs Grover and for the baby, and things for Captain Grover, too. I remember there was a pair of silver candlesticks for Mrs Grover, and about six rattles for the baby, and Captain Summers' gift was a big brass ornament, like an engraved plate, for Captain Grover's cabin aboard ship. It showed a lad in sort of rustic clothes handing a bunch of ribbons or something like that anyway, to a lass, and across the foot of the plate were the words *The Pretty Fairing*. Captain Summers had it engraved specially, found someone who'd do it while he waited.

'And somebody else, I don't know who, gave Captain Grover another gift for his cabin – the oddest thing, but Captain Grover was very pleased with it. A set of lanterns, it were. All with bronze frames. They were just simple candle lanterns but they all had coloured glass – red, green, blue, yellow. Well, they'd make a lit cabin pretty, Captain Summers said, and I think he thought they were a bit of nonsense, but Captain Grover was mighty pleased with them. I hope he enjoyed them, for the little while he had them . . . Oh, my God!'

He gulped brandy. 'I can't stop remembering. It was all so happy and Captain Grover was so full of how glad he'd be to see his wife and his new baby . . .'

'Go on,' I said, realizing that although reliving the memory was painful to him, he needed to do it.

'When we got back from the Indies, we fell into each other's company again, not entirely by chance, I think. I believe the two captains had made a rendezvous and hoped to keep it, wind and weather permitting! Well, it did and we set off to sail home together. We was off the Cornish coast. It was night, the *Fairing* was just ahead of us, and we were tacking in towards the land. We were taking care; that stretch of coast is all rocks, much like here and it was a dark night – overcast – but we could see another ship further away, ahead of us both, still making in towards the land so we knew we were all right, or we thought we were, but then the clouds parted and out came a full moon and oh, my God . . .!'

He had gone white. 'I hope never to see or hear anything like that again. The lights of the third ship, so far ahead, they weren't a ship's lights at all, they were lanterns. We could see that they were being carried by men on the shore. They were moving . . . pretending to be a ship's lights, drawing the *Pretty Fairing* after them, and us as well and at that moment, the *Pretty Fairing* hit the rocks. There was nothing we could do! She was – what? – a hundred yards ahead, no more, but we couldn't get to her. We lowered two launches – I was in one of them – but it was no good, there were rocks all around; the launch I was in was holed and sank. There were four of us in it and somehow the men in the other one kept clear of danger and hauled us out of the sea. We lived by a miracle! We couldn't help the *Pretty Fairing;* she was jammed tight, cocked up, one end standing into the sky and the other under the water, and the tide was rising round her, crashing over her, great white breakers with teeth . . . we could see her crew trying to escape, climbing the masts, only then there were the men on the land, running to the sea, and not so as to rescue anyone!'

'You mean . . .?' Susie had gone white too, as understanding came.

'Yes, I do mean!' John was full of rage. 'Those crewmen on the *Fairing*, that didn't drown, they were clubbed to death, we were near enough that in between them crashing waves, we could hear screams! We could hear them dying! As for the cargo – we saw boxes and kegs being snatched, or floating away and those devils hauling them back; they had nets to throw over them. There was cold-blooded murder done that night and we'd have been murdered too if we'd got any closer. Then the moon went in again . . . seemed like it had come out just to show us what we'd missed . . . it was no use, in the end, we just rowed back to the *Eleanor* quick as we could . . .'

He nearly broke down then but after a sob or two he commanded himself and said. 'We could only get away. Next day, Captain Summers took a couple of us and we put into the next port and reported what we'd seen and I dare say someone will try to do something but what? We couldn't describe what any of that gang of . . . what any of the gang looked like, we were too far away for *that*, and we didn't know exactly where we were at the time, anyhow.'

'There's never been anything of that kind along our coast,' Susie said thankfully, replenishing his glass. 'What wickedness! What awful wickedness!'

'What happened next?' I asked.

'We sailed off again and that's when the storm came up! We just about made it into Minehead. The sea was getting into the hold and there were bales of flour and sugar kegs there that got ruined. Captain Summers is heartbroken, and he's had to inform Mrs Grover that she's a widow and her son is fatherless, and on top of that, Captain Summers lost so much cargo that there'll be no profit on this trip. Some men,' said John, 'long to be ship's masters but I'm damned if I do. Too much responsibility. Mr Duggan's seeing to the *Eleanor*'s repairs and he's making two new launches. We lost them both. One was the one I was in, that sank, and the storm got the other one – just wrenched it loose and flung it overboard.'

'When did you reach Minehead?' Susie asked.

'Oh, two weeks ago. There were things to do aboard ship, the smaller repairs and such, and there was a funeral I wanted to attend.'

'A funeral?' I said.

Old Memories

John drained his glass and set it down on the mantelpiece. I watched him thoughtfully. My younger son looked very like James, just as William did, but – also like William – he did not think like James. Life at sea, with the constant travelling and contact with other places and people, had probably given him plenty to think about, too.

The easy way he had accepted my reappearance was proof of that and so was his attitude to Rose and Henry Hannaford. When he heard how they had cut themselves off from me, he shrugged and said: 'Rose always was a prig and that man Hannaford is worse. We can do without them,' and left it there.

But now, he was eyeing me as though something about me worried him.

'What is it, John?' I asked him.

'I went to the Duggan boatyard with a message. There was something Captain Summers had forgotten to say when he gave the order for the new launches . . .'

'Oh, *John!*' Susie was reproachful. 'It would have bin best if 'ee hadn't gone there, now wouldn't it?'

'Susie, sweetheart, I'm an able seaman. If my captain says take this here note to Duggans Boatyard, I can't say to him, sorry, I can't do that, due to some old mix-up with the Duggans and my family. I say *Aye aye, sir*, and do as I'm bid. Anyhow, I went there and I found Mr Ralph Duggan in a great state of upset, worse than Captain Summers, even. Mrs Duggan was taken bad at New Year – got caught outside in the storm that nearly did for us. She came home drenched and was in a high fever next day and dead two days after that.'

'*Harriet!*' I said, distressed. Harriet was the only Mrs Duggan at the boatyard. Bronwen had died two years before. The Darracotts had told me that.

'Yes. When I went to the boatyard, Mr Duggan was getting ready for the funeral next morning. Poor man. He kept saying . . . Oh, look, Ma, I know, we all know, that he once meant a whole lot to you . . .'

'We were young then. We've long since got over all that and got settled in our lives,' I said. 'What did Mr Duggan say?'

'That his wife was the best of women and it was cruel of God to take her the way he had and he couldn't bear it. His son Charlie and the three daughters, they were there and in a state as well. It was a house of mourning if ever I saw one. I asked permission to attend the funeral, as a mark of respect. I've met Mrs Duggan though I never thought I ought to talk of her to you, Ma. I liked her.'

'Everyone liked her,' I said steadily. 'Harriet was a good woman. So you went to her funeral? Ral . . . Mr Duggan let you?'

'He said, the more folk were there, the better, that it would comfort them all to see a lot of people come to say goodbye to her. So I went. Mr Silcox and Edmund Baker were there too.' He paused and then said: 'But that's not all.'

'What else is there?' I asked. Susie, who had started to make tea, also heard the curious note in his voice, and looked round in concern.

'Mrs Duggan was buried in St Michael's churchyard,' said John. 'But when we were all standing round afterwards, the way people do, I heard some talk. I heard a name. Reckon you'll know it. Laurence Wheelwright.'

'Wheelwright!'

'Aye, that's him. Him that's said to have murdered a girl years ago, though Mr Ralph Duggan's younger brother was accused of it, first. This Wheelwright fellow left Somerset and no one knows where he went but he came back flush with money, and a big sum was paid to the girl's parents all of a sudden and now everyone thinks that he was the one as murdered her, but the money's kind of bought him out of it. No one's after him any more and the Duggan chap is settled overseas, seemingly. This Wheelwright has a ship's chandlers in Minehead and he's got a sailing boat – the

Summer Dawn, she's called, smart little thing, apparently, red sails and a little cabin and all, and he goes out fishing in her now and again. Well, folk were standing about and gossiping about him and sayin' – Charlie Duggan was sayin' – that it was on this Laurence Wheelwright's account that his mother died. You see, the free tradin's started up again. This Wheelwright fellow began it – found he'd got likely customers among them as used his shop and he soon found others who were willing to join him, and after a bit, Ralph Duggan did too. Charlie Duggan was saying that he couldn't think how his father could work with Wheelwright after that murder business, but Mr Duggan said the past was all over and Philip was happy in Antigua . . .'

Involuntarily, I said: 'Oh, Ralph, Ralph!'

'Anyhow,' said John, taking no notice, 'seems Mrs Duggan had heard somehow that the Revenue knew there was to be a landing, and where. Someone laughed when Charlie told us that, and said Mrs Duggan used to take tea with women friends and one of them was a Revenue man's wife and women's tongues wag, don't they, and never tell a secret to a woman! Anyhow, Mrs Duggan had heard something that scared her and out she rushed to catch her husband before he could get into his boat, to warn him that he mustn't sail that night. Charlie wasn't home that evening, or he'd have gone.'

'Did she catch him?' Susie asked.

'Yes,' said John. 'She did, and he didn't sail. He probably couldn't have, anyway, because of the weather. But the storm blew up all of a sudden as Mrs Duggan was going home and, well, she died. This Wheelwright wasn't at the funeral, it seems. I heard something about that, too; someone said he probably felt he'd best not show his face. I was all ears, I can tell you.'

'You must have been sprouting them,' I said, as lightly as I could. 'From head to ankles!'

'Mr Silcox and Mr Baker weren't in the group that was talking about Wheelwright and free trading,' John said. 'They was talking to Mr Ralph Duggan and the vicar, in the church porch. Charlie and his friends that were gossiping about

Wheelwright stopped when they saw the vicar bringing them over. But like I said, what Charlie Duggan said, was that his ma caught her death warning her husband not to go out smuggling that night.'

'Do you think this Laurence Wheelwright really did kill a girl once?' Susie asked. 'I've heard the story. Her name was Maisie Cutler, wasn't it? But why would he do such a thing?'

'Oldest reason in the world. She preferred another man – the younger Duggan boy, probably. I reckon Wheelwright did it, yes,' John said.

'Yes, he did,' I said. 'I've known for years. Let's get settled in the parlour with tea and scones and I'll tell you this tale, too.'

So Susie and I got the tea and scones together, and once we were seated and private in the parlour, for the first time ever, I told the tale that Daniel Hopton had told me, as we sat in the gig out in the Bristol Channel, waiting in the moonlight for the *Moonlight* to arrive. Susie and John listened with much astonishment.

'It was because of that night,' I said, 'that James sent me away. He was angry that I should want to warn a free trader and he suspected that something happened between me and Ralph Duggan that night. Which it did. As you both know already. I did wrong, and yet at the time it seemed to be right. I am not able to regret it.'

'It doesn't worry me,' said John. 'The past is the past. Maybe Mr Duggan had the right of it there.'

'It worries me!' said Susie. 'I can't put a young girl's murder in the past, just like that. I'm thankful it wasn't me, having to decide, should I break the law to save my husband! I wouldn't know what to do.'

'I find it confusing, too,' I said. 'Very. But we can't undo what's over and done with. Only I feel very sorry about Harriet. I'm glad you were at her funeral, John. Poor Harriet. Poor Ralph.'

But while I was saying, *Poor Harriet; poor Ralph*, another voice, a treacherous voice, of which I was ashamed, was speaking inside me. Old memories were awake.

Ralph, you are a complete fool, said the voice. *Getting entangled in the free trading again! You idiot!*

And . . .

Ralph Duggan is a free man now, it said.

Midsummer

The year went on, bringing springtime and sunshine, and a plenitude of work. Harry was now much more manageable but as if to make up for this, little Michael, small as he was, was developing a streak of inquisitiveness that meant he had to be constantly watched if he were not to fall into the well or get into the stables and irritate a horse into kicking him, or eat poisonous berries or overturn saucepans in the kitchen. Then, in the spring, Susie announced that she was expecting again, and her pregnancy was very obviously a strain for her. Most of the childcare seemed to devolve on me.

As June approached, with its shearing and haymaking, I found that for the first time ever, I couldn't enjoy them. I was fifty now, would soon be fifty-one and my body had just passed its great change. Now that it was over I was not as vigorous as I used to be. Now, I could only think of the extra cooking to be done, day after day until both shearing and haymaking were over, as well as making sure that the children were kept well away from the shearing and watched over during the hay harvest. Neither Harry nor Michael would be safe anywhere near a pitchfork.

The weather that year was uncertain and was complicated by the Darracotts at Standing Stone, who, having arranged to cut their hay on a certain Tuesday, asking Marsh and Foxwell for assistance, changed their minds at the last moment. It wasn't the first time. They had done exactly the same thing at the same time the year before. Just as we were all honing our scythes in readiness for them, they decided at five minutes' notice to sell off a couple of cows they thought weren't giving as much milk as they should, and buying some others, and they wanted to attend to that first.

This time, they didn't even offer the excuse of being too busy with their cows, but simply sent word that they'd put their haymaking off for a week. It threw us all into confusion though it did work out well in the end – for us, that is. We got our hay in at once with help from Marsh and another farm, and had a patch of good weather in which to do it, while the vacillating Darracotts were not so lucky. They cut their hay the following week and then had it soaked in a downpour when it was supposed to be drying in the field. The Darracotts were the losers, not us. But it was aggravating at the time.

When it was all over, I felt as exhausted as though I had personally sheared and scythed and thatched the haystacks. The sheep, looking oddly small now that their woolly coats were gone, were back on the moor. The first evening after it was all finished felt like a magical pool of calm. I could sit in the parlour and take the weight off my feet, not that they had any excessive weight to carry. My busy life had kept me from growing fat. I could still get into dresses I had worn years before.

But I wondered, as I sank down into an armchair and hoped that Jenny wouldn't take too long to bring me the tea I had asked her for, how much longer I would be able to go on working as I had. I had got through this year's June, but at the thought of next year's, I found myself wilting.

The tea came and I poured myself a cup, wishing that now I could have a less physical life, could sit back and do something that would occupy my brain. My modest bookshelf was handy, next to the fireplace, but everything on it I had read a dozen times. I ought to buy something new, I decided. Why not buy a set of Shakespeare? I could read *Antony and Cleopatra* again! I hadn't read the play since my schooldays. It would be interesting, something to do.

The parlour windows didn't overlook the farmyard and since we so rarely used the front door, nearly everyone who called on us came in through the yard gate. So when a visitor arrived, I knew nothing of it until Jenny came to the parlour door again and declared in her broad Somerset voice that someone had called to see me.

And then Ralph Duggan walked in.

There was a moment when everything seemed to stop: heartbeat, breathing, time itself. Then I said: 'Thank you, Jenny.

Will you bring some fresh tea? And I think in the larder there are some of the cakes that Annie made yesterday. Bring those as well.'

Jenny disappeared and Ralph just stood there, looking at me. It was as though he didn't know what to say. I didn't, either. I just gazed back at him, thinking that he was older, thinner than I remembered, and noticing with sadness that there was grey now in his black hair.

Finally, abruptly, he said: 'I meant to wait a year. To do the proper thing. And I do still mourn for Harriet. I expect part of me always will because no man could have had a better wife. But Harriet isn't there any more and . . . I had to come. There are things to talk about.'

'You're welcome,' I said. 'Sit down and be comfortable. Did you ride from Minehead or take your boat round to Porlock?'

'I rode. Ned Webster is taking care of my horse. I caught sight of Charlotte as I dismounted – mucking out a stall. She didn't see me and I didn't call to her. I know I have no rights in the matter, but' – he took a chair as invited but didn't relax in it – 'though I realize I shouldn't just walk in here and start talking like this, Charlotte is partly why I'm here. I've been worrying about her. I couldn't . . . attend to her very well while Harriet was alive but it's different now, and as I rode in, I saw how remiss I'd been. I should have done more than just send you money for her. It gave me a shock, seeing my daughter all grubby, wearing boots with mud and worse on them and bits of straw on her dress. I don't want to offend you. It's not your fault; just circumstances. Are you offended?'

'No. I feel the same. So do Mr Silcox and Edmund Baker. She goes to school in Exford. They have suggested that she should take up teaching, and begin by being a pupil-teacher for them when she's old enough. I'm considering it. Charlotte isn't far off fourteen. It's been on my mind.'

I had in fact been trying to make plans, albeit vague ones, to see that when she was older, Charlotte should meet the kind of people who might provide a suitable husband, by which I meant a man who would take her into a gentler world than that of Foxwell, and would look after her, so that she could have her own children and not have to make do with other people's. Life as a teacher could be bleak in some ways, unless one had a true vocation for it. I didn't want Charlotte to enter it unless she had such a vocation, any more than I wanted her to be a farmer's wife when she disliked farm life. I wanted her to marry well.

Jenny arrived with the cakes and the fresh tea and while we ate and drank, I shared my ideas with Ralph, who sat nodding. 'I shall give this a lot of consideration,' he said. 'Leave it to me for a while. I know a good many people. She's young yet.' Then, as I poured his second cup of tea for him, he said: 'There's something else, though I didn't know it when I started out from Minehead but on the way here . . .'

He stopped and we looked at each other, and then, suddenly, we were laughing.

'We're still ourselves,' Ralph said. 'For a moment, I felt as though I'd called on a stranger. I thought you'd changed. But you haven't, not really. Have you?'

'No. Not much. I'm older and I know more than I once did,' I said. 'Have you changed, do you think? Was it hard, getting used to life without Harriet?'

'It was dreadful at first,' said Ralph, and I saw that he meant it. 'But one does become accustomed. What was I saying just now? Yes. On the way here, I decided to look in at Standing Stone first, to see how it was doing. Well, now that I'm no longer their landlord, the Darracotts talked to me more freely than they would have done in the past. They're not doing well and they wish they'd never taken on this tenancy. They want to give it up and go back to what they were doing before – keeping a shop in Minehead. What do you feel about that?'

'They've a perfect right to give up their tenancy if they want to,' I said. 'And it's true they're not doing well though some of that's their own fault. I do go over there sometimes and I have had to advise them on occasion, not to say bully them.'

'How do you mean – their own fault?'

'Mr Darracott's forever changing his mind about things – when to start haymaking, for instance. He's done that two years running and created some fine muddles for the neighbourhood. And he fidgets his cows.'

'In what way?'

'Cows like a quiet life,' I said. 'They like to graze with companions they're used to, and they don't like having to absorb strange cows into the herd every five minutes. It upsets them and that affects the milk yield. Darracott keeps on selling off cows he thinks aren't good enough, and bringing in others. So he never gets the milk yield he expects. I've tried to tell him but he doesn't listen. He doesn't like being advised.'

'There are new shops opening in Minehead and Dunster now,' Ralph said. 'Both places are well on the rise. I suggested to Mr Darracott that that this might be his chance.' He grinned. 'There's that ship's chandlers in Minehead that Laurence Wheelwright has. He doesn't have much competition, and Mr Darracott was a seaman during the war with the France. He would take to life running a chandler's, I think. He might set up as a rival.'

'Does Wheelwright still engage in free trading?' I said. I probably sounded distasteful, but free trading had wrecked my marriage and killed Harriet. I had once taken it for granted; now I knew I hated it.

'Yes. We both do, even together sometimes,' said Ralph. 'Never mind about that. The thing is, there are possibilities there for the Darracotts. And that opens up possibilities for you. Do you know how worn out you look? I saw it, the moment I walked into this room. Would you like to escape from here? Because if so, if the Darracotts go, what's to stop you from moving into Standing Stone, taking it over for yourself?'

'To live there alone?' I said. 'To run Standing Stone on my own?'

But the thought of getting away, not from Foxwell exactly, but from the life that had become so disturbed and exhausting was tempting. I had been so happy to come home but now . . . yes, I was tired through and through, not just the tiredness of a busy day but all the time, deep inside, even when I woke in the morning.

Sarah was capable. She could take charge of William's family. Only, did I want to be alone quite that much?

'You wouldn't be alone,' Ralph said, reading my mind. 'You would have Charlotte with you, at least for the time being. There are also two young maidservants at Standing Stone and a big fat cook and several farmhands, including the foreman Dickie Webster and that lively family of his. You would bring your knowledge to the place, but other people would do the work. That applies to Charlotte too. This could be the first move towards improving her prospects. Besides . . . it need not be for too long. It would be good for Standing Stone to have you there for a while, perhaps till the end of the year, straightening it out, but then, well, there are other possibilities.'

Across the decorous display of tea and cakes, our eyes met.

'You have eyes the colour of rich, dark molasses,' Ralph said. 'I remember noticing them, the first time we danced. You know why I really came here today, don't you? Yes, I wanted to see Charlotte, and yes, I must have had Standing Stone in the back of my mind, at least. But the real reason . . . when I have given Harriet her due, by waiting a whole year, will you marry me, Peggy Bright?'

The evening was coming on and when we stepped out of the kitchen door to stroll in the open air, it was growing cooler. Ralph had suggested that I fetch a coat. I had it over one arm while the other was comfortably linked in one of his.

The world was quiet. All our hands had gone home. William would make a last careful round later on, after supper. For now, no one was about. As we walked across the farmyard towards the hay barn, Ralph said: 'When we were young, and you stayed with us in Minehead, I used to long so much to be allowed to make love to you. I knew I never would be, not until we were married. And I had another ambition too, one I knew you wouldn't let me fulfil even after we were married. But now . . . I wonder.'

'Ralph, what in the world are you talking about?'

'I didn't just want to make love to you. I wanted to do so as lads and lasses have been doing since the first hayfield in the world was mowed. I wanted to love you, illicitly, in a hayloft.'

I said: 'I have a coat to keep the hay from prickling, and there's no one watching. Oh, and there is no danger now of any unwanted results.'

'In that case,' said Ralph, 'what are we waiting for, sweeting?'

In those far-off days of our youth, I had sometimes wondered what it would be like when first we came together. Then it had happened, but in such a curious way, in the night, with fear and danger behind us and perhaps ahead, and it was a frenzied business, on cold ground, under the trees of Culbone Wood, encircled by the rustles and mystery of a woodland in the unearthly darkness that precedes the dawn.

This was quite different.

The new hay, mingled as it was with clover, smelt sweet and felt soft. There was a window, for formerly some of our farmhands had slept there and James had made sure that the place was comfortable. Slanting sunshine came in, turning the hay to gold, showing the motes that danced in the air around us. And Ralph, dear Ralph, was with me and I had been waiting for him for so long, and he for me.

If it was nothing like our union in Culbone, it was nothing like any of my unions with James, either. They had never been fully satisfactory. This began slowly, gently, and then burst into an eagerness that was both fierce but also kind, ending in a climax like the sudden rain that bursts forth in a thunderstorm. When we parted, gasping and laughing, we were spent, yet filled with energy; amazed and yet quite certain that this was how it ought to be, and should have been, long since.

We tidied our clothes, shaking the hay out of them, resuming things we had taken off. We combed our hair with our fingers. And then, after peering warily out, just as though we were still two young things who must make sure their parents didn't catch them, we descended the ladder and walked to the house as we had left it, arm in arm.

Annie was in the kitchen, stirring stew. She turned as we came in and although I don't know what she saw, something about us made her eyebrows rise, and caused a smile to hover at the corners of her mouth. She didn't speak, but her face did it for her.

Only . . .

As we sat down in the parlour to talk for a while before I went to the kitchen, there were things to be said. The golden tide in which we had been drowning had receded. 'Before we went out,' said Ralph, 'I asked you to marry me. You didn't answer. Will you give me an answer now?'

'I would have to let Standing Stone again,' I said. 'If I joined you in Minehead.'

'Yes. We shouldn't actually marry until it's a year since Harriet died. You could stay at Standing Stone for a while as I said and get it into order. Then you would live with me in Minehead. I'm not retiring from the boatyard yet.'

'And the free trading?' I asked. 'You would continue with that?'

'I don't do as much as I did before the war,' Ralph said, grinning. 'But it's still profitable, if one goes about it rightly. Not as profitable as it was – but it brings in a fair amount, just the same.'

'It killed Harriet!' I said. 'And one day . . . think what happened to Luke and Roger Hatherton! That could be you! And the worry I would have, just as Harriet had . . . Ralph, I can't marry you while you're still free trading.'

I hadn't known I was going to say that. It came out by itself. I couldn't face it; that anxiety, knowing, every time he went out to sail after contraband, what he was risking. I would be frightened all the time and not just while he was at sea, but also afterwards, when we had contraband in our possession, in the cave or in our own cellars. Always afraid of the hammering on the door, the arrival of the law . . .

'You surely don't mean what you're saying,' Ralph protested. 'Darling, my beloved Peggy, after what we did in the barn just now . . . you can't mean . . . you can't refuse me! We belong to each other, you know we do!'

Yes, we did. But . . .

I tried to tell him. About the fear I would have to live with, about my longing for quiet, for repose now that I was no longer young. He himself had said I was tired – could he not understand that to be married to a free trader would be even more exhausting?

No, he didn't understand. And so, for the second time in our lives, we quarrelled.

We were reasonable, middle-aged people. Well, we had not been either reasonable or middle-aged in the hayloft, but in returning to the parlour we had in some way returned to our everyday selves. Our dispute was therefore not noisy, at least, not at first. It was no less bitter for that.

I tried to explain that I could not bear to live with the fear, every time he went out to fetch contraband, that he would not come back. I tried to explain that Charlotte would have to share that fear, would worry as much as I would.

'To find her father, and then live in dread of losing him!' I said.

'I haven't been caught yet!' said Ralph, as though I had insulted him. 'Wifely fears are natural enough,' he added loftily. 'The wives of honest fisherman feel them too. The sea can be every bit as dangerous as any Revenue vessel. Harriet stood it. Why can't you? Never mind about Charlotte – it's *your* fear we're discussing.'

'Perhaps I'm just not young enough any more.'

'You were no doddering ancient in the barn just now.'

'No, but . . .'

'But?'

I made a serious mistake at this point. I said: 'Free trading – smuggling – is against the law, and people these days are starting to feel differently about it. If you were imprisoned or transported, Charlotte and I might be pointed at. Might be . . .'

'Rubbish! Of course you wouldn't be. You would just be imagining it – because you were ashamed of me? And who has protected you and Charlotte all these years? Because of me, you have been able to keep untouched the money your father left you, a bulwark against an uncertain future, and safely hidden from James – oh yes, I saw the letter your father left you, saw how he warned you about the law. And how did I manage it? Through free-trading. I could never have afforded it, but for that. Have you ever really loved me, Peggy dear, or was I just a passing passion, which accidentally resulted in Charlotte and so bound you to me?'

'Of course I loved you! I always have, I still do – oh, Ralph, can't you see that it's *because* I love you so much that I can't endure the fear, the sleepless nights, awaiting your return, dreading to hear the law pounding our door . . .'

'Harriet endured. She accepted both the proceeds and the fear . . .'

'She *never* asked you to give the smuggling up?'

'Hinted at it once or twice. But nothing more. Harriet was a good, obedient, faithful wife . . .'

There was a faint emphasis on the word faithful. Very faint, but it was there. And that was *his* mistake. 'And I wouldn't be?' I snapped. He stared at me but didn't reply. 'Because I was unfaithful to James?' I demanded. He still didn't speak. 'Well if I was,' I shouted, 'it was with you! You were unfaithful to Harriet then, or have you forgotten? There's a saying that people in glass houses shouldn't throw stones!'

Our voices had risen after all. 'So you're turning me down,' Ralph barked. 'Even after what happened this evening! Because of the trade that's helped you and Charlotte all this time. My God, you hypocrite!'

'I could say the same of you!' I shouted. 'I've been as true to you as I could be. I never forgot that I promised myself to you in the first place – before we were wrenched apart.'

Ralph picked up his hat, which had been lying on a stool. 'Charlotte's allowance will continue,' he said. 'I will not take it out on her. It will go on until she is twenty-one or wedded. And Standing Stone is, of course, legally yours. When I give, I do it with an open hand. I'm off now. I've never in my life been so hurt, so disappointed. I'll find a room for the night at the inn in Exford. Goodbye!'

'*Ralph!*'

It was a cry of despair but he had already gone out of the door. Moments later, Annie came in, saying that Mr Duggan had gone out to the stable; was he just seeing to his horse or was he leaving? She had supposed that he might stay the night.

'No,' I said bleakly. 'He – won't be staying.'

The Summons

I cried myself to sleep that night, grief-stricken. I told myself I was behaving like a lovelorn maiden of sixteen instead of a woman of fifty but I didn't feel like a woman of fifty and certainly hadn't behaved like one during that episode in the hayloft. I felt hot all over when I remembered that. How could I . . . how could I possibly have . . .?

Only I had, and I had loved it and if only Ralph had been willing to give up the free trading, I would have married him without a second thought. When I was younger, I might have borne the worry and strain of life with a husband who could be transported to Van Diemen's Land at any moment. Now I could not. Even Harriet, who *had* been younger, had been worn down by it. Had died in the end because of her fears for her man.

Tossing restlessly, I thought about Charlotte. I would have to tell her something of what had passed. She had still been out somewhere on the farm when Ralph left but she would soon hear most of it. Annie or Sarah would let it out to her. They were both gossips.

She was thirteen now and had become a woman two months ago. She was old enough, I hoped, to understand, at least up to a point. Better that she should hear it from me. That her father had asked me to marry him and I had wanted to say yes, but could not face life as the wife of a free trader. I thought she was capable of understanding that.

Ralph had promised to continue her allowance. Thank God for that. But if I had agreed to marry him, he could have done so much for Charlotte. Oh God, should I have refused him? Why must Ralph be such a fool? If only he had given me one kind word as we parted.

If only . . .

Towards dawn, I slept. In the morning, I got up and got on with things. I did talk to Charlotte and she, sensible child that she was, did seem to understand, though she was clearly unhappy. 'I wish we could have gone to Minehead,' she said sadly. 'It's so disappointing.'

Yes, in a way, I had let her down. I tried to explain what it would be like when there were contraband landings, waiting and worrying, always with the shadow of the transport ships, of being parted for years, perhaps for ever, from a husband, a father. She seemed to understand, yet the disappointment was still there.

The summer passed. I tried not to think about Ralph. I did not hear from him; nor did I hear of any changes at Standing Stone. The days shortened as September advanced. And then . . .

Looking back, I think of it as a summons. I had always believed that the day that I rode on into Culbone Wood, looking for cows that I was sure were not there, I was in fact responding to a mind-to-mind call from Ralph. And I think that my sudden decision, one September day, to go to Minehead to look for Shakespeare's plays was no coincidence, either. The corn harvest had gone well and was in. I had piled as much of the kitchen work as I could on the other women, and felt the better for it. I was taking my ease in the afternoon, sitting in the parlour and getting on with the woollen jersey I was knitting for William. It struck me presently that I would like to put the knitting down and read something, except that I had no new books in the house. I remembered how, earlier in the year, I had planned to buy a set of Shakespeare.

And with that, I rose to my feet at once and went to change into the clothes I used for riding, along with leggings and boots, a coat and a waterproof leather hat. One never knew with Exmoor weather. Then I collected a pair of saddlebags, put in nightwear, a change of clothes and shoes, a warm shawl, washing things and my knitting and, of course, the knife that James had taught me to carry, so long ago. I made sure there was money in my purse and then I was ready.

I went downstairs. Annie was surprised to hear that I suddenly had an errand to Minehead but I cut her short when she tried to ask questions

'I shall stay the night in the Wellington Hotel,' I said. 'I might even be there for two nights. I don't know how long my shopping will take. I'll take Glossy, since no one else is using him just now.' Goldfinch and Copper were dead, but we had bred from Goldfinch and the gelding Glossy was her son. 'Let William know when he comes in from the fields,' I said. Then I set off.

It was a warm day but not hot and without the flies which bedevil the summer. It took me the rest of the afternoon to reach Minehead and it was too late to go looking for a bookshop. I did wonder vaguely why I hadn't at least tried Dunster first but from the start, the word *Minehead* had been imprinted in my mind. I would settle into the Wellington, I said to myself, and go to the shops in the morning.

I dined early, and then, because the evening had turned cool, I sat in a small lounge, where there was a fire. There were others there, three women and two men. They were all quiet-spoken and well dressed but did not look wealthy. They were obviously a family group and seemed to consist of two married couples and someone's sister. They were talking animatedly together and took little notice of me beyond a few polite nods to admit me to the gathering, as it were. There was a free armchair not too far from the fire. I sat down and brought out my knitting.

Listening to their talk, I gathered that the party had come from Lynmouth, the port along the coast thirteen or so miles beyond Porlock. They seemed to be here on business of some kind in Minehead, but proposed to travel on to Taunton to deal with further business the next day, making an outing of it.

The business, in which the two men were evidently partners, apparently concerned household goods such as glassware and saucepans and cutlery which they sold at their shop in Lynmouth. They wanted to expand and were looking at possible shop premises in Minehead and Taunton. I listened with half an ear, while I clicked my needles. A waiter came in to ask if anything was wanted and one of the men asked for a brandy. The other one laughed and said no, he would have a cider, and perhaps the womenfolk would like wine? I shook my head when the waiter glanced at me. The order was taken and the waiter went away.

The man who had chosen cider said that brandy these days came too expensive. 'Pity the free traders are almost a thing of the past,' he observed.

And then, making me suddenly alert, ears no longer casual but on the prick, the other one said: 'They aren't quite. That fellow Ralph Duggan's still bringin' in a drop or two, so I've heard. Based in Minehead, b'ain't he? Still runnin' his old *Moonlight*. Might be an idea to call on him while we're here.'

One of the women said: 'Bert, I don't like that kind of talk, you know I don't. Don't matter to me what the free traders get up to but I don't want us gettin' mixed up in things like that there.'

'Oh, come on, Bet; half the countryside still buys the odd bit of contraband. It b'ain't the customers as run the risks.'

Bet frowned, which didn't at all suit her broad, good-humoured face and with air of detaching herself from the conversation, she rose to her feet as the waiter came in, to help distribute the drinks. Bert, however, was continuing to talk. 'Well, I wouldn't mind a chance of some good brandy at easy prices. Who would? And if Ralph Duggan's the man to talk to, well, why not?'

Unexpectedly, the waiter broke in. 'Beggin' your pardon, sir, I wouldn't talk like that, not just now, or here.'

'What d'you mean?' Bert's business partner was annoyed. 'This here's just private chat in a private room.' He clearly didn't count me as mattering.

'Chances are, the cargo the Duggans are bringing in tonight'll be their last. There's talk in the taproom that the Revenue are on to 'em. Seemingly, there's someone in the crew that the Duggans shouldn't have trusted. There's to be a landing somewhere and the Customs men know of it. I'd keep well clear of the Duggans if I were you.'

He went away again. I realized that I had stopped clicking my needles, and I hastily resumed. My companions were now talking about family matters. I remained quietly knitting until I felt that I had waited long enough to allay any suspicion. Then I put my knitting into its bag, said goodnight, received

civil if absent-minded goodnights in reply − I think they had
forgotten that I was there at all − and went upstairs.

I changed back into the stout dress and boots and leggings I
had worn for the ride, and put on my countrywoman's hat,
the sturdy leather-lined affair I used when riding or working
out of doors. I put on my warm shawl and pushed my purse
into a pocket on my dress with a few other oddments, including
my knife. Then I slipped down a back staircase, fortunately
managing not to meet anyone on the way, went quietly out
of a back door and out into the night.

I made haste, on foot, along the cobbled main street to the
shore. The street was empty, which was a relief, because a
woman on her own, after dark, was always something to stare
at. A dog cart passed me, going away from the sea, the horse's
hooves ringing on the cobbles. When I reached the shore I
turned quickly left and hurried on towards the harbour. The
night was clear and the moon, nearing the full, was rising; I
could see my way well enough. To my right, the sea murmured
with a low voice. I hastened on, cursing inwardly because it
seemed a long way along the track above the beach, until I
reached the harbour wall.

The harbour was, and is, fair-sized, and the wall curves out
into the sea like a crooked forefinger. It breaks the force of
the sea and keeps the harbour sheltered. I paused to examine the
scene and then, feeling my heart and stomach, both together,
plunge down into my boots, I saw what I had dreaded.

Ralph was on his way. There was the *Moonlight*, under sail,
making use of the light wind to manoeuvre herself away from
the quay. I was just too late. Tears rose up in me. It had all
been no use; my swift response to that strange imperative; my
sharp ears and careful reactions in the hotel lounge, my hurried
dressing, my rapid walk.

Or was I too late? With a surge of hope, I saw that I was
standing above one of the steep stone stairways down inside
the wall, giving access to the water and the boats. Just below
me, quiet on the peaceful water of the harbour, some small
boats were moored. Because the wind was so slight, the *Moonlight*
was moving very slowly. I might just do it.

I started down the steps.

It was dangerous. The moonlight might be bright but it was also misleading. The steps were rough, narrow and slippery and although there was a rail of sorts along the wall side, it was a shaky affair and as slippery as the steps and on the other side there was nothing but a sheer drop. I clutched at the rail, groped carefully for a sound foothold at every step, and muttered things under my breath that no lady should ever mutter. I must get there, I must reach the *Moonlight*. I must, must, get to Ralph!

I was down and scrambling into a boat. I found her mooring rope and discovered that it was attached to her by a seaman's knot. I couldn't get it undone. I was crying with frustration when I remembered my knife. Once more, James' precaution against the unexpected proved itself. *Thank you, James.* Seamen hate cutting ropes. I had once heard Josiah Duggan say to Ralph: 'You never know when you might need a good length of rope, to repair damaged rigging with, or to haul a man to safety if he falls overboard. *Never* cut a rope unless you have to.'

I did have to. I attacked the rope without a second thought, sawing frantically at it, for it was stout. I pulled in some buffers of thicker rope that were hanging over the sides, in case the boat should bump against one of its neighbours. They were heavy and I was gasping as I struggled with them. Then I sat down and seized the oars, thankful that I had learned to row during my long-ago stay with the Duggans, praying that I could still do it and determined to do it even if I *had* forgotten how. I would just have to make myself remember.

I did remember. I rowed, splashing deliberately, to attract attention, and calling out between splashes. '*Moonlight* ahoy! *Moonlight* ahoy! *Ralph! Ralph! Moonlight ahoy!*'

I was catching up. The *Moonlight* was tacking and it was taking time. I hailed her again and again and then at last came an answering hail and a glimpse of pale, moonlit faces looking towards me. '*Ralph Duggan! Ralph Duggan!*' I bawled.

I was alongside. The *Moonlight* was hardly moving now. The sails had been adjusted. Something – a rope ladder – was flung over her side. I stood up, wobbled, nearly fell in but managed to grab the ladder instead and begin to clamber up, and then someone with strong hands was helping me aboard, and there were orders being shouted about lowering gear to bring up the boat I'd used, and then I was on the deck, damp from spray, shivering with cold and with my arms aching from the unaccustomed rowing but otherwise none the worse.

Things were being done to the sails again and the ship was under way once more. And there was Ralph, a lantern held high in his hand, looking to see who had come aboard and open-mouthed with astonishment when he recognized me.

'*Peggy!*'

'I came to warn you! Once again! Don't land any contraband tonight! The Customs men are on to you! I overheard talk in the Wellington Hotel; you'll sail right into their hands if you try to pick that cargo up . . . you've got someone untrustworthy in your crew and he's reported your plans and . . .!'

'Peggy!' His voice was that of the old Ralph, the one before that dreadful quarrel. It was as though it had never happened. He was laughing. *Laughing?* I had come to save him, but after the things we had said to each other at our last meeting, I was chilly inside, fearing that he would reject me. But no. It wasn't like that. His laughter had relief in it; he was glad that whatever we had said in the past, I was still concerned for him. So was I.

'My dear, dear Peggy, good soul that you are! Well, how were you to know? I'm in no danger from the Revenue. I was the one who had that rumour put about – at least, Daniel Hopton did it for me. I told him to find a public house where he might be overheard by the wrong people, get drunk and let things out.'

'Aye, and so I did.' A face, vaguely familiar though older than when I last saw it, but adorned with well-remembered large ears, appeared behind Ralph's shoulder. 'Best task I ever was given. Enjoyed that, I did.'

'Good evening, Mr Hopton,' I said faintly.

'He was to hint about a landing at the cave,' said Ralph. 'The old cave that had the path opened up by the landslide. Where you once came to find me. The Revenue'll be hovering round there tonight. While the *Moonlight* is somewhere else and I'm attending to something quite different. I don't want the law interfering so I've made sure it won't, only this time, I'm doing the law's own work for it.'

'But – what do you mean? What I heard . . .'

'Was the echo of Mr Hopton's efforts. Oh, hell!' The ship had cleared the harbour now and her sails were filling. 'I ought to put you back ashore but I don't want to waste time. Getting in or out of the harbour takes so long. You'll have to stay aboard. You can go below when . . . well, when things come to a head.'

'Come to a . . .? Ralph, what do you mean?'

'You'll see.' He studied me in the lantern light. His face was grave now, the laughter gone. He said: 'In a way it's right that you're here. You and I were both victims.' He put out a hand and touched one of mine. 'When we last met, we argued,' he said. 'I am sorry. As I said, we have both been victims. We ought to feel for each other.'

'Yes, I know. But, Ralph what do you mean about . . .?'

'Whose boat did you steal?' said Ralph interrupting. Then he called to someone behind me: 'What name's on that boat?'

'*Cockleshell!*' someone replied.

Ralph grinned. 'Poor Mr Hayward's going to be annoyed tomorrow. Never mind. He'll get her back and I'll make it up to him somehow.' He turned back to me. 'Come below, Peggy. I've some good wine in the cabin; reckon you'll be glad of it. It's a chilly night and always colder on the sea. You'll soon see what all this is about. Come.'

The Overdue Reckoning

A second lantern appeared behind Ralph. 'Let me lead the way,' said a familiar voice.

'John?' I said, startled.

'Yes, he's here,' Ralph said. 'Lead on, my lad.' As we moved towards a companionway, he added: 'It was John who began all this. He has to be here. Mind your footing.'

Down below, things were dark and cramped and smelt fetid. However, in the small cabin to which John led us there was a kind of comfort, as there were lanterns, a table and chairs and a bench along one wall. From a cupboard, John and Ralph produced glasses and a bottle of wine. I sat on the bench and sipped and felt much warmer than when I was on deck. But still bewildered.

'Just what is going on?' I asked.

'It will all become clear, once we're well out to sea,' John said. 'We don't want to talk about it till then in case the wrong person happens to overhear something.'

Ralph said, in a low voice: 'Take it that we're planning a very nasty surprise for someone.'

John said: 'Ma, you look tired. Mr Duggan, can she lie down in your cabin for a while? It'll be an hour or more before we're far enough out.'

Ralph agreed, and showed me the way. I sank down thankfully on his bed. 'I had no idea that John's ship was in port,' I said.

'She's been across the Atlantic and back, this time,' Ralph said. 'There are always repairs after a voyage like that. That's how all this came about. John had an errand into Minehead and . . . you'll hear, later. Try to sleep. I'll leave a lantern.'

I was indeed tired but I didn't expect to sleep. I did, though. Only seconds seemed to pass between seeing Ralph leave the cabin and the moment when I heard John urging me to wake up. I got up, still bemused with sleep, but shook myself

awake and followed my son up on deck, to learn the meaning
of the mystery.

The ship had heaved to, and was rocking gently on an easy
sea. On deck, extra lanterns had been hung up to make a pool
of light. In the middle of this was a table on which stood a
large wooden box with a lid. All the men seemed to be gathered round. There were seven altogether. As well as Ralph and
John, Daniel Hopton was there, and a youngish man whom I
realized, because of their resemblance, was probably Ralph's
son Charlie, and two that I didn't know at all and one more
whose face did seem dimly familiar, though I couldn't place it.

There was an atmosphere: tense, grim. I found that I was
nervous, though I did not know why. John guided me to a
place between him and Ralph and then Ralph said: 'This is a
solemn business and as we have no padre aboard, I'll have to
take his place, the way captains do when, as sometimes happens,
they marry people. So I think we'll start with a prayer. Almighty
God, we beseech thee, please to look with favour upon this
humble attempt to set right a wrong and bring justice about,
however late in time it comes. Amen.'

Everyone dutifully said *amen*.

It was then that I noticed that of the seven faces I could see
in the lantern-light, six seemed quite calm, if unsmiling, but
one looked puzzled. That was the man I thought I had seen
before. I found that I was now not just nervous, but afraid.

Ralph said: 'No more delay, now. Mr John Bright has something to tell us and to show us. Mr Bright?'

John said: 'My ship, the *Eleanor Browne*, is in Minehead for
the usual repairs after a long voyage. Nothing big – her crew
are seeing to them. We're all working hard and I had to get
permission to be here tonight. But Captain Summers granted
it because he has a stake in this. He did not think it proper
to be present himself but he said I might do so, and he also
swore never to speak of it to anyone, not one soul. My fellow
crewmen think I have been sent ashore on ship's business.

'We've been in port over a week now. On the first day, I
was sent to the ship's chandlers in the main street to buy new
ropes and some paint and I did so. We have the proprietor of
that shop here with us, since he also sails with the free traders

at times. There he is. Mr Laurence Wheelwright.' He pointed, briefly, at the man I had half-recognized, and then recognition flooded back, all the way from the inquest, long ago, on Maisie Cutler. Of course! Laurence Wheelwright! Her other beau.

The other man who was suspected of her murder. The man who was almost certainly guilty, as Daniel Hopton had once told me.

The man who had paid weregild for her.

I looked at him and saw that his face had gone rigid.

'He wasn't there that day,' John said. 'Just his assistant, a young lad, but most helpful. You have a good young fellow there, Mr Wheelwright. It's a good shop, well stocked and there's a shelf at one side with decorative things on it: things to adorn a captain's cabin or make a gift for a girl. I saw this, and bought it.'

He leant over the table, took the lid off the box, and got something out of it, which he held up for us to see. It was a brass ornament about two feet tall, and looked like a plate fastened upright on a plinth. John tilted it under the light and I was close enough to make out the lettering engraved across the plinth.

The Pretty Fairing.

'I'll pass it round,' said John, and did so. Each of us in turn had a chance to study it. I remembered John, in the kitchen at Foxwell, a brandy in his hand, describing it. It had a pleasant engraved picture of a youth handing a bunch of ribbons to a girl. It was surely the gift that Captain Summers had presented to his brother-in-law to mark the birth of Captain Grover's baby son.

John, in fact, was saying so at that moment. He was describing the celebration party and the other gifts that he had seen along with this one. He was saying how odd it was that it should turn up in Mr Wheelwright's shop in Minehead.'

'I got it in Cornwall!' said Wheelwright. 'There's a fellow there I know, a fisherman that makes a bit of extra money beachcombing. He said he'd found this on a stretch of beach. It were half-buried in the sand. I bought it from him cheap and shined it up to go in my shop.'

But Wheelwright's voice was high and scared. I saw now

what this gathering was all about. Wheelwright was being accused of something and not, apparently, of murdering Maisie Cutler. This was something else.

'You must have known where it came from,' said Ralph stonily. '*The Pretty Fairing* was a Minehead ship. And she was destroyed by wreckers. We all know the story.'

'Yes, yes, but what does it matter? It's a pretty thing, what would be the point of just leaving it in the sand? I thought, someone might buy it for old times' sake! Someone who'd known the *Fairing* . . .'

'I bought it and called on Mr Duggan on the way back to the *Eleanor*,' said John. 'Mr Ralph Duggan wasn't there but his son, Mr Charles Duggan, was.'

'Aye,' said the man I had identified as Charlie. 'So I was, and a bad shock it gave me, seeing that brass ornament and hearing that it had just been bought in a shop like lawful merchandise. Contraband we do run here, when we get the chance, but wrecking, no, and *Fairing* was the victim of wreckers. Made me think, that did. Mr Bright here was thinking, too. So he and I, we hatched a plan, and when my father came back, I talked to him. We got Daniel Hopton to help.'

'Aye,' said Daniel.

'We tried the chandler's shop first,' said Charlie. 'Wheelwright lives above it, don't you, Laurence? You were away somewhere in the *Summer Dawn* when John bought this pretty ornament and you were still away. John here begged some time off – that's when he told Captain Summers about all this – and then we went to the shop and got your assistant outside by having a pretend accident in the street, a collision between two carts. John and Daniel saw to that while Dad and I nipped into the shop and did some searching. We didn't find aught but next day, home you came in the *Summer Dawn*. We reckoned it was worth trying again. Mr Bright, go on.'

'This is all nonsense. What are you saying I've done? I don't understand!' Wheelwright's eyes were slewing from side to side, as though he were a trapped animal wanting to escape.

'That night,' said John, 'us four met at the harbour after dark and slipped aboard the *Summer Dawn*. Nice little vessel, she is. Got a cabin down below, well furnished. Has a rug on the floor. We got the rug up and some of the boards below looked funny and we had them up, too.'

Once more, he delved into the box and this time brought out a set of four lanterns, one after another. He put them on the table and asked for a light. Charlie Duggan lit a spill from one of the ship's lanterns. It seemed that the ones on the table all had candles in them. One by one, he lit them. It was then clear that they all had coloured glass in them. They cast beams of blue and yellow, red and green across the table.

'Those were also among the gifts that Captain Grover received when he celebrated the birth of his child,' said John. 'I saw them myself. Were they also found by an innocent Cornish fisherman looking for flotsam in the sand? How do you account for them turning up under the deck in your ship's cabin, Mr Wheelwright? They weren't the only things there, by the way. There were quite a number of pretty gew-gaws, some of them valuable. There were pieces of women's jewellery, for instance. Not for sale in your shop, I should think – you no doubt had other outlets for such things.'

'This is ridiculous! I . . . I . . . .!'

There was, of course, virtually nothing that Wheelwright could say in his defence. Even by lantern light, I could see that his face had turned to a greyish-yellow colour. His eyes were huge with fright.

Ralph spoke. 'Most of us believe – to the point of knowing – that many years ago, Mr Wheelwright, you murdered a girl called Maisie Cutler, because she preferred someone else to you. You apparently paid for that – paid money to her family – and have since been free of the law. Indeed, we are not here to try you for her murder. All the same . . .

'When the *Pretty Fairing* was attacked, Captain Grover, her master, died with her and his death has caused great grief to his wife and child and also to Captain Summers of the *Eleanor Browne*, his brother-in-law and his friend. That is why John Bright here was granted permission to join us tonight. Captain Summers would like to see justice done. And even though you bought yourself out of the grip of the law when you paid Maisie's parents for her loss, others suffered loss through her death, as well as her own family. My brother Philip was nearly arrested for her murder, except that we got him away. You would have let him hang. At the time, also, I was about to be married.'

He did not look at me, or need to. Probably everyone present knew the story. 'Because of the suspicion that attached to my brother Philip, my marriage never came about,' he said. 'And that, too, caused much sorrow. You have much to answer for, Mr Wheelwright. You left Minehead for a while after the Maisie Cutler business and you came back well supplied with money. You've been well supplied with it ever since. The *Summer Dawn* is quite a luxury vessel. Where have you been making all this nice money? Would it, perhaps, be as a member of a wrecking gang in Cornwall?'

There was silence, except for a gobbling sound from Laurence Wheelwright. His head turned this way and that, seeking a way out, seeking a friendly face. Finding neither.

'You may speak in your own defence,' said Ralph. 'If you can explain how the objects on this table came into your possession, and thereby clear yourself, then do so. We will all be glad to hear that explanation.'

'I . . . I . . . oh, God!'

'Have you really nothing to say on your own behalf?' asked Ralph, and then a murmur began among the other men.

'Course he hasn't . . .'

'Like to hear it, I must say . . .'

'B'ain't no doubt . . .'

'We got ropes, ain't we? And a yardarm?'

'No! *No!*' Wheelwright screamed the words and turned as if to flee, even though there was nowhere to flee to, unless he were to throw himself into the sea. Charlie Duggan and one of the men I didn't know, had seized hold of him.

Ralph, raising his voice above Wheelwright's cries, said: 'Is it the opinion of you all that this man is guilty of the crime of wrecking? A show of hands, please!'

All hands were shown, except that the two men who were holding Wheelwright, had no hands free and shouted *Aye*, instead.

I too raised my hand. I could do nothing else, and hideous as the outcome of this must be, justice to the dead insisted on it.

'In that case,' said Ralph, 'there is nothing for me to do but pronounce sentence of death by hanging and may God . . .'

I suppose he ended by saying *have mercy on your soul*, but the words couldn't be heard above Wheelwright's frantic shrieks. I looked at his face, so distorted by terror that he scarcely looked human, and remembered the fear on the face of Augusta Waters as her fathers prepared to beat her. That, I thought, is what blind terror does to people. It reduces us to petrified animals. Then John put his hand on my shoulder.

'Ma. Best go below.'

So I didn't see Laurence Wheelwright die. But I heard. Even with my hands over my ears, I heard; the pleas for pity, the wild babbling and the horrid sound of a man crying; then an unintelligible scream, suddenly cut off by a choking noise and then thuds and scrabbling against the door to the companionway, the beastly sounds of kicking feet, until they weakened and ceased.

I was by myself until it was over, and then John came to me. 'I had to be there. We all had to be, Ma. We had to witness what we had chosen to do. But I'm sorry you were alone. Are you all right?'

'Yes, John. What has been done with . . .?'

'Weighted and put overboard,' John said.

I remarked: 'It's a pity you didn't get the names of his fellow-wreckers out of him before you . . . did it.'

'We'd only have done that by bargaining with him for his life and we weren't going to do that. Mr Duggan will lay information in Cornwall, about Mr Wheelwright and the *Summer Dawn*, though. Without mentioning tonight's events, of course. Mr Wheelwright had an accident at sea, that will be the story. His boat will be found empty and adrift, and things discovered inside her when she was brought into harbour, things that aroused suspicion. That should lead to an enquiry and very likely, that enquiry will find out who his associates were, which dubious characters were his friends; times when his boat was seen in the area. I think his companions in crime will be brought to book before too long.'

'What now?' I asked wearily.

'We make for port,' said John. 'I must rejoin the *Eleanor*

tomorrow – no, today, now. Ma, you had better go back to wherever you were staying . . .'

'The Wellington.'

'We'll try to get you there in time for breakfast and you can pretend you went out for an early morning walk. I should stay there today, if I were you, and get some rest.'

The door creaked as Ralph pushed it wide and came in. 'And in the evening,' he said, 'perhaps I may have the pleasure of giving you dinner at the Wellington, Mrs Bright. And before you answer, I think I must tell you – free trading is in the past for me now. I am leaving it behind. I think you and I may have things to talk about. Please agree to dine with me.'

Completion

I could, of course, have said no. But tonight, everything had changed. My bitter parting from Ralph had faded into a misty past. I only knew that here was Ralph, just as he had always been. *Ralph*. And that was enough.

Besides, there was still Charlotte. I had been protecting her as much as myself when I refused to commit the two of us to life with a law-breaking husband and father, but if he had truly left free trading behind, he would have much to offer her and they had a right to know each other, to be truly father and daughter.

And so, that evening, we sat opposite each other in the Wellington dining room, our faces lit by the branched candlestick on our table. We had had time to rest, to put on tidy clothes, to think. Now we studied one another, our faces serious.

'Last night,' I said. 'It was dreadful.'

'It was necessary,' said Ralph. 'The law might well have been too slow, too cautious . . . and we might have had some difficulty in explaining our own actions. Wheelwright, in the hands of the law, might have done some bargaining. He might have handed over a gang of free traders! No, it was best as it was, Peggy, and it was just.'

A waiter came to ask for our order. We made our choice. It felt extraordinary to be free to do this, to dine in public with Ralph, knowing that no one in the world would object.

But there were things to be said, that must be said. When the waiter was gone, I came straight to the point on which my whole future might turn.

'Ralph, did you mean it when you said, on the ship, that you were putting smuggling – free trading – behind you?'

'You want to hear it again, out loud, in a more definite way, don't you? The answer is yes, I am. Peggy, when I left you – so unkindly, at Foxwell – I was full of hurt, of rage. You knew me, you had once been ready to marry me; the free trading didn't matter then; why should it matter now? Those were the thoughts that dominated my mind. I didn't, couldn't, understand you. And then something happened.'

'Yes?'

'In my work, I meet seamen. A sailor came to the boatyard to collect a new boat and we did a little gossiping. He had once been a deck hand on a prison ship bound for Australia. It was the one the Hathertons, Luke and Roger, were on. He remembered them; they'd been angry, aggressive, made a to-do . . . but they never reached Australia. Dysentery broke out on the ship and over half the prisoners in the hold perished, as well as some of the crew! Both the Hathertons died. Luke first. His son tried to look after him, but two days after Luke had gone, Roger went as well. The sailor,' said Ralph, and I saw his mouth twist as though he had tasted something repulsive, 'said that the conditions in the hold where the prisoners were, were beyond belief.'

'Squalid?' I asked.

'Worse! The hold stank anyway, he said, but when that disease came, well, a healthy man would start to retch if he as much as opened the hatch leading to it. They were bound for an Australian port called Botany Bay. They limped in like a plague ship. They *were* a plague ship. The port authority wouldn't let them ashore until the sickness had run its course. All the dead had been buried at sea, of course. More were buried in Botany Bay itself. Eventually, the survivors were allowed to land. This sailor managed to change ships and get back home as a hand on a cargo vessel that didn't smell of anything worse than cheese. And Peggy, that's when I began to think.'

'What exactly do you mean, Ralph?' Two waiters had now appeared, one with the wine, the other with soup. I had forgotten what soup I had chosen but it turned out to be oxtail, thick and brown. I remember it so well.

'I suddenly realized that I was not quite the young adventurer you fell in love with,' Ralph said as he took up his spoon. 'I began to see that if you had changed, so had I. The Hathertons were fine, strong men, but they couldn't withstand the conditions on that prison ship. Would I? I cringed at the thought of trying. Then I saw that after all, I did understand your fears.'

I wanted to say *thank God* but held my tongue.

'I found,' said Ralph, 'that after all, I shared those fears. I don't think I could endure transportation, Peggy. I think I would just die. Even if I survived the voyage, I'd have to face forced labour in a strange land. I thought about that too. I never really had before. Transportation was a disaster that happened to other people. But then I remembered hearing that many convicts die, even if they get to Australia safely, because of overwork and homesickness. I'm not adaptable enough now, even if I ever was.'

'Ralph,' I said. 'What do you think made me – twice now – come to find you, to warn you, but fear for you? For what capture might do to you.'

'I know. I *do* know, Peggy. And a prison here in England would be not much better,' he added grimly. 'I've realized that, too. I've warned Charlie to lay off the free trading as well. He has a family to consider, even if he's willing to risk his own freedom. Our smuggling days are done, Peggy. Besides, there's much less money in it now. The government is learning sense, bit by bit. And so, partly because of you, but partly because I'm not quite the Ralph Duggan I was, I have decided to turn respectable. You can have it in writing if you wish.'

'I'd like that. Yes, please.'

We drank our soup after that without talking. The plates were removed and replaced by beefsteaks, along with an array of vegetables. Ralph said: 'Honest trade with America is proving valuable. I am already building ships to carry imports. These tomatoes stuffed with mushrooms – we owe the tomatoes to America. It's pleasant, having these new things on the table.'

'Yes. It is.'

There was another silence while we ate. Then, suddenly, Ralph laid down his knife and fork. 'Peggy.'

'Yes?'

'I haven't thanked you properly for twice warning me. You kept your oath to my band of smugglers. I respect that.'

I said: 'I did it for you.'

Ralph smiled, and stretched a hand to me, across the table. After a moment, I reached out to clasp it. Everything that needed to be said was said then, when our hands met. Although it did still need to be put into words.

Ralph said: 'I really do believe you love me. Peggy, the last time I was at Foxwell, I asked you a question. You said no. And I shouted at you. I said insulting things that I didn't mean because your refusal hurt me so much that I wanted to hurt you back. I'm sorry, sorry, sorry – and even sorrier about the way I turned my back on you and walked away. Can you forgive me – really forgive me? And now I ask you the same question again . . .'

He paused. I waited.

'If this time the answer is no,' he said, 'then that is the end, for ever. But will you marry me, Peggy Bright?'

'Of course,' I said.

Over apple pie and clotted cream, we got down to practicalities.

'The Darracotts have had all they can stand,' Ralph said. 'They just can't manage at Standing Stone. They're losing ground. Dick Webster does all he can with them but Darracott always has some new idea or other for improving things and his ideas never work. But now Wheelwright's Ship's Chandlers is available! That would be ideal for the Darracotts. We could get things arranged and be ready to move into Standing Stone in a matter of weeks. I learned a bit about agriculture in Antigua, and you know plenty and so does Dickie Webster. You can run things between you while I learn.'

'The Darracotts have black cattle,' I said thoughtfully. 'An old, well-established breed, but I like Red Devons better. We could start by buying some heifers, a different bloodline from the Foxwell herd, and mate them to my bull . . .'

Ralph began to laugh. 'You're a real farm lass, aren't you, my Peggy? How many ladies, dining in a smart hotel, would accept a proposal of marriage and then start discussing cattle breeding?'

'I used to be impatient with James for being too practical,' I said. 'But perhaps I learned something from him after all.'

'Being practical can be useful.'

And we were both laughing, and the world was warm around us.

Six weeks later, at long last, we stood side by side at the altar of St Salwyn's in Exford and became man and wife. Charlie Duggan was best man and Mr Silcox, though he was now very frail and leaning on a stick, gave me away. William had declined, not because he disapproved of the marriage, but because he said there was something not quite right about sons giving their mothers away. Indeed, he was far from disapproving. He was pleased to think that I would have a good farm of my own, and he liked Ralph.

We laid on a feast to remember, back at Foxwell. Annie and Mattie and Jenny, aided by me and Charlotte, had toiled over the preparations for days. Jenny helped with a will, though she had no love for the institution of marriage. She knew what it led to. A houseful of bawling brats, that's what, she told me.

'There's no danger of that for me,' I told her, amused. She meant it, though. She is still at Foxwell, well into middle age by now, and cheerfully unwed.

We enjoyed the feast and afterwards, danced to the music of the Exford band. Few of the players were the ones who had played for the dance at which I accepted Ralph the first time, but the instruments were the same. But while the dancers were still gliding and prancing in the parlour, which had been cleared of all furniture to make room for them (actually, it was quite a squash to get the dancers in as well as the band), Ralph and I slipped away.

We were to leave for Standing Stone the next morning. That first night we spent in the room that once I had shared with James. I hoped that his shade, if it existed anywhere and knew what was happening, would not mind too much. But soon, I had put him from my mind, as for the first time, Ralph and I lay in each other's as man and wife, as lawful lovers.

That was thirty years ago. The first twenty of them, we had

together. We saw our daughter Charlotte married and Ralph had the pleasure of giving her away to a good husband.

They met, by chance, when she and I were at a market in Dunster, and for them, as for Ralph and myself, it was an instantaneous thing. He is a farmer, so Charlotte did end up as a farmer's wife after all, but I had dowered her well and she has never had to work on the land. Later, when Ralph was gone, they gave up their tenancy and moved to Standing Stone and here, too, hers is the life of a lady. Her children have met and made friends with the children of my estranged daughter Rose, their cousins. I heard that Rose and her husband were outraged by this, but it pleased me greatly.

The children of William and Susie have all turned out well, even Harry. He's a family man himself now, and has the tenancy of a farm near Taunton.

Twenty years, and then it was over. But when Ralph died, it was mercifully easy. A hateful shock for me, but not for him. He had not been ill. He went out one morning with Dickie Webster to repair a leaning gatepost at the entrance to one of our fields, and then Dickie came rushing back, to say that all of a sudden, Ralph had just fallen over and lain still 'and when I went to 'un to see what was amiss, he was . . . he was dead, missus. Just dead. But all quiet like and he never cried out nor nothing and so I don't think he ever knew what happened . . .'

That was ten years ago. I am used now to life without him. After all, I was without him for most of my life. I regret those lost years still. We could have had so many more, except for Laurence Wheelwright.

And yet, in that case, William would never have been born and nor would John . . . dear John, lost at sea the year after my wedding to Ralph, but a wonderful son while I still had him.

Sometimes, I think about William and his children, and I think about Charlotte and how I came to bring her into the world, and about Ralph's useful capital that took care of us while he lived and became mine when he died. That useful capital was the fruit of some thoroughly unlawful transactions, but I don't brood about these things because, as I have so often felt and said, it's all too complicated to worry about.

What those unlawful activities did do, as Ralph intended and I thankfully accepted, was to preserve my secret hoard. Over the years, once free of the fear that James might seize it, I used some of it. Some of it went to provide Charlotte with her generous dowry, and both Standing Stone and Foxwell now have red Devon herds which are famous. Each has a pedigree bull whose services are widely sought.

The rest I retained and still retain, but when I am gone, William and Rose will both benefit. Yes, Rose too. Perhaps then she will feel more kindly towards me.

Meanwhile, much as I miss Ralph, I remember that I had him for twenty years. I have memories to treasure. Let that be sufficient.